Misogyny

A
Fake News
Mystery

By Gary Engler

Cover by Frank Myrskog

RED Publishing

203 32nd Street West, Saskatoon, Saskatchewan, S7L-0S3

1.

The first time Waylon Choy talked to Emma Murphy was the same day he inadvertently learned his daughter Samantha was sexually active. He was sitting on the second floor toilet, reading the sports section of *The Province* when he heard Samantha walk into her room while talking on her cellphone. Choy could understand everything his daughter was saying despite the closed bedroom and bathroom doors. The walls in this part of the house had not yet been renovated and 130-year-old uninsulated plaster and lath were an inadequate barrier to the sound of an excited, recently turned 16-year-old telling her best friend about a boy she had just met.

"He's like so intense," Sam was saying. "His eyes, you know they're green, I love green eyes, they make me melt. Makes me all gooey inside when he looks at me."

This seemed very unlike his daughter, who he had never before heard talk like this. She was usually serious, earnest and powerful, not silly girly or airheaded. In fact, the two of them had had a conversation a few weeks earlier in which Sam had made fun of a friend "whose entire existence revolves around attracting a boyfriend."

"He's an anarchist but really heavy into the environment and feminism, so I can live with the anarchism part of it," Sam said. "I haven't told him I'm a Marxist socialist yet, but that should be okay. At least we both hate capitalism."

Since when is my daughter calling herself a Marxist or socialist? It has to be that damn drama and ecology teacher at Templeton High School who she is always quoting.

"Of course we kissed. His tongue was in my mouth and was so delicious. He's by far the best kisser I've ever ..." she laughed at something, then continued in a lower, more serious tone that made exactly what she was saying difficult to distinguish.

While Choy was only moderately certain she said the words "his hand" then "buttons" and "my breasts" he reacted badly. Flushing the toilet and turning on the pipe-screeching hot-water tap guaranteed he could no longer hear what his daughter was saying and revealed his presence nearby. Then a vigorous closing of the bathroom door and stomping down the hallway to the staircase made clear his displeasure at what he heard. Or not. Perhaps Sam thought the noise came from her brother Ben who was going through a post-pubescent growth spurt that made his movements even more like those of a grizzly bear after waking from hibernation.

What did I expect? That Sam was never going to be interested in sex? That she was going to become a celibate nun? All 16-year-olds talk about sex.

Still, maybe he should call Helena.

And say what? That I was snooping on Sam's telephone conversation?

Maybe Sam had told her mother something. Obviously a girl is more likely to open up or ask for advice from her mother. Had they talked about ... what? Sex? Of course they had. What about age-appropriate sexual activity?

And what exactly is that?

A 16-year-old almost certainly would have a different opinion on the subject than her father and mother.

What do 16-year-old girls in the age of Internet porn think normal sex for their age is?

He'd read stories about teenaged girls being pressured into all sorts of stuff, from "golden showers" to threesomes to anal sex because boys of their age had seen something on a website.

By the time he reached the living room, Choy had worked himself into a frenzy of fantastic, frantic thoughts about the horrors of teenaged pregnancy, sexism and 21st-century sexual practices. He paced elliptically around his favourite couch. Should he talk to Sam about what he had just heard?

What would I say? 'I was sitting on the toilet and I couldn't help hearing …'

That would make her paranoid about privacy in her own bedroom. Maybe wait for an appropriate moment and ask her, straight up, 'what do boys nowadays expect from girls when you are necking?'

Do they still call it that?

Or maybe dig out that story about boys pressuring girls into sex and ask if any of her friends have experienced anything like that? That might work.

Maybe such a conversation would lead to asking about her new boyfriend, and even if it didn't, at least I would know Sam is aware of the problem.

But experience strongly hinted such a conversation would go badly. Two months earlier Sam had reacted negatively and aggressively to suggestions she start wearing a bra to school after a call from the school principal to Helena about breasts that were distracting boys. In fact the "talk" with her mother had completely backfired. Going braless had become a point of principle with Sam, an act of resistance against a "patriarchal system that wanted to control women's sexuality".

And of course Sam is already aware of the problem about boys pressuring girls into sex.

She had long been the one her friends called for advice about everything. She was the feminist and political activist in her crowd. And she was more than capable of handling herself. He'd heard previous phone and in-person conversations in which Sam had given good, solid, even conservative advice.

On the other hand, raging hormones could do crazy things to any teenager's judgement. He vaguely remembered himself at that age. He had an intense crush on Susan Smith who was in drama club with him and was the most beautiful girl he'd ever seen. He still remembered the shape of her body — long legs, pronounced hips, athletic chest and arms with sexy smallish breasts and short golden hair. Funny he couldn't picture her face, although he remembered deep blue eyes that sparkled whenever she smiled, something that happened a lot. He had never asked her out, never really talked to her, but longed for her, dreamed of holding her hand, kissing and walking down Templeton's hallways with his arm around her shoulder. Why did he never work up the courage to ask her out, or at least talk to her?

Because I've always been scared of women.

This guy Sam likes is probably older than her.

He remembered how rotten older guys could be. He remembered what had happened with Susan, how she started dating that Grade 12 basketball player from Tech. Thompson Lee, that was his name, or maybe it was the other way around. The guy had a name that could work both ways, something he thought cool, much better than his embarrassing moniker that made people think he was Chinese, a big deal in East Vancouver in the late 1980s.

Sixteen is an awful and wonderful age. Everything is scary and exciting at the same moment. All grown up and still a child.

Sam is a good, responsible young woman. She always does the right thing. I don't need to worry about her.

At the moment he came to the same conclusion he always did after a panic attack about Sam, his office phone rang. He entered the long narrow room across the hallway and picked up the black handpiece on the old rotary machine he had found in a basement cupboard.

"Hello, this is Waylon Choy. May I help you?"

"I hope so," said the woman's voice. "I've spent the last two days trying to convince the police, but they don't seem to care or understand."

"About what?" asked Choy after a silence that seemed strange given she had called him.

Maybe this is one of those people who find it difficult to talk to strangers.

He'd interviewed a few people over his years as a reporter at the *Vancouver Sun* who were pathologically shy. Sometimes they had an amazing story to tell but getting it out of them required patience and tact.

"These guys I've been looking at, incels, you know, like the terrorist in Toronto who drove up on the sidewalk and killed 15 people, almost all women, I first found them on 8chan where I pretended to be one of them, then I was invited to this chatroom — you wouldn't believe the vile, violent stuff they write and I found out where one of them lives — here in Vancouver, well out in the Valley, in Abbotsford so I decided to fly from Calgary — that's where I go to school, even though I'm not in school right now — I finished all my exams in April and still have a few weeks until hockey schools start — I'm on a scholarship at the University of Calgary and we can make extra money by working the schools over July and August."

Hockey schools? I wonder if she's a goalie who might offer me some advice?

"But like I said that's not for a few weeks so I flew out here to visit my aunt in New Westminster and get a sense of who he is, the incel who let it slip he lives in a third floor apartment across the street from a parking lot for Abbotsford Collegiate and I looked on Google Maps and there was only one building it could possibly be so I decided to come, you know in person, take his picture, whatever, and it took me three days to find Barry, the only young guy living alone was in Apartment 331, and I followed him and he went to this gun club across the river in Mission, then he met up with two other guys to fly a drone, kind of creepy to think of incels flying this thing to take pictures in people's backyards or outside bedroom windows, then the three of them went to a coffee shop and I went in and listened to their conversation — it was frightening, both what they were saying and spying on them — but when I went to the police …"

Choy interrupted because she hadn't taken a single breath in her run-on sentence. Maybe she wasn't shy, although in his experience nervousness sometimes displays itself through excited talking. "You tried to report what you learned about this guy to the police, but they weren't interested?"

"They acted like I was a crazy girl stalking an ex-boyfriend or something," she answered, finally slowing down. "But when I explained where I was from and how I got into the chatroom they finally listened and I told them what I learned."

"Which was?"

"They're planning something violent."

"The guys in the coffee shop?"

"I'm not sure."

"What do you mean?" asked Choy.

"Well, they talked about how all of them 'had taken the black pill', which is their code for saying that women rule the world and agreeing that it will take violence to overcome men's supposed oppression, but when they were talking about some big event coming up that 'will make all the Staceys and Beckys and Chads finally take notice' and 'maybe even move the government to consider 'forced sexual redistribution' it was not clear if they were talking about themselves or some other guys in the chatroom."

Choy had read a little about these women-hating losers after the van attack in Toronto when it was all over the news, and knew they were considered a fringe element of the men's rights movement, but 'forced sexual redistribution' was not a term he had heard before.

"I told the cops these guys might be planning a mass killing, but the Abbotsford police told me to call the RCMP and the Mounties gave me this number in Ottawa and the guy I spoke to told me to get off the site because it's dangerous."

"That's all he said?"

"Essentially."

"Essentially?"

"He said the RCMP and FBI were already monitoring the site, so not to worry. But when I asked when charges would be laid he said jurisdiction is complicated because the guys using the chatroom could be anywhere in the world and some countries don't have laws against hate speech and even in Canada getting a prosecution is tough. Then he said if these guys found out I was a woman they'd come after me, so I should just drop what I'm doing."

"Which is?"

"You're a journalist, you should understand," she said. "The people behind sites like these, who put ideas into the heads of vulnerable, pathetic mentally ill men — the ideological and financial backers — need to be exposed. Don't you agree?"

"I'm sorry, I didn't catch your name."

"Emma, Emma Murphy. I'm the granddaughter of one of the women killed on that sidewalk in Toronto. She had gotten off the subway and was walking to a doctor's appointment when that women-hating piece of shit smashed her skull with a rented van because no girl wanted to fuck the pathetic, sick loser."

"I am so sorry Emma for your loss."

"I'm sorry for being so crude."

"You have every right to be angry."

"Will you meet me so we can talk and then write a story exposing whoever is behind this?"

"I'll meet with you, but until I get more information, I can't promise a story."

"I don't have any money to pay you."

"That's not necessarily a problem. You play hockey. Are you a goalie?"

"Yes, why do you ask?"

"Would you give me some pointers?"

"You mean like trade services?"

"I want to play goal in a men's over-50 league. It's my latest project. I never played the position as a kid; I was a forward up through midget. I want to be a decent goalie by the time I turn 50. I've got a year and a half to learn the position."

"Your website says you charge a minimum of a thousand dollars plus expenses to write a story. There's no way I could offer that much in goalie advice."

"Depends on how good you are," said Choy.

"I'm pretty good," she answered, then paused before continuing. "But I know what you're thinking."

"What am I thinking?"

"You're thinking 'pretty good, for a girl'. 'She claims to be pretty good, but she's a girl goalie', that's what you're thinking."

"Not at all," said Choy defensively. "I was thinking it would be great to have a goalie I could talk to. And I was also thinking that I've learned most people who can afford to pay a thousand dollars want me to write boring stories, usually nothing but advertising trying to disguise itself as news."

Boring, but easy and pays well.

"So, you're like independently wealthy and don't need the money?" she asked.

"I need money like everybody else, but not necessarily now and not necessarily for every story I take on. I got a buyout from the *Sun* and sold my house. I'm living with my father so my expenses are low, except for the renovations we're doing. If it's a good story, a lack of money isn't going to stop me from looking into it. And if you can offer goalie lessons, that's a bonus."

"Advice you said, not lessons. I've got to head back to Calgary in a few days."

"You're staying with an aunt in New West?" he asked.

"Yes."

"I could take the SkyTrain out there. We could meet at the market. You know Freebird? It's a food stand there and their Hainan chicken is excellent."

"I can find it. I've been to the market. My aunt's townhouse is close by."

"Noon tomorrow? They only have a few tables and despite my name I don't look Chinese. I'll be carrying a greenish pannier, bike bag."

"Okay."

"I'll see you then."

Despite his positive words, Choy was not enthusiastic about taking on this story. He was in a comfortable routine. His book about the war on drugs was selling well, both in Canada and the USA and had earned him more than a few well-paid speaking gigs.

Violent incels? Do I really want to get back into that kind of stuff?

***

The first time Choy saw Emma Murphy he guessed she was a lesbian.

During the SkyTrain trip with his bicycle, information gathered the previous evening swirled in his brain, creating a vague outline of who she might be. According to the University of Calgary's women's hockey website Emma was a multi-sport athlete, excellent at softball, lacrosse and hockey, who was enrolled in the Theatre Department and hoped to become a Broadway actor after playing women's professional hockey. Her grandmother had been a moderately successful stage actor beginning in the 1960s in Toronto and Stratford, Ontario.

When Choy read this he immediately thought of Claire, his best friend during the last two years of high school, who was a fantastic athlete, his female lead in three drama club productions and the first lesbian he ever met. In a basement bedroom during a cast party in Grade 11 Claire had told him she was gay when he kissed her. As far as he knew, she confided in no one else at Templeton; the secret shared created a bond that was deep and unbroken through graduation and even into university despite her attending UBC while he had gone to Simon Fraser University. They were so close that Claire had even helped him attract his ex-wife Helena, who he first met in a fourth year history class at SFU. Helena was very good looking, out of his league he thought at the time, but Claire both convinced him that was not true and devised a plan that resulted in a date. Claire, who was at least as good looking as his ex-wife, had draped herself all over him at a Friday Margaret Benston Student Union pub night that Helena regularly attended. He would never know for certain, but Choy believed this display of his masculine desirability had led to Helena agreeing to go out with him the following week.

When Choy saw Emma sitting on one of three chairs surrounding a utilitarian metal table with her short "butch" haircut, muscular body and asexual T-shirt and jeans she seemed to exactly fit a dyke stereotype that he and Claire often joked about. So, when he approached her table and said: "Are you Emma? I'm Waylon," it was with positive feelings towards her perceived sexuality.

She, on the other hand, it immediately became apparent, had a chip on her shoulder. "Hello," she said, holding her hand out to shake. "I should maybe have told you this last night, but I didn't so I need to now, before we go any further."

"I told you," said Choy, assuming he knew what she was talking about. "I don't care about the money, even the expenses. If the story is good I'll work for free. You just give me some goalie advice."

"Something else," she said, uncomfortable but trying to act cool. "I'm gay. A lesbian."

That's it?

Choy smiled, then shrugged. "And I'm straight. So?"

"I've had bad experiences when people learn about me. The cop I talked to in Abbotsford — pretty sure he was an evangelical Christian — seemed to think my sexuality meant I hate all men and that's why I want the police to look at these incels."

"My best friend in high school was a lesbian," said Choy.

"So?" said Murphy.

"So, you remind me of her. I trusted her completely. We acted together on stage."

"You know about my interest in theatre?"

"And your grandmother's."

After a moment she smiled. "A good journalist always does his research?"

Despite being a 20-year-old lesbian hockey player, she reminded Choy of his daughter who hated sports and, given the previous day's telephone conversation, was unlikely to be gay. Both young women had fire in their eyes.

I should invite her over to meet Sam.

"Here," she said handing him a stack of papers. "I printed out some stuff I give to my teen goalies the first day at hockey school. My philosophy of goaltending, drills, and the psychological aspects of playing the toughest position in all of team sports."

"Thank you."

"Read through it and then we can talk. I'll answer any questions you might have."

"This looks like good stuff," he said, quickly scanning the material.

"You say the chicken here is really good?" said Murphy, picking up the menu. "I see it's organic, free range. I like that."

"Me too. Tastes better and better for the planet."

"Better for the chickens too," she said smiling. "At least in the short run, even though they pretty much end up in the same place, organic or not."

He liked her.

Smart, opinionated, feisty, but a little unsure of herself, thinks about how to make a better world; exactly what everyone should be like at her age. And willing stop pucks shot at her head.

***

The third time Choy spoke with Emma Murphy was the following Saturday when his phone rang at 7:30 a.m. while he was still on the street returning from his daily run.

"Did you hear what happened?"

"Emma?" he said, catching his breath as a result of an interrupted final sprint.

"Two women were raped last night in Abbotsford. I just heard it on the radio."

"Two?"

"It was them, the incels, Barry and the other two. I know it was. That's what they were talking about."

"Raped?"

"The radio said two women were picked up on a street, blindfolded and taken to an undisclosed location where they were sexually assaulted, then released hours later."

"That's terrible."

"I'm going back to the police station. Can you meet me there?"

"Now? I'm just finishing my run."

"Later this morning?"

What to say?

While running he'd been thinking about how to tell her his decision not to help.

I shouldn't feel guilty. I've done my share of stories about violent, crazy people.

"I can't today," he answered. "I need to drive my son Ben to his baseball game in an hour and a half then I'm playing slo-pitch in a rec league and we always go out drinking afterwards."

"You can't miss it one time?"

I could but I don't want to.

"What are you going to tell the cops you didn't tell them already?" he said.

"If a man comes with me, a reporter, maybe they'll listen this time."

"You don't have anything, not really."

"I know it was them. They talk about rape all the time in that chatroom. They hate women and see rape as a political act asserting their manhood."

"You already reported that."

"If the cops search Barry's apartment they'll find something."

"They're not going to search his apartment based on over-hearing bits and pieces of a conversation in a coffee shop. You don't even know for sure he's the guy in the incel chatroom."

"You don't care about those two women who were raped?"

"That's not fair, Emma."

"I'll tell you what's not fair! It's not fair that those women were raped despite my warning the cops. If they had knocked on Barry's door, these guys would have been scared off."

"You did what you could do. You tried."

"Have you?" she answered, directing her anger against him.

Why should I feel guilty?

"I'll go with you Monday, if you still think it makes sense repeating yourself to the cops."

Silence.

"Emma?"

"My plane leaves tomorrow for Calgary. I told you I was only here for a week."

"You try the cops today and I'll bug them again Monday. If you thought the cop assigned to this was a sexist pig that might be better anyway."

Silence.

"Sure."

She was angry and disappointed.

What if it was Sam who had been raped?

"I'll talk to them Monday, I promise."

"Thank you Mr. Choy."

Mr. Choy, not Waylon.

"I read all the goalie material you sent me," he said. "It is exactly what I was looking for.

"You don't have to pretend you're going to help me," she said.

"I never said …"

"I understand. Like you told me, investigating these right wing violent types is dangerous. You've got two kids to look after."

"I haven't decided one way or the other."

"Good-bye, Mr. Choy."

As she hung up, his sense of guilt grew.

***

The fourth time he heard from Emma Murphy was a text message a week later. It read "Got ur email. Sorry for anger. Glad you started work on this. May have real breakthrough. Meeting with key figure today. Will call later."

Then, when the following day Choy saw the Calgary area phone number pop onto the cellphone screen along with his Strauss waltz ringtone he immediately thought it was Emma reporting on her breakthrough, but the voice was male.

"Hello," the voice said. "This is Detective Peter Sullivan of the Calgary police."

"Yes?"

"A text message was sent from Emma Murphy's cellphone yesterday to this number."

"Yes."

"Your name is Waylon Choy?"

"It is. What's going on?"

"There's been an assault."

"Of Emma?"

"I'm afraid so."

"Is she okay?"

"She is in hospital, unconscious, with very serious injuries."

"What happened?"

"That's what we're trying to piece together and why I'm calling you."

"I'll tell you all know, but … Is she going to be okay?"

"We don't know. She was hit on the head with a blunt object, maybe a goalie stick and suffered a severe trauma. She's in a coma and the doctors have operated once already … It's up in the air …"

2.

The cop's voice trailed off, which Choy took to mean the doctors didn't know if Murphy was going to live or die. Then a foreboding guilt overwhelmed his consciousness. "Was she raped as well?"

"Why do you ask that?" Sullivan said without answering the question.

"Because she was meeting with someone yesterday who might have information about an incel chatroom where guys talked about raping women as a political act against feminism. I'm a journalist and she wanted me to investigate."

"Are you? Writing a story?"

"Yes."

He hadn't decided to do it for sure until that moment.

"I guess this assault will be good for you then. And if she dies it will be even better."

"What's that supposed to mean?" said Choy angrily.

"Just making an observation about what makes a good story for journalists," said Sullivan with a smug tone. "Will you be coming to Calgary?"

Not to see you, asshole, were the words he would have liked to say. "I don't know. Maybe. Maybe not. Depends."

"Upon?"

"Look, I'm busy here."

"Did I hurt your feelings?"

"Yes."

Choy imagined a white, with a slight pinkish tone, fiftyish, overweight, kind of a slob cop on the other end of the line that really wasn't a line anymore in the age of cellphones and computer networks.

"I like to rattle the chains of reporters, that's all, but nothing was meant by it," said Sullivan. "Hey, I'm sorry, it was a stupid thing to say."

"She's a really nice kid, a lot like my daughter. Very strong willed and tough."

"A girl hockey player. A goalie."

What is this cop saying?

"Do you know if she liked boys or girls?" said Sullivan, clarifying his intent. "I can ask her mother, who says she's coming here from Ontario, or maybe her teammates, but it might be a little less awkward if you know the answer."

A legitimate question for a cop investigating an assault to ask.

"She told me she's a lesbian. It came up because she had just spoken to a sexist cop out here, in the bible belt suburb of Abbotsford. He didn't take her seriously because of stereotypes about dykes. Are cops in Calgary as homophobic, sexist, racist and right wing?"

That feels good.

"Haven't you heard, we've got the most progressive mayor in Canada. He and the chief ride in the Pride Parade, if that turns your crank and makes you feel more comfortable."

"Love a parade," said Choy.

"Look, I said I was sorry for the crack about journalists," said Sullivan. "I'm a pretty conservative guy and I might have voted for Donald Trump if I lived it the States, but people tell me I'm also a good cop and this girl has been assaulted, which pisses me off. I want to find out who did it and if you have any information that can help …"

"I'll tell you everything I know, but only if you stop talking like all reporters are scum."

"That will take some work on my part, but it sounds like a fair deal," he answered.

"And you tell me exactly what happened to Emma."

"Cannot do that."

"I promise not to tell anyone or write about it or in any way jeopardize your investigation. I'll only write about it if you give me permission."

"Cannot do that."

Silence.

He's got me because I want to help him and he's got no reason to help me.

"Okay, I'll tell you everything I know," Choy said. "Then you decide if you want to tell me anything that might help in my investigation."

"I'm listening and have the recorder running."

***

"Have you ever heard of 8chan?" Choy asked his daughter.

"The website where the Nazis and crazies go?"

He nodded.

"Some people call it infinitychan," Samantha continued. "It's like for people really into conspiracy crap."

"I've been looking at it for a story I'm working on. People on there write some pretty vile stuff."

She gave him one of those looks that transmitted the message 'I can't believe how stupid you are' which 16-year-olds specialized in, especially with their parents. Choy ignored her adolescent version of condescension and proceeded to tell Sam what he knew about Emma Murphy and a little of what he had read on 8chan.

"I don't know what to do," he said. "What do you think?"

His daughter stood up from her chair nearest the window above the kitchen table and headed straight to the fridge as she spoke.

"You've got to go to Calgary to check out how she is," said Sam, as she pulled out a container of yogurt, stripped off the tinfoil lid and grabbed a spoon from the drawer. "But first go to Abbotsford and find this Barry guy. I could help with that."

Choy looked at his daughter with his best stern parent visage.

"What?" said Sam.

"You think I would allow you to get involved with an investigation into violent men suspected of raping and beating young women?"

"Those guys don't scare me."

"They scare me."

"They're pathetic losers."

"Violent pathetic losers who hate women."

"But you're going to investigate them just like you've investigated and written stories about neo-Nazis and drug lords."

"That's different."

"Why? Because you're a middle-aged man and I'm a young woman?"

"Because I'm a trained journalist with over 25 years of experience. You are in Grade 10."

"All your experience until less than two years ago was writing fluffy features about Gwyneth Paltrow's favourite Vancouver restaurant or the sad demolition of an old Chinatown gambling parlour. You learned how to investigate these right wing nutbars by doing it, just like I would."

The hardest part of parenting is when you must pretend your child is wrong even though a part of you thinks she is right.

"Your mother would get a restraining order against me ever seeing you again if I let you help on this."

"When in doubt blame it on a woman," said Sam with that annoying 16-year-old, know-it-all smirk on her face. "It's always the mother's fault."

"Come on, be serious."

"I am."

"Be fair. I'm your father. I'm supposed to worry about your safety."

"You're supposed to teach me how to be an independent adult — and I quote: 'when it's time to fly the parents must let the little bird leave the nest regardless of how scary it is' —you told us that when I was 11 and Ben was not quite nine. Are you taking it back now?"

"That's really not fair," protested Choy, as he realized once again it was a mistake to argue with the 16-year-old daughter of a lawyer and a big-mouth journalist.

"Why? Because I quoted you?"

"Because you use my quote out of context. I was trying to convince you to sing that beautiful song you had learned for the recital. You were scared of going up on stage."

"It was true then and remains true today. The only difference is the identity of the scaredy-cat."

She is right, but still wrong. How to explain?

"Look, I'm proud as hell you have the self-confidence to think you can do this, and you probably could. Probably nothing bad would happen. Probably these guys I'm investigating are pathetic losers inhabiting dark corners who, once the light of scrutiny is shone on them, will go scurrying back to their underground lairs. But 'probably' only means a better than 50 percent chance. 'Probably safe' can mean there's a 49 percent chance these guys are violent and dangerous. And my job as a parent is to keep the risks you face to a reasonable minimum. My judgement — and I agree this is subjective, maybe even unfair — is that the risk of you helping me find this Barry guy is too high for a prudent parent to allow."

"Dad!"

"When you're 18 and in university you will be the one assessing risk for yourself, but until then it's your mother and I who have that job."

She walked to the sink and rinsed out the yogurt container before dropping it in the recycling bin. While doing so she gave her father a well-practised pouty look that he interpreted as 'not happy, but not mad and besides I'll do what I want anyway.'

Can't blame her. If I was in her shoes that's what I would be thinking too.

"I may need your advice though," Choy said as her little brother Ben entered the kitchen.

"What's going on?" Ben said, reading his sister's face. "I have the all wise mind. If it's advice you're after the guru is here."

"I need a young woman's perspective," said Choy. "Last I checked that's a little outside your comfort zone."

As Sam shook her head at him, Ben began to do his impersonation of a 16-year-old girl. "Oh, did you see how Brock looked at me! Oh! Oh! He is so cute! I need to go home right now and shave my legs! Oh. Oh! Do you think he's going to kiss me? Oh! Oh!"

Choy tried his best but couldn't stop a slight smile from appearing on his face. Sam glared at him and then back at her brother before stomping out of the room. Father and son stared at each other for a moment.

"What?" said Ben.

"You don't think that was a little over-the-top and sexist?"

"Her and her friends are the ones acting like airhead bimbos."

"Honestly, that's a fair portrayal of your sister?"

"I think it was an extremely accurate depiction of Sam and her friends. You should have heard Morgan and Kara on Saturday when you were off drinking with your friends after slo-pitch. They were here for three hours and I swear the entire time they were talking exactly like that!"

"You were listening in on them?"

"It's kind of hard to avoid hearing them when they're in Sam's room and I'm in mine."

The front half of the second floor definitely needs to be the next target of renovation.

"Some girls go through a silly stage about boys," said Choy. "Sam has actually been a lot better than most."

"She's gone all gaga googoo about this Grade 12 guy from Van Tech. 'Like he's so brilliant, so profound, so green-eyed.' She and her friends acting like bimbos are the ones giving girls a bad rep, but I'm the one accused of sexism by mimicking them?"

"You and your male friends never talk about girls like that? Or worse?"

Ben immediately switched from his smartass 'I'm more mature than you think' attitude to his embarrassed 'I don't want to talk about it' look. Then he changed the subject.

"It's so unfair. You're always worried about me being sexist, or something, but girls are allowed to make fun of boys and tell us how stupid we are but that's okay."

"What are you talking about?"

"Did you know I'm the only guy in the top-10 of marks in my entire grade? Girls get the best grades and when they make fun of a guy for being dumb, no one says anything, but if some boy tells a girl she's not good enough at soccer to play with us, the teachers get all excited, like we shouted Heil Hitler or something."

This was a revelation. His son had never before voiced such a concern and with such passion. Clearly this perceived double standard bothered him.

"You think the school is prejudiced in favour of girls and against boys?"

"Ya!" answered his son like it was the most obvious thing in the world. "Especially against the guys who like to run around and do stuff with their hands, you know the ones who can never sit still."

"You mean like we talked about in Grade 3? Remember when you told us Mrs. Beasley hated boys? Is it still like that in Grade 7?"

"It's worse," answered Ben. "Now the girls are almost all bigger than us, you know, more mature, but the teachers still act like boys are the problem, like with bullying, talking about sex and all that stuff."

"Maybe the teachers are trying to correct a historical problem?"

"By favouring girls over boys? That's not fair."

"It's still a hell of a lot more common for men to rape women than the other way around, right?" said Choy, trying to maintain eye contact. "Men still earn more than women for doing the same job, right? Lots of boys are brought up to think a man should be the boss of his family, right? How many of your friends think that way?"

"Mom has always made more money than you," he answered tentatively, but then became more self-assured as he continued. "Neither you nor grandpa ever raped anybody, right? Mom has always been more like a boss than you. And you guys brought us up to believe that everyone should be treated equally, no matter who you are, men or women, right?"

Choy had to answer his son's challenge with a nod of affirmation.

"So, why does Mr. Nielsen pick Emily Chow for the oratorical contest and not me," said Ben, who suddenly looked as if he was about to burst into tears. "My speech was better than hers, everyone says so."

"That's what this is all about?"

"He picked her because she's a girl. He even told me I was a better speaker than her, but 'she needs to win more than me'."

"He said that?"

"It's not fair," Ben said nodding.

"But it is a pretty big compliment."

"A compliment?"

"Of course it is."

Ben gave him a look of disbelief, as only a-soon-to-be-14-year-old could manage, that combined confusion, pain, self-doubt, naivety and aggression.

"Mr. Nielsen is saying you are more mature, more self-confident than Emily so she needs to practise speaking in public more than you and the fact that he talks to you about his reasoning means that he trusts you are smart enough to understand. It's a huge compliment."

While only partly won over by the logic of his father's words, Ben no longer looked pained or displeased, even when he mumbled: "It's still not fair."

"Mr. Nielsen is also recognizing that you have a big heart and want to help people," Choy said, putting his hand on his son's shoulder. "He knows you understand how much Emily will benefit so you will be fine with a little bit of disappointment."

"Her big sister is in Grade 11 and is like the top student in the entire school. Emily always compares herself to her."

"That must be tough."

"Ya, good thing my marks have always been better than Sam's," Ben said, a sly grin suddenly making an appearance on his pubescent face.

Choy returned the smile even though he understood his son was taking advantage of the situation to gain some sympathy for his last, or perhaps next, report card. The truth was his older sister's marks had also been hard for him to live up to.

***

On his drive to Abbotsford for an appointment with the detective in charge of the sexual assault investigation Choy had a difficult time preparing for the conversation. His thoughts were dominated by Ben's resentment about the way school was designed — more suited for girls in his experience — and how most boys were shut out of the ranks of top students. He remembered similar feelings of resentment in earlier grades, but his son was in Grade 7, a time when, in his day, boys had started to catch up, mostly because girls seemed less interested in competing with boys and more in competing for them. He wondered if this had really changed. Certainly his old newspaper, the *Vancouver Sun*, had been full of stories in the past 25 years about how more females than males were going to university, about how more of them now made the cut for prestigious programs that had once been dominated by men, like medicine, law, dentistry and pharmacy. There had also been features about boys being left behind in early grades because women teachers valued the ability to sit still and punished those students who disrupted class by their physical wandering. He remembered doing a story five years earlier about a group of mothers in North Vancouver who were complaining to the school board that their sons were being discriminated against by a particular female principal who was "too much of a feminist" and maybe even "hated boys". He had always dismissed such stories as the reaction that always accompanies progressive change. But maybe there was something to it? Had schools gone so far in the direction of empowering girls that boys were being negatively impacted?

Bullshit. All the statistics still show women being paid less than men, that most directors of companies are men, that most people who get rich are men. Almost everybody in positions of power are men.

How could someone see this evidence of structural sexism against women and yet claim the problem we should focus on is discrimination against boys? Still, that didn't mean every school in Canada was doing all they could to help boys learn and become productive citizens. Maybe some discrimination against boys was happening. Maybe this was especially true of boys who weren't gifted academically. Maybe Ben had a point.

Maybe there is some connection between what Ben is feeling and these incels.

Certainly once you enter the teen years everything about gender and sex is confusing. That was true when he was young and probably even more confusing today. What if you had parents who taught you boys were better, more valuable, than girls but then you confronted a school system where the opposite seemed true?

Definitely a recipe for resentment.

The truth is at a certain point in your life it's easy to be resentful of girls. They control access to something you really, really want. Choy remembered his early teen years. At 14 he was certainly interested in sex, but it amounted to nothing more than looking at Playboy and Penthouse magazines and masturbating two or three times a day while imagining touching breasts. Girls weren't even tangible at that point — they possessed objects he desired and hence, in so far as sex was concerned, they were simply a theoretical means to satisfying powerful urges. Girls were an abstraction, definitely not real in the sense of being "like me" and having independent needs and desires.

It wasn't until a few years later, maybe when he was 16 that girls and sex achieved some measure of reality, when he actually spoke to and touched a member of another gender. He remembered going to a party where there must have been a few dozen kids more or less his age in the basement of a 1950s bungalow in Renfrew Heights. Everyone but him went to Van Tech — he had no recollection of who invited him — so he didn't know any of the girls, but somehow ended up on a couch with one of them, necking. That was the first time he touched a breast and it felt good.

What was her name?

Maybe he never knew it. All he really remembered was French kissing and moving his hand up her tight T-shirt and she wasn't wearing a bra! Momentarily his bare skin touched hers, felt a nipple and — that was it. The sensation was permanently locked in his brain, but not her name, not her face or anything else about her. Just the electric current that travelled from his fingers to his private parts. To this day he recalled the experience down there, rather than in a more rational part of his anatomy.

Who was she? Does she remember me, my name, what I looked like?

There was absolutely no doubt this was an absolutely clear cut example of objectification. The fact that he could remember nothing else about her proved she was nothing but an object of sexual gratification, such as it was when he was 16. For years afterward he could summon that sensation when a Penthouse letter or picture was not available.

Is it still like that for boys today? Samantha's boyfriend? Of course it is. How could it be any different?

That thought was troubling. Not so much the touching, but all that went along with the objectification. He remembered thinking that Van Tech girl might have been willing to let him go further, if he had just tried. He even discussed the subject with Max Labret, the resident Grade 10 sexual braggart who claimed to have had regular sex since he was 12.

"Girls want it," he said. "They're turned on by real men who take what they want. A real man would have gone all the way."

Even back then the words had seemed wrong — an invitation to rape — but he remembered thinking later that maybe Max was right. 'Maybe that is what girls want. Maybe that's why so many of them like older boys. Maybe that's why I'm a virgin and he's not.'

Of course, even before becoming a father, he never could have forced a girl to have sex because that's not how he had been brought up. He was taught to respect them and that meant asking if they wanted to, even back then. He'd always asked permission, even if it was not always in so many words.

Why was that? Who taught me that? A teacher in sex ed class? Definitely not my father. He never talked about anything related to sex. Not Mom either; she was sick by then and ... maybe it was the memory of her.

Maybe he saw women as frail, easily broken, and therefore you had to be nice to them. You certainly would never use violence to force yourself upon them.

The thought of violence and sex together — it's a definite turn off.

But he knew some men, maybe even some women, had a different opinion. Rape was all too common. Books, movies, newspaper stories, real life. A few months back he'd read a history of rape and war. Mass rape had often been a weapon used to terrorize entire populations.

The truth was, as he and Helena told Samantha when she turned 13, rape takes many forms and the men who do it come in all sorts of guises. The thought of it back then had scared him into trying to scare his daughter into taking the threat seriously. But it was a "bogeyman" sort of fear, not real the way it seemed now, because of these two women in Abbotsford and Emma, who was lying in a hospital bed barely clinging to life. What kind of men would do something like that?

It seemed ironic, given the macho culture surrounding the sport, but visualizing Emma's goalie drills and thinking about her philosophy of goaltending was the means by which Choy emptied his brain of thoughts about rape.

He focused on the movement of Shuffle Drill #1. Shuffle forward from the goalpost, then left, left again and again. Then back to the post. Repeat.

It takes 10,000 repetitions to get good at anything. Who wrote that?

Goalie drills were like ballroom dancing. Learn the moves and then practice. Empty your mind of all other thoughts so that you can live in the moment. Just be a goalie, or a dancer, or a bridge player, or a rebuilder of an old car.

Has that been the object of all my 'hobbies'? Achieving a sort of Zen state of consciousness?

More likely a way of taking his mind off stuff he'd rather not think about. His deteriorating marriage, that's when his hobbies first began. It felt good to be transported to a simpler world. The car. The part. Cleaning the part. It was all a means to take his mind off unpleasant realities. A way to escape.

Sometimes I need that.

And that was Emma's advice in the Psychology of Goaltending chapter. Learn to clear your mind of all extraneous thoughts and focus on the moment you are living in. Follow the puck. Anticipate the puck. Be the puck. Then stop it.

***

Detective George Folk of the Abbotsford police was ex-RCMP. Like many of the cops who worked for the few municipalities in the Lower Mainland that had their own forces, rather than contracting out the work to the federal police, he had spent 20 years as a Mountie moving around western Canada, before being hired as a detective by the fast growing city of 150,000 about 80 kilometres east of Vancouver in the Fraser River valley. Turns out he had worked for the RCMP in Burnaby for almost a decade and he remembered being interviewed by Choy.

"You wouldn't take no for an answer," said Folk, trying to be friendly despite the aloofness towards civilians that was drilled into them at the military-like cadet training academy in Regina, Saskatchewan, that all Mounties attended. "You wore me down. Somehow you got my mother-in-law's telephone number and called me while we were having Sunday dinner."

"I remember now," said Choy. "Someone found a duffel bag with about $20 million in counterfeit money. I happened to be in the office on that Sunday transcribing notes from an interview I'd done with Bono and I was the only reporter around."

"And you wanted the story for the Monday paper, even though I told you I didn't work weekends."

"I do remember that. I interviewed the guy who found the bag, but the managing editor wanted someone from the police to confirm the information and you gave me the details. It ended up being the line story. Feature writers don't get many of those, so I probably owe you a thank you."

"It's funny," said Folk. "But I always pictured you as Chinese, I mean with the name and all. Kind of surprises me to see …"

The guy had started a sentence that was likely going to end with a racist observation, but realized what he was about to say might be offensive. Choy, with his name and lack of Chinese features, had been getting a lot of that lately. It was as if people were more attuned to the inappropriateness of always zeroing in on strangers' ethnic backgrounds but couldn't completely contain their curiosity.

"I get that a lot." The truth was he'd rather answer questions about the discrepancy between his name and appearance than think that someone wondered about it but was afraid to ask. "The name comes from a great-great-great-great-great grandfather who came to B.C. during the Cariboo Gold Rush, but he was my last fully Chinese ancestor."

Folk nodded and offered a modest smile before he turned officious. "You wanted to see me about the sexual assaults? You have some information?"

"Did Emma Murphy speak to you?"

"The young woman from back east trying to play detective?"

"She made a report to the Abbotsford police about overhearing three young men in a Mission coffee shop talking about doing something violent towards women just a few days before those two women were raped. She had the name and address of one of them. A guy named Barry. She wanted you to search his apartment."

"This is why you asked for an appointment?" Folk said, making it obvious that he was annoyed. "What's your connection to Emma Murphy?"

"She came to me with information and wanted me to write a story about incels — involuntary celibates, like the guy who killed those women in Toronto, one of whom was her grandmother — who she was worried were plotting to do something violent."

"You don't work for the *Vancouver Sun* anymore, do you?"

"No. I'm a freelancer. I get a good story I sell it to whomever is interested or sometimes I write a book."

Folk glared at him in that military-talking-to-a-civilian style for a few seconds before speaking. "Did you really think I'd tell you anything about an ongoing investigation?"

Choy shook his head.

"So?" said the cop, about to stand up.

"You probably haven't heard and I thought you'd want to know," said Choy, returning the cop's glare.

Two can play this game.

"What?" Folk finally asked.

"The day after she talked to you Emma Murphy went back to Calgary where she is attending university on a hockey scholarship and she texted me two days ago that she was continuing her investigation into this incel chatroom and was about to make a breakthrough."

"And?"

"And then this morning I get a phone call from a Calgary police detective that she was beaten and is in a coma in hospital. She may have also been raped. They think she was hit on the head with a goalie stick. They don't know if she'll ever regain consciousness."

Folk settled back into his chair and "scrunched" his face like some people do when they are upset, but don't know what to say.

"I kind of feel like I owe Emma," said Choy. "She wanted me to come with her to see you, but I had a baseball game and knew you'd probably just brush her off anyway. I mean what did she really have? And I didn't want to get involved in investigating potentially violent young men. So now I feel guilty. The least I can do is follow the story she was following."

The cop said nothing but Choy could see he was making a decision.

"Barry Archibald," Folk said quietly as he looked around the coffee shop to make sure no one could overhear the conversation. "A very troubled kid. Socially awkward and into computers, exactly like that incel guy in Toronto. No police record. But he's the nephew of my boss."

"Your boss?"

"If he ever finds out I told you, my job is …" Folk stood up, pulled a couple of toonies from his pocket and placed them on the table then took out a notebook from his breast pocket, ripped a page out and wrote on it. "The names of Barry's two friends are Brian Grayson, from Mission, and Michael Turner, from I'm not sure where, no one seems to know exactly."

Choy stared at the cop.

"Here's Archibald's and Grayson's contact information." He looked around carefully again as he held out the piece of paper.

"Thank you," said Choy.

"Someone else will be taking over this case so never contact me again. And this meeting never happened."

Choy nodded, but the detective had already begun walking away.

3.

"For these Trump supporters truth is personal and subjective, not something objective," said Allison Bouchard, as she and Choy drove in his car to the Sumas First Nation administrative office near the northern edge of Sumas Prairie, 11,000 acres of farmland that stretched into the United States, formerly the bottom of a lake that had been drained in the 1920s.

"If you're brought up on fairy tale bible stories as the literal truth and told faith is required to get into heaven what do you expect the result will be?" answered Choy, thinking Bouchard shared his negative views about religion.

She had worked over 20 years at the *Abbotsford Times* before the twice-weekly paper closed five years earlier when the two companies that had once competed against each other across the province swapped "properties" so that each ended up with local monopolies. Choy had met the reporter/photographer almost 15 years earlier on the picket line when a strike for union recognition became ugly and dozens of Local 2000 members from the *Sun* and *Province* newspapers marched in solidarity with the 20 or so *Times* employees. Bouchard and he became friends because of a shared interest in duplicate bridge, one of Choy's serial passing fancies, a two-year-long passion that followed attending games at every Major League Baseball park and predated restoring a 1965 AMC Ambassador 990 convertible, ballroom dancing and his currently growing obsession, becoming a goalie. The two journalists had made a good, if at times at-each-others'-throats, pair: she was a by-the-books bidder and no-nonsense declarer, while he relied more on instinct and feelings, especially after his intuition-led bidding landed them in difficult contracts. The contrast confused opponents, but alas, along with some success at regional tournaments, their bridge partnership was fraught with the same sort of tension that destroyed Choy's marriage: women found him too much of a dilettante, a dabbler, unable to commit to anyone or anything. It was certainly like that with bridge, after a year he was having less and less fun and became wilder and wilder with his bidding to make the game more exciting. His partnership with Bouchard ended after his gut feeling led them to a six No Trump slam, doubled and redoubled, which resulted in a spectacular "down seven" when their principal rival, seated to his left, ran off eight straight diamond tricks. Bouchard was so angry they didn't speak for a few years, but more or less achieved peace when she heard about his marriage break-up and called to offer him a sympathetic female, non-sexual shoulder to cry on.

Alison was one of those unemployed-against-their-will journalists for life who still knew everyone and everything about her community and had maintained a blog about the goings on in the "bible belt" community where she had lived for over 30 years after emigrating from the States. Bouchard was the first person Choy thought of when considering who he might enlist to help with the story.

The second person Choy thought of was a not frequent collaborator, and someone he had never actually met, who went by the name of TwoSpiritPhoenix and insisted on gender neutral pronouns. Ze was transgendered and maybe Indigenous, given the nom de plume. Ze had first contacted Choy and offered to help after he began working for a transsexual person who had transitioned to a female. Ze was a brilliant computer hacker, who seemed able to access almost any computer system. If anyone he knew could retrace Emma Murphy's steps in infiltrating the incel world it would be zir.

Given his recent experiences while working on other stories and Emma's assault, Choy had informed both potential collaborators of the dangers they might be facing, but neither backed away from helping or expressed any fear. Regardless, he was determined to learn from past mistakes and be more careful when investigating dangerous people, especially given the climate created by a U.S. president who labelled anything he disagreed with "fake news", which emboldened the already violence-prone to employ a strategy of "shoot the messenger" as an effective means of ensuring no negative news coverage.

"I don't think it's fair to blame religion for these right wing crazies," said Bouchard, in response to Choy's negative comments. "I know many very good religious people — kind, thoughtful, informed about the world."

"I never said all religious people don't know what the truth is," Choy responded. "I said if you're brought up believing the bible is the literal word of God then you're more likely to link truth and faith, which is just another way of saying truth is subjective."

She didn't look convinced, penetrating his defences with those big brown motherly scanner eyes, just like he remembered from the bridge table.

"What?" said Choy, reacting to her look. "Now you're into defending religion? Spending too much time in the Bible Belt has finally rubbed off on you."

"My husband and I sponsor a Syrian refugee family and three-quarters of the people in our sponsorship group are Mennonites."

"So?"

"So don't make ignorant generalizations about religious people."

"I was making a generalization about bible literalists. Not even a generalization, an inference. And it wasn't ignorant, it was an informed, logical inference."

Her stare continued as he pretended to keep his eyes on the road.

"How many bible literalists have you even met?"

"Too many," Choy said, remembering a dead journalist and other events in Nevada the summer before Donald Trump was elected commander-in-chief of the biggest military force in the world.

"You're so full of bullshit," she said, shaking her head and then smiling.

"Yes, I am," he said, trumping her smile with a goofy grin. "But I stand by my analysis regarding bible literalists."

Choy liked how this woman always challenged any whiff of hubris. It was strangely comforting, even while a little annoying. It was good to have someone keep him in line, like Helena had once done. Without that he had a tendency to shovel ever bigger steaming piles of bullshit. And that had undoubtedly contributed to the end of his marriage then the murder a year ago of the only woman who seemed nearly perfectly compatible and had actually enjoyed his company. Bouchard was like a big sister who never lets you get away with being stupid.

"Let me do the talking," said Bouchard as they turned off the freeway towards the Sumas border crossing. "You heard how reluctant Stacy was on the phone."

Stacy Smith worked for the Sumas First Nation and was a cousin of one of the women who had been abducted and assaulted. During their short telephone conversation she seemed well past "reluctant" to Choy. A better characterization would be mad at the world, to the point where stereotypes of radical angry young Black or other minority women came to mind. Of course it made sense for Bouchard to lead the interview. She was a woman, had interviewed Stacy for previous stories and even taught a class about dealing with the media to the band council that employed her.

At first Smith seemed nothing like the stereotypical image that had stuck in his brain. Instead of blue jeans and a T-shirt, she was conservatively dressed in a white blouse with an embroidered Haida design, beautiful enough to have been a Dorothy Grant original, although Chow knew that was unlikely because years ago he had written a story about the incredible prices her one-of-a-kind pieces of clothing sold for, and a plain black skirt.

"How is your cousin?" asked Bouchard.

"Sarah hasn't gotten out of her bed since she made it home from hospital. I'm the only one she'll talk to. I don't think she'll ever recover."

"And how are you doing?" said Bouchard, giving the thirty-ish but tired looking Smith a hug.

"Terrible. I haven't slept since the attack."

"You and your cousin are close?"

"She's like my baby sister. I changed her diapers and looked after her. Her mother and my mother ... used to go on binges," said Smith, obviously emotionally frail. "I promised myself I wouldn't cry anymore and I won't. I can't. I'm all cried out."

Bouchard hugged her again. This time holding her close for such an extended period that Choy felt the need to say something.

"I'm so sorry," were the words that finally came.

Smith pulled away and stared at him for a few seconds. "Who are you and why are you sorry?"

The words "I'm sorry" almost slipped out again, but instead he looked uncomfortably down at his feet.

Why did I open my mouth? Just keep it shut.

"This is Waylon Choy," said Bouchard, annoyed eyes glaring at him. "He's a former *Vancouver Sun* reporter who writes books and magazine articles now. He's working on a story about a woman hockey player in Calgary, who was also assaulted three days ago, and who ten days ago was in Mission and overheard some guys planning a rape. She was the one who asked Waylon here to write a story."

The look on Smith's face changed from generalized anger to a piercing rage as Bouchard continued to speak.

"This woman also contacted the Abbotsford police about what she heard but they said it was nothing they could act on and ignored her," continued Bouchard.

"The cops knew someone was planning to rape Sarah, before it happened?" said Smith, looking straight into Choy's eyes.

Bouchard also looked at her partner.

"To be fair," said Choy hesitantly, "what she actually overheard the three guys saying was a little vague."

Smith glared.

"It was more of a hunch based on some other stuff Emma knew about the three young men, some stuff she learned by joining a private chat room and pretending to be one of them."

"One of whom?" asked Smith.

"Have you heard the term 'incels'?" he asked.

"Involuntary celibates. Like the guy who killed all those women in Toronto?" Smith said.

Choy nodded and said: "Emma's grandmother was one of his victims. That'as why she infiltrated the incel chat room. She pretended to be a young man who was angry that no women would have sex with him. She gained access to some private chatrooms where all sorts of violent fantasies were discussed. But Emma didn't believe they were just fantasies. She was especially concerned with one young man who identified himself as being from Abbotsford. She found him and followed him."

"To Mission?" said Smith.

"She listened in on a conversation that three men had in a coffee shop before your cousin was attacked," said Choy. "Emma couldn't hear everything they said, but she was convinced they were planning some sort of attack against women. She wanted me to write a story exposing them and about the cops ignoring her information. The next morning she phoned me after hearing about your cousin and her friend being attacked and asked me to go with her back to the cops. I couldn't, so she went alone and had to go back to Calgary the next day. A few days later she called and said she made a breakthrough in uncovering who was behind this group of incels and was meeting somebody. Then yesterday I got a call from a cop in Calgary telling me Emma had been beaten with a hockey stick and was in a coma. She might not live."

"Jesus Christ!" said Smith.

"Jesus Christ is right," said Choy. "I've told you the outline of pretty much all I know and we were hoping you could tell us something that might turn out to be a good lead."

"We're hoping your cousin said something that might help us identify the men who attacked her," said Bouchard. "Maybe details that would either reject or confirm the possibility that the three guys who Emma suspected were, in fact, the ones who did it."

"Who are they?" said Smith, decidedly angry and determined.

Choy shook his head. He had guessed this would be her response and had thought about the best way to explain why they couldn't give her the names. "Do you want whoever did this to be caught and found guilty of their crime?" he said. "Because, if we tell you the names we have, it will make that much more unlikely to happen. A defence lawyer would use …"

"I get it," said Smith, quickly. "I'm not stupid. Anything you might find out as a result of what I tell you, a lawyer would argue had been tainted by the fact I wanted to get the guys who I already thought were guilty. I've watched enough court dramas on TV. But where are the cops in all this? Didn't you give them the names?"

"They have the names," said Choy.

"And?"

"They haven't been able to prove anything so far."

"But they are trying, right?" Smith stared at Choy for a moment. "What aren't you telling me?"

The silence was uncomfortable.

"The cops are not taking it seriously because the victims were two Indians?" Smith spit the words out. "Right?"

Bouchard, who knew the real reason, shook her head.

"Right?" Smith repeated, even angrier. "Just two more squaws who got what they deserved because they were drunk and probably trying to sell themselves. Right?"

"No," said Bouchard. "That's not it. Or at least that's not the most important reason, if it is a factor at all."

This time Smith stared at Bouchard.

"We know some things we can't share," said Choy. "I'm sorry, but if we told you …"

"We will tell you when we can, I promise," said Bouchard.

"You've told her everything you know?" said Smith to Choy.

"Yes."

"Okay," said Smith, studying Bouchard for a few seconds. "I trust her."

The two women hugged again.

"Now you need to tell us everything you know," said Bouchard. "Everything your cousin told you about what happened. Every detail you can remember."

***

Bouchard had been right to insist on interviewing Stacy before paying visits to the two men for whom they had contact information. Among the many horrific details of what happened to Sarah and her friend before, during and after the attacks, a few stood out and shaped what the two journalists needed to do next.

"Sarah told Stacy three men were hassling them in the bar, being all friendly at first, trying to pick them up, but then calling them 'fat squaws' and laughing after being rejected," said Bouchard. "She said two of them were medium height, plump, dark haired and looked like nerds and the other, the really mouthy one, was at least six-foot-four, with dirty blonde hair, bad skin and very skinny. If we find the guys we visit match any of her descriptions, that should be enough to take this to the police."

"It won't be them," answered Choy, who, as in his bridge playing past, was prepared to follow his instincts rather than obvious logic. "If it was anyone in the bar it will be the table right next to them with the quiet guys."

"But there were only two of them."

"Another guy joined them later."

"Why them?"

"'Both short and the kind of guys you really don't notice,' Stacy said Sarah told her," Choy answered. "Wouldn't two quiet guys you didn't really notice fit the persona of incels better than ones you did?"

"Maybe, but how does that help us? If it's them we don't have any descriptions to match up. And they didn't do anything in the bar that would make the cops believe they were suspects worth checking out."

"True, but what if the bar has surveillance cameras? My bet is they do."

"I know the owner of that bar," said Bouchard. "He owns a couple of other businesses and ran for city council last election. I've heard he plans to run again."

"So the guy will want to do journalists some favours. If we can get a decent look at the table beside the two girls and any of the guys on the incel list look like the guys in the video …"

"You think the cops might have already confiscated the bar's surveillance tapes, if they have any?" Bouchard interrupted.

"Based on my discussion with the detective, the Abbotsford police are doing as little as possible on this one."

"Well, maybe we'll get lucky then," said Bouchard. "Let's head to the bar. Turn right at the next lights."

As Choy started driving, he thought of something else Stacy said Sarah told her. "You know what she meant by one of the guys who assaulted them 'smelled like the terrible TV commercial'?" he asked, making the right turn as instructed.

"I think she meant Axe deodorant," Bouchard said. "The brand with all the commercials from a few years back where girls absolutely can't resist a man wearing the scent? They were way over the top, almost self-parody."

"Haven't watched much TV the past six or seven years, what with rebuilding this car, ballroom dancing, looking after my kids, starting to freelance, renovating our house and taking goalie lessons," said Choy. "Would you recognize the scent?"

"No, but we can stop at London Drugs and have a sniff after stopping at the bar. There's one a few blocks from where the first guy lives."

"Sounds like a plan."

***

As soon as he opened the apartment door Choy knew Barry Archibald was one of the two guys the surveillance camera caught sitting next to Sarah and her friend at the bar. The nephew of one of Abbotsford's top cops was short, with light brown hair, a moderately bad complexion and had the look of a deer caught in headlights when he saw the two journalists in the hallway. He was clearly expecting someone else and like a forest animal crossing a highway, froze from surprise.

"Are you Barry Archibald?" asked Choy.

"Who are you? And why do you want to know who I am?"

"We're journalists, working on a story about a fight in the parking lot across the street from your apartment window," said Bouchard, who had come up with this part of the plan. "The apartment manager gave us your name. He gave us the names of each of the people in the apartments with the best views of what happened."

"A fight? When? What happened?"

"Last Tuesday, about 7 p.m." said Bouchard. "Were you home?"

"Probably," he answered, thinking about it. "Yes, I was home, on my computer."

"Did you hear anything? There was a lot of yelling."

"Maybe."

"There were two large groups of teenagers, one mostly white and one mostly East Indian."

"Ya, I remember now. I heard it and went to the window."

"What did you see?"

"A bunch of teenagers standing around, yelling at each other."

"Nothing else?"

"This one big Paki seemed to be the one causing it all," said Archibald. "He was yelling the loudest and was waving something around in his hand, something shiny — I couldn't see too clearly, but the sun reflected off whatever it was."

"You saw someone who looked East Indian yelling and waving around something shiny?" asked Bouchard.

"A Paki," he answered defiantly.

"What makes you say that?"

"He was wearing a turban."

"Most people from Pakistan don't wear turbans," said Choy.

"Sikh people wear turbans and most Sikhs who live here originally came from the Punjab region of India."

"India, Pakistan, they're all Pakis to me."

A misogynist and a racist. Figures.

"Did you see or hear anything else?" asked Bouchard.

"No, I went back to my computer and put on my headphones."

"You didn't hear the police?"

"No, I was playing video games."

"Okay, thanks," said Bouchard.

"Do you know someone named Michael Turner?" asked Choy, going with a gut feeling, instead of their plan.

Archibald once again looked like a stunned ruminant mammal as Bouchard gave her partner a disapproving look.

"Do you know Michael Turner?" Choy repeated, more insistently.

"What's ..." Archibald's voice was faint and fluttering. "I ... I ... don't ..."

"He goes by the handle 'GuyPower' on the same incel site you've posted on at least a hundred times," said Choy. "You and Brian Grayson were seen outside the Sneakers bar with him last week."

"Who ... why ... you can't," Archibald sputtered, the panic in his voice proving that confronting him was the right tactic.

"What did you guys do after leaving the bar?" Choy continued to push. "Where did you go?"

"Nowhere," he answered quickly. "Back here to play some video games, that's all."

"The three of you? Straight here?"

"Ya, we were here for hours."

"All three of you?" repeated Choy.

"Ya."

Choy stared at Archibald for a moment, then glanced at Bouchard, his eyes suggesting it was time to leave. Then he looked back at the 20-something kid. "You're a terrible liar."

The two journalists turned away and walked down the hallway. As they reached the elevator, Choy looked back. Archibald was frozen in the same spot, looking down the hallway at two tormentors who had tricked him into saying something he now understood he should not have said.

***

"Why did you ask him about his friends?" said Bouchard. "That wasn't part of the plan."

"I was improvising."

"Like when you bid seven no trump?"

"It was six no trump," said Choy, annoyed.

"The important point being you improvised and the result was the only time in my bridge playing career that I went down eight, doubled and redoubled."

"It was down seven and you know it."

"Down seven is so much better than down eight."

"What's your problem with what I did in there? It worked didn't it? We got confirmation that the three of them were together that night. We never would have gotten that if we had stuck to the plan. I saw how flustered he was and realized pushing him a little might get us the information we need. And I was right."

"I don't know why I agreed to help. You can never do what we plan beforehand. Do you realize how stressful it is to work with someone you don't trust?" Bouchard shook her head as they walked out of the elevator and through the lobby to the parking lot.

"Why do you make this about 'trust' and doing things according to a plan, instead of praising me for the creativity that got us some critical information, which we likely otherwise never would have gotten," Choy answered.

"We're right back to our bridge playing days," said Bouchard, "when we talked to each other like an old married couple who had forgotten how to be civil."

After walking quickly to the car, she stood at the passenger side door and composed herself. After Choy unlocked his door and opened hers they sat silently for a few seconds.

"I'm sorry," she said. "From the moment I met you on the picket line I felt like we were kindred souls, we got along and understood each other. But you're like my younger brother, you frustrate me. Your goddamn flightiness frustrates me. What you call creativity and I see as irresponsibility makes me want to steal your favourite toys and hide them in the attic."

"So, you see me as family?" Choy said and smiled. "A brother and sister in journalism?"

She shook her head and sat silently for another moment.

"So now that we no longer have a plan, what do we do next?" she said, changing the subject.

"Barry confirmed what I thought, he's a mouse. And from what we know the two of them did in the bar — nothing — Brian Grayson is also a mouse. Which leaves us with Michael Turner being the cat."

"What are you talking about?" she said.

"We go to Brian Grayson's house as quickly as we can and try to do to him what I did to Barry. As soon as Turner gets a chance to sit down with both of them, neither of them will talk anymore."

"Okay."

"So how do I get to the Mission bridge from here?" Choy said.

***

Brian Grayson lived in a tiny, 100-year-old, definitely not yuppified, wooden millworkers house a few blocks from Mission's historic downtown. In his mid-twenties, short, already balding and wearing glasses held firm with an elastic binding, he was rough-housing with a large young pit-bull-type animal in a small front yard strewn with dog toys when the two journalists pulled up across the street in the convertible. Choy saw him look up, but only momentarily, as if a quick glance that no one noticed might protect him from having to speak with strangers. He was definitely the no-eye-contact type of shy person.

"Brian," shouted Bouchard while getting out of the car as if she knew him, taking the lead in the confrontation they planned on the 15-minute drive that took them across the mighty Fraser River.

He looked up a second time, but again tried to pretend he hadn't by rolling over with the dog in dried mud. Bouchard pushed the gate open and walked straight towards him.

"Brian," she repeated, her tone insistent, slightly unfriendly and authoritative. "You need to speak with us, right now."

As Choy closed the gate behind him and carefully eyed the large adolescent female cross between a pit-bull and something moderately less threatening, Grayson finally acknowledged the two strangers in his yard.

"Who …"

"If you don't talk to us, right now, you will regret it," said Bouchard, interrupting him as she stood within a foot of where he was lying on the ground.

Choy thought he heard a low growl, but even the dog seemed intimidated by Bouchard's display of authority, seeking refuge in its master's arms.

"We talked to Barry and he claims you were the one who chose those two girls to grab," said Bouchard. "I'm not sure I believe him because from the look of the video we saw of you two in the bar, it seemed he was the one staring at those girls the most."

Grayson looked up at his accuser, trying to figure out what to say or do. He managed to form one word, "who"— repeating what he had already said.

"Personally, I don't give a damn which one of you takes the most blame," said Bouchard, her feet only a few inches away from his head. "As far as I'm concerned you're all equally guilty, but that's not necessarily the way the law looks at these things, especially when it comes to punishment. The way it works in court is the one who helps the Crown get its convictions usually ends up with the lightest sentence."

Grayson continued to hold the dog, pressing it tighter to his chest.

"Come on, be a man, stand up," shouted Bouchard. "You look like a little girl, lying there, whimpering and hugging your little doggie."

Choy, still standing by the gate, in case the dog became aggressive, marvelled at how well his partner was playing the role assigned to her. She clearly revelled at playing the dominatrix to this guy's submissive wimp. But would the game work? Would he break?

"Stand up," she repeated, even more aggressively.

As he began to get up, Grayson left the dog on the ground. It sat at attention in front of Bouchard, sensing who was in control. She put her hand on its head, then patted its side. Seeing the dog following her orders, Grayson momentarily looked up at Bouchard, but the eye contact was brief; almost immediately he looked straight forward, like a soldier at inspection.

"So, who was it?" Bouchard said. "Was it you or Barry who picked out those two girls?"

"It was Barry," he answered, his voice barely above a whisper. "He's always had a thing for squaws — Indians, I mean."

"I knew it," said Bouchard. "Is that Axe deodorant I smell? It is, isn't it? It stinks and you've used too much!"

She glanced at Choy, giving him a slight nod.

"But …"

"But what? What are you trying to say?"

"Michael …"

"What about Michael?"

"He was the one." Grayson sat back down on the caked mud surrounding him, defeated. He held his arms out to the dog, who remained beside Bouchard.

"He was the one who what?"

"I … We … I … can't."

"What are you trying to say?" said Bouchard, who gave Choy another look, this time suggesting if he had any ideas about how to proceed, he should speak up.

"He's trying to tell you that Michael is the one who had the idea to attack the two girls, right Brian?" said Choy. "It's Michael who tells them what to do. He's the one who should face the most punishment, right Brian?"

Grayson tried not to react, but his head nodded regardless.

As Choy walked towards his partner, the dog emitted a low growl once again. Bouchard patted the animal's head to calm it while Choy retreated back towards the gate and saw a car drive up to take the empty parking spot in front of the house. Barry Archibald was in the driver's seat while another guy, who Choy immediately guessed was Michael Turner, quickly got out of the front passenger door, marching into the yard as he surveyed the scene.

"Grayson!" he barked.

"Sir," responded the frightened man sitting on the ground.

"What are you doing on the ground?" shouted the man Choy assumed was Turner.

"I'm sorry sir," said Grayson, getting to his feet and coming to attention.

"Who are these people in your yard?" he said, looking first at Bouchard and then at Choy.

"I don't know sir."

"They are media scum! Did you invite them onto your private property?"

"No sir!"

"Well then, perhaps you should tell them to leave."

"Yes sir."

Grayson looked at Choy and then at Bouchard. "Please leave my yard."

"You heard him," shouted the other man.

"We know what you did, Mike," said Choy to the man in charge. "Your boys talked."

"My name is Michael," he answered.

"We know your name Michael Turner and we know who you are, as well as what you did," said Bouchard as she walked past the smirking man and motioned for Choy to follow her.

When the two journalists were seated in the car, both looked back across the street, watching as Turner ordered the other two men around like he was their drill sergeant.

"What did we just see?" said Bouchard.

Choy shrugged.

"They're playing military?"

"Looks like."

She shook her head. "This can't be good. Incels playing soldier."

"Not good at all."

4.

After what the two journalists had learned about incel involvement in the Abbottsford attack then witnessed in Grayson's front yard, they decided it was time for another visit to the police, but the new detective in charge of the sexual assault and kidnapping case was unimpressed. In fact, he was hostile, claiming they were endangering his investigation. This was no surprise — cops never liked reporters digging for stories about active cases — but the possibility that one of the perpetrators had a high-ranking protector inside the force made the situation even more delicate.

Rather than press the issue they decided to back off and retreat to a restaurant where everyone, waitresses, cook and customers seemed to be friends with Bouchard. After many hugs and other exchanges of pleasantries, the two journalists discussed what to do next. Bouchard was in favour of pursuing the sexual assault case by talking to a RCMP contact she had become close to over the years, but Choy was more interested in expanding the inquiry to follow the wider political implications. What were the connections between involuntary celibate young men making threats in an Internet chatroom, Emma's assault in Calgary, the kidnapping and sexual assault of two women in Abbotsford, and Michael Turner ordering his two friends around as if he were their drill sergeant? It was time to go all in on the investigation, the hell with fear. He'd stood up to violent right wingers before and could do it again.

They decided that each of them should pursue their preferred strategy so Choy dropped Bouchard off at her house and drove back to Vancouver. Internet searches and a few phone calls revealed Michael Turner was a "three-percenter" — a member of a right wing, anti-Islam quasi militia group that claimed to have hundreds of members across Canada, mostly in Alberta, which was associated with similar groups in the United States. While the American "three-percenters" openly carried weapons while parading or during demonstrations and bragged of their military training, the legality of such activities north of the border was questionable, so the Canadian branch of the self-proclaimed U.S. "national organization made up of patriotic citizens who love their country, their freedoms, and their liberty" carried cattle prods instead of guns when in public. Turner, like a significant number of this and similar groups, had once been in the Canadian Forces. Turner was described on the group's Facebook page as leader of the western Canadian branch.

The "Three Percenters", who took their name from the supposed proportion of the U.S. population who fought against the British in the American revolution, had first been exposed in the media a year earlier when it mobilized over a hundred members to gather in front of Calgary City Hall to "protect" an anti-Islam speaker from the mayor, the first Muslim elected to lead a big Canadian city. The group claimed to engage in military-style training and when Choy called the freelance reporter who had written the first published story about them, he learned that the Calgary group had recently bought a 2,000 acre ranch a few hours southeast of the city, near the U.S. border.

"I'm told they're opening a centre where recruits will drill and get firearms training," said Jennifer Dubinsky, the freelancer who was two years out of Ryerson J-school and had sold her work to the CBC, *Calgary Herald* and Vice website. "No one is saying anything, but the rumour is they're bringing up military grade weapons from across the border."

"Where did they get the money to buy the land?" Choy asked, always interested in following the money.

"Member donations, they say, but what exactly that means I'm still looking at. Is there one rich member who made a big donation? I don't know, yet. I've spoken to one former *three-per* who tells me there's an important oil industry exec who is the moneybag, but so far he's invisible, if he exists at all. I haven't really dug around for the past few months though. I've had to take on some corporate PR work to pay the bills."

Another good reporter forced by economics to abandon journalism.

When he asked whether or not she had heard anything about incels in the Three Percenter milieu, Dubinsky said no, but this was the line of enquiry that felt right to Choy because it offered the possibility of leading back to Emma Murphy. So, he called Bouchard and they agreed she would continue to pursue the story in Abbotsford while he would head east to Calgary to chase down links between what Emma had learned in the incel chatroom, her attack, Michael Turner and the Three Percenters.

***

It was Round 9 in the battle over automobiles, with his daughter in the opposing corner, and he was behind on points so there was no choice but to go for a knockout punch.

"Are you really going to drive that car through the mountains to Calgary?" she said, each syllable a jab to his body. "Do you know how much carbon a car like that releases into the atmosphere every kilometre you drive?"

"You asked me this before and I told you, no I don't, but I would be interested in finding out," said Choy, throwing his hardest punch yet. "Have you figured out the answer yet? Of course not, because you're only asking rhetorical questions and not really interested in serious solutions. If you took a scientific approach to global warming you'd realize that guilting individuals is pointless because the only way we're going to solve this problem is by social and economic policy. Collective approaches to a complex collective problem."

He'd been planning this response for an entire day after deciding that a trip to Calgary was more necessary than ever.

"I need to go to Calgary to uncover the truth about what happened to Emma and I doubt you can take a rented electric vehicle all the way there," said Choy. "Maybe you can, but how do they generate electricity in Alberta? A little wind, a little solar, a little hydro, but most of it is from burning natural gas or coal, so how does that help the atmosphere? I could fly, but that is also terrible for the environment. There's no train anymore, so that leaves the bus, but what do I do when I get to Calgary? It's as bad as Los Angeles for needing a car to get around. I need an automobile to do my work. Is that a good thing? No. But it is reality. I could buy a new car that was more fuel efficient, but is bringing another car into the world really a good idea? What about all the carbon spewing fuel that goes into building a new one? The way I see it, relying on a 1965 AMC Ambassador 990 convertible that I rebuilt myself and have only driven less than a thousand miles, other than that trip to Las Vegas, in over two years, while riding my bicycle as my primary mode of transportation makes me one of the good guys in the battle to control global warming, not some vile evildoer who needs to be lectured by his daughter."

Samantha glared, which meant his punch had caused her knees to wobble and she was having trouble regaining her balance to launch a counterpunch.

"You were just waiting for me to say something about the car, weren't you?" she finally said. "How long did it take for you to come up with that argument?"

"Am I right or not? Is individual or collective responsibility the primary way to solve the global warming problem?"

"Both," she said quickly, recovering slightly. "The world needs collective solutions, but that doesn't excuse all individual responsibility."

"I said 'the primary way to solve global warming', not the only way."

Again, she glared, then repeated: "How long did it take for you to come up with this argument?"

"It took me the best part of 24 hours after we decided one of us had to go to Calgary," he said, smiling. "I played it over and over in my head before I said anything to you. It was pretty obvious how you'd react."

His daughter's glare turned into an almost polite stare.

"I'm leaving first thing tomorrow and I needed to let you guys know," said Choy. "Or would you prefer I don't tell you? Just show up every two weeks when it's my turn to look after you?"

Sam shook her head. "You just decided yesterday to go to Calgary?"

He nodded. "Bouchard is going to continue working on the story here. But too many pieces of the puzzle have 'made in Alberta' stamped on the back."

He had to go and he would drive the Ambassador, but he did feel guilty. Sam was right about global warming.

***

Choy had completely forgotten that he had agreed to accept an intern from the Langara Journalism Program. Or, more accurately, he had purposely put it out of his mind because he was uncomfortable with the idea of an unpaid temporary worker, the result of writing at least a half dozen stories over his years as a reporter at the *Sun* about the exploitation of young people who wanted to get a foot in the door of various gaming, animation, software development or other high tech companies that had appeared like hallucinogenic fungi in Vancouver over the past few decades. But a long-time friend and some-time collaborator who was working as a professor at the J-school was convinced he had the perfect intern for Choy, a young woman who wanted to be an investigative journalist but didn't expect to earn a great living from it. She worked a few days a week as a registered nurse to support her writing habit and would continue to do so. She certainly sounded intriguing, so he'd told Doug Tait to have her call when she was ready to work with him.

But that had been a month earlier and the actual call from Balinder Rodriguez the night before he was leaving for Calgary caught him like an uppercut from a sparring partner the time he had written a feature about the old gym and boxing club in the basement of the Astoria Hotel on East Hastings. It was both disorienting and something to be avoided by any means necessary. The good thing was he didn't need to make up an excuse or outright lie. The truth was his best excuse. He was leaving in about 12 hours and didn't know when he would be back in Vancouver. Choy told her that he was in the middle of a fascinating story — chatting for at least ten minutes, telling her all about it — and wasn't it too bad that he was leaving the next morning because it would have been the perfect story to have a young woman intern help him out with.

Even more disorienting and painful than the call itself was her response. She would drop everything and go with him to Calgary. She asked when he planned to leave and promised to be at his house five minutes earlier. Before he could come up with a further excuse she hung up and at 7:30 the next morning, a 23-year-old-who-looked-16 bundle of sleep-deprived energy, wearing a nurse's uniform from the overnight shift at Vancouver General and carrying a duffel bag, as well as a small back pack, knocked at his front door.

"Hi, I'm Balinder Rodriguez — everyone calls me Bal — my grandfather was Chilean thus the last name, but my mother is Irish and she loved Bollywood movies so named me after a minor Indian star. Geez, you don't look Chinese at all. But I guess my blond hair and blue eyes don't fit very well with Balinder Rodriguez either. So, now that we got that all out of the way, can I throw my bags in the trunk and hop in the back seat. I need to sleep really, really badly."

***

A summer trip from Vancouver to Calgary has to be one of the most beautiful 1,000-kilometre drives in the world, especially in a convertible.

Even if I am contributing to global warming.

Of course, the beautiful summer weather sprouted long lines of campers and boats, pulled by trucks, and cars that meandered on and off the highway, causing jams of slow-moving traffic, especially on the two-lane stretches that began 50 kilometres past Kamloops or just after Vernon, depending on the route chosen. Not that Choy wanted to drive as fast as possible to the four-lane highway that began again in Alberta. He would be content to linger behind the semi-trailers and Winnebagos that laboured on the steeper grades and kept to the speed limit on infrequent flat stretches. The trip could be made in ten hours but eleven or even twelve hours might be productively spent reflecting upon the various strands of information that had been uncovered so far. So long as his back seat passenger continued to sleep.

The first half hour was city driving during which he switched on the CBC early morning program to catch up with the latest news, then an hour of crowded freeway traffic required a level of concentration not conducive to the improvisational thinking that always produced his best results. Instead he thought about the young woman sleeping in the backseat.

I'm not a teacher.

The truth was, despite all the times he had said or thought variations of the theme 'those who can do, those who can't teach', being good at helping other people learn was a rare skill. He thought of all the teachers he had had in 12 years of grade school, four years of university and the one-year journalism program at Langara. Very few had the gifts of excellence at motivating and illuminating that were at the core of educating. The ones who did were special people.

The best he could offer was illustrating by example. He could let her watch how he investigated and then wrote a story. He could answer her questions and offer her access to his thought process.

Is that enough?

It wasn't until he left the last Hope exit behind, where the Coquihalla Highway began its climb into the mountains, that he was able to really focus on where the investigation was at. During the one-hour drive to Merritt, as the landscape changed from mountainous coastal rain forest to interior highland dryland he played what had happened and what he had learned back and forth in his brain's video replay centre. By the time he pulled into the cowboys and millworkers town in the beautiful Nicola Valley to top up his gas tank and check the car's oil he had consolidated his scattered thoughts into a summary statement: Emma had pretended to be a young man to infiltrate the incel chat room; this had led her to Abbotsford and Barry Archibald. Following him she overheard three men in a coffeehouse talking about attacking some women and the next night two women were kidnapped and sexually assaulted by three men. Two of those three all but confessed to the crime, which Choy and Bouchard were prepared to testify to, but the Abbotsford police were ignoring them as suspects, probably because one of them had an uncle high up in the department. Or maybe because there was not yet strong enough evidence linking them to the crime. Perhaps the cops were just being cautious, a not unreasonable course of action given who was involved. Everything could be seen as reasonably straightforward if one accepted that the attack on Emma Murphy in Calgary was in no way related to the crime in the Fraser Valley a thousand kilometres away. But that seemed a much too convenient coincidence. The answer he needed to search for now was to the question: Too convenient for whom?

The hour drive up the Connector over sparse high mountain landscape that separated the Nicola from the Okanagan valleys passed in a flash of thoughts that ranged from attempts at justifications for driving a gas guzzling, carbon spewing car, to reasons why it wasn't his fault that Emma was in a coma, to an item he heard on the CBC morning program about a woman who had screamed "speak white" to a pair of young Quebecers in a Medicine Hat roadside café. While he didn't believe more people were anti-immigrant or anti-French or racist than decades earlier — in fact the opposite was almost certainly true — the current POTUS, Donald Trump, had emboldened loud, obnoxious nativists and racists, even in Canada, to spout their hatred in public. The incident in an Alberta diner illustrated the intelligence level and almost pitiful malevolence of the perpetrator, but also the social licence that politicians and the media covering them gave to these sorts of people. Would this coverage ultimately be seen as a good thing or a bad thing? The question that really intrigued Choy was: Is it better or worse when these sorts crawl out from under the rocks where they had once hidden?

Will writing about these incels reduce their number or give them publicity that aids their recruiting?

The early cherries were in season and he stopped at a fruit stand on the north side of Kelowna to buy a small bag. It was pleasant to pop one in his mouth and a few seconds later spit out the pit into the wind that blew over and around a topless automobile. While Samantha was right about the environmental impact of a transportation system based on the private car, it sure felt good to be cruising down the highway in a convertible.

First thing they had to do after arriving in Calgary was visit Emma. She was in the Foothills Hospital, which, according to the Google map he had consulted was very close to the motel he had booked for the first night. Which, now that he had Rodriguez with him, would be awkward, even if it was a room with two beds. She was a young woman, only seven years older than Samantha, and very good looking. Ten years younger he might have been interested in her and she might have been drawn to him, but now even thinking about her in that way seemed inappropriate. Especially because she was his intern, which created a power imbalance in their relationship and was why universities banned professors from having sex with their students.

Strange to be thinking about having a relationship with a woman again. How many months has it been since Joy died?

Even the thought of thinking about seeing another woman was painful, so Choy made himself stop.

Plan what you're going to do once we get to Calgary.

They had to talk to Emma's family and friends. He wasn't really sure she had any family, but the Calgary detective mentioned a mother. They needed to check out the university hockey rink to see if anyone there knew who she was talking to the day before she was assaulted.

Choy knew a retired reporter who might be willing to help. Frank Polansky had worked for almost a decade at the old *Albertan* newspaper then 20 years at the *Calgary Herald* before being one of the senior reporters who lost their jobs as part of the settlement of a long strike that began in the last millennium and stretched into this one. Then he spent 15 years with some business publication before semi-retiring. He was a good guy and knew his city and province extremely well. It would also be fun to buy Frank a drink, catch up and commiserate about the miserable state of Canadian journalism.

When he stopped in Sicamous to once again top up the gas tank and check the oil — the rebuilt engine was still not burning any — he discovered that TwoSpiritPhoenix had sent him an email, reading "This is going to take more time. Will get back to you as soon as I can."

The next part of the trip, the 350 or so kilometres to Banff during which he would pass through Mount Revelstoke, Glacier, Yoho and Banff national parks, was breathtakingly beautiful and he planned to enjoy the view, breathing in the crisp mountain air, taking a few scenic rest stops and trying his best to empty his mind of all thoughts about global warming, who and why someone would swing a hockey stick at Emma's head, or what the connection was between that and the assault of two young women in Abbotsford. Thinking too much about ugly bad people gave them a victory in an important psychological skirmish; it was better to live the truth that the world is also full of beauty, goodness and hope.

But as he was pulling away from the pumps, the young woman in his back seat woke up. "Where are we?" she asked. "How long did I sleep? Geez, I'm hungry. Is that a restaurant? Can we get something to eat? When did you put the top down? We're in Sicamous, right? There, that's a good restaurant. We always used to stop here when I was a kid and we were driving to Calgary to see my grandparents. Can't believe I slept right through you putting the top down, but my shift in the emergency room was absolutely crazy. Never got a single break. We had six ODs. Two died. Don't understand how people can put that junk into their bodies. It's like they're committing slow motion suicide. This woman Emma we're going to see in Calgary, she is clinging to life, desperately wants to live, but these other people, they act as if they don't care at all if they live or die. I could just run in and order a sandwich to go if you want to get back on the road quickly. I didn't tell you but I don't have a driver's licence — took lessons and know how, but never got around to the test — so here's hoping you didn't expect me to take the wheel. Want me to order a sandwich for you as well?"

***

There was a woman reading a book sitting next to Emma's bed in the Foothill's Hospital.

"Hello, I am Waylon Choy, a writer from Vancouver," he said. "Emma came to see me just before ..."

"I'm her mother Caroline," she said, standing as she offered her hand. "The police told me about you."

"The one outside the room or the detective?"

"The detective," she said, motioning for him to sit in the chair beside her.

"This is Bal Rodriguez. She's my intern and is going to help me gather information."

Rodriguez smiled, but received no response.

"What did the detective tell you?" he asked.

"Not much. That Emma texted you just before ..."

"How is she?" said Rodriguez, surprising Choy.

"No change. She could wake up any minute, or never. She may need another operation, but the surgeons think for now it is best to wait."

"You've been here the whole time since it happened?" said Choy, realizing he may have been rude by asking about the police before Emma.

"I got here as soon as I could, the day after her first operation."

"Emma never told me where she grew up," he continued.

"Hamilton. Dundas actually, just outside Hamilton, which is close to Toronto."

"I've been to Dundas. Lovely old late 18th and early 19th century buildings," said Choy. "And her father, has he been here as well?"

"He's not been in our lives since Emma was two."

"I'm sorry."

"I'm not."

Choy felt a little uncomfortable and was not sure what to say next.

"I never guessed Waylon Choy would look like you," she said, smiling awkwardly. "I pictured someone more ..."

"Chinese?" he said. "I get that all the time."

They made eye contact for a moment, each self-conscious and embarrassed.

"Does it annoy you?"

He nodded. "Sometimes."

"I'm sorry then."

"It is a quite insignificant annoyance."

"Nevertheless ..."

"Especially compared to how you must be feeling." Choy regretted the words, while he was saying them, but they came out regardless.

"It doesn't excuse my insensitivity." She looked embarrassed. "I'm a nurse at McMaster University Hospital and we've been given sensitivity training, so I should know better. It's wrong to make assumptions about people's backgrounds or place of origin. It's just that, as a nurse, I find it more efficient sometimes to come out and say what's on my mind, rather than steer the conversation slowly around to ask what I need to know. I work in the recovery room and it is important to understand a person's background because, in my experience, this can be a strong indicator of how a family will react to certain situations, like death or permanent paralysis. Still, I'm sorry, about what I said."

"Do you want to know why?" Choy said after a few seconds. She seemed to be a nice woman living through a horrible nightmare and he wanted to be friendly. And his intern was also clearly curious.

"Why? I'm not sure what…"

"Why my name is Choy, but I don't look Chinese."

"If you don't mind telling me," she said quickly. "I am curious."

"My great-great-great-great-great grandfather went from China to the California Gold Rush and then less than ten years later to British Columbia for the Cariboo Gold Rush. He married a Metis woman and never went back to China even though he had a wife there as well. He was the last completely Chinese person in my family."

"I see. And you've had people asking you that same stupid question all your life?"

"Emma told me she was a lesbian, the first time I actually met her," said Choy, first regretting the words then realizing they were in response to Caroline's point about getting to the point.

"She has always been impulsive, like me."

"A straight shooter, rather than beating around the bush," he said, quickly correcting her. "I liked that about her. Better than having people wonder, but afraid to ask."

Their eye contact this time was genuine and friendly, producing two smiles.

"Is there anything else you can tell us about your daughter?" said Rodriguez, interrupting the nice moment, earning an annoyed glance from Choy.

"She loved hockey. From a very young age she resented the idea that hockey was a man's game. From a very young age she had a chip on her shoulder about men in general. I always thought it was because of my ex-husband leaving and all."

While no words were spoken about it, Choy assumed Emma's father had been in some way abusive. More abusive than just abandoning a two-year-old daughter.

"She wants to be an actor like her grandmother and a hockey player, like, I don't know who. It seems such a strange combination, but that's what she has wanted since she was 12."

Rodriguez nodded and put her hand on Caroline's wrist.

"You're an experienced journalist?" she said, looking at Choy, then back at Bal.

"I'm a nurse like you, at Vancouver General," said Rodriguez. "But I'm also going into my second year of journalism school."

"I worked 25 years for the *Vancouver Sun*," said Choy.

"Is that like the *Toronto Sun* with its naked women?"

"No," he shook his head vigorously. "That's a tab. There's no Sunshine Girl in the *Vancouver Sun*. It's more like the *Hamilton Spectator* or a cross between the *Toronto Star* and the *Globe and Mail*. A serious newspaper."

"Good, I hate the *Toronto Sun*," she said.

"I've spent the last almost two years working as a freelance journalist, investigating important stories that people bring me and I write articles or books, exposing bad people or systemic problems. Primarily my goal is to make readers think."

"Think?"

"I give readers the facts I uncover, present some ideas that might plausibly make sense of those facts and ask people to think about should be done."

"Do you have any facts or ideas about who did this to my daughter? The police seem stymied, or perhaps they're just not telling me anything."

"Your daughter uncovered many interesting facts that are almost certainly connected to what happened. I have dug up numerous related details and have a number of ideas that might explain them."

"But the police …"

"The police know most of what I know, but details are not necessarily evidence."

"Which means?"

"Journalists are not the police. They have the job of collecting evidence that can be used in courts of law to determine the guilt or innocence of people charged with crimes. My job is to uncover the truth. Or at least that's one of a journalist's jobs."

"And you want to uncover the truth about what happened to my daughter?"

"She came to me for help. She wanted, wants, to uncover the truth about a certain incel chatroom where young men were making inflammatory comments about women. She wants to understand what happened to her grandmother. She wants to expose the motivation or thought processes of the young man who drove the van up on the Toronto sidewalk."

Suddenly Caroline appeared even sadder. "That's what she was doing when … ?" Her voice trailed into silent tears.

"You didn't know?"

She shook her head almost imperceptibly. A few tears flowed down from her eyes.

"Emma was trying to make sense of what seemed senseless," said Choy. "I really admire her for that."

"Admire? I lost my mother and now I may lose my daughter because she wanted to make sense of what happened to my mother? I … What is there to admire in that?"

"Your daughter was acting like a journalist. We, or at least the good ones, have a need to make sense of what people say is senseless."

"I never understood my daughter, not even when she was a little girl and I understand even less why she put her own life at risk so soon after my mother died," said Caroline, looking deep into his eyes again.

What can I say to that?

"Emma loved her grandmother more than she loved me. Do you know how painful it is for a mother to know that?"

She looked at her daughter, laying on the hospital bed with tubes attached to her arms and face, then looked back at Choy.

"She never talked to me, not really, not in the way she talked to her grandmother. I thought maybe my mother's death would bring us closer together, but after the funeral she only stayed in Dundas a few days and then came back here to Calgary. She said it was for her summer job, the hockey schools, but now you tell me it was really to investigate these men who hate women. What good will that do anyone? It won't bring my mother back."

"Maybe it will help prevent what happened to your mother from happening to anyone else," said Choy, trying to respect this woman's understandable grief, but still defending Emma, as well as journalism.

"It put my daughter there," said Caroline, angrily pointing to the bed beside her. "It didn't help anyone."

Imagine if it was Samantha lying there. I'd have a hard time seeing any good that might come of that.

She began to cry again. The display of grief triggered a long dormant sense memory. Choy was 15 and in a Cordoba Street funeral parlour three days after his own mother died, determined not to show any emotion. He was angry at his mother, not sorry she was gone, or so he told himself. She was a drunk who drove his father to gambling, to get out of the house, to avoid the pitiful spectacle of her splayed on the living room sofa, unable to utter a comprehensible word, but feeling a need to speak, nonetheless. She was embarrassing. She embarrassed him and prevented him from allowing his friends to visit his house. What kind of a mother does that? His mother. And then he had begun to cry, just like Caroline now in the chair beside him, uncontrollably, accompanied by loud pain-filled moans that were a symptom of the sorrow that filled his very essence. People were looking at him, his father was staring at him. He ran out of the room, out of the funeral parlour, onto the sidewalk then across the street to the Powell Street Grounds, a place that always made him feel sad and now he remembered why.

Minutes later when he returned to the present Choy could feel tears running down his cheeks and Caroline was holding Rodriguez's hand.

"I'm sorry," Caroline said. "My daughter must have been very passionate about discovering the truth about these incels to have contacted you. She has never been one to seek help. She's always been stubbornly independent. But now …"

Caroline looked like she might start crying again, but instead squeezed Rodriguez's hand tighter before looking back at Choy. "This must have meant a lot to her and I can see it means a lot to you."

Their eyes connected again.

"Please find out who did this and why. Please. For my daughter's sake. If she never opens her eyes again, at least we will know that if she does, we will be able to tell her we have found what she wanted to know."

5.

Rodriguez, who had decided to stay with Emma's mother at the hospital, opened the hotel room door at 8 a.m., just after Choy had returned from a half-hour run in the neighbourhood of 1950s bungalows across a moderately busy street from Motel Village, which seemed to be the name attached to the cluster of a dozen or so tourist hotels that fronted the TransCanada Highway, less than a kilometre from Foothills Health Sciences Centre.

"You stayed with Caroline all night?" said Choy, sitting at the small desk, having just looked at a few files from the incel website that TwoSpiritPhoenix had sent him.

"She wanted to talk, then there was a little emergency with Emma …"

"What happened?"

"Turns out it was a problem with a monitor, and probably wouldn't have been noticed in most cases, but when a patient's mother is a recovery room nurse, it turned into an exciting few hours. She's upset and hasn't been sleeping."

"I'd be going crazy if it were my daughter."

"She blames herself for Emma being in Calgary. They had a fight — something to do with Caroline's mother's will — then Emma left Dundas early."

"Families fight over the stupidest things," said Choy. "Like the last time Sam and I talked was an argument about my car's carbon footprint. If that were to be our last conversation … it's hard to put into words how I'd feel."

"Caroline's not a writer and she absolutely could not put it into words. Mostly a lot of crying and holding hands. She needed someone to listen and be there."

"I never could have done that," said Choy.

"She never would have done it with you," answered Rodriguez. "It's not something women do with men, at least not men they don't know."

"It helped her, right? Made her feel better?"

"It's going to be a long time before she feels better," answered Rodriguez.

"But your being there was something Caroline needed?"

"You're trying to justify my spending the night with her? Like that's not what a real journalist should do? Too personal?"

"I never said. But, yes, I guess that was my point. Does that sound heartless?"

"Sounds like a man," she said, quickly.

Choy found it impossible to read her look. Was she angry? Disgusted? Were the words a putdown or a simple statement of fact?

"Don't worry," she continued, reacting to his look of bewilderment. "It's not a criticism. Men simply don't have empathy the way women do."

"Isn't that kind of sexist?"

"I'm 23-years-old and in my entire life, when I was hurting or feeling bad about something, it's always been women who comforted me."

"You're saying we can't?"

"I'm saying you don't."

She's awfully lippy for an intern. I like that. Even if it's also kind of annoying.

"Probably true," he said, trying to smile. "Maybe that's why we tend to focus more on the narrative, rather than the description or the emotional journey — and probably why I'm a journalist rather than a novelist."

"What are you saying?" came her quick, angry response.

"Nothing." He lifted up his hands in surrender.

"You're saying a good journalist has to be emotionally crippled like a man? In order to focus on the story."

Where did she get that from?

"I'm not saying that at all. I was trying to agree with you. Expand on your notion that women are better at empathy than men. That's it. Honest."

She looked at him carefully before speaking again. "I've been up all night and only slept four hours yesterday. Makes me kind of labile."

"I get it. Don't worry, really, I understand."

Despite his words she scared him. There seemed to be an absence of necessary filters. She was an intern, supposedly following him around to learn what investigative journalism was all about. She should be deferential, not aggressive. Her behaviour was not appropriate.

On the other hand, this might be how Sam would talk to her boss if she were an intern.

"I'm sorry," she said.

"Like you said you haven't had enough sleep." He would try to ignore this outburst, but it would inevitably be filed somewhere on the side of a ledger reading 'Reasons Not to have an Intern.'

"I did learn some stuff about Emma," she said, vaguely apologetic "There were no signs of sexual assault. No bruises, no attempted penetration, nothing."

"Caroline told you that?"

"First one of the nurses, then she confirmed it."

"It could be an important indicator of who might have done it," he said. "Or at least it rules out one motive."

"It still could have been attempted rape," said Rodriguez. "The way you described these incels, maybe whoever did it wanted to force himself on her but couldn't."

Something he had just read from the material TwoSpiritPhoenix had uploaded to his computer suggested that scenario was plausible.

"What else did you learn?"

"That as far as her mother knows, Emma wasn't having a relationship with anyone. In fact, at her grandmother's funeral Emma was complaining that she had no friends at all in Calgary. According to Caroline, this drove Emma to get more and more political, because the only places she found people to talk to were in environmental, women's and antifascist meetings. Apparently she thought most of her teammates were 'shallow, ignorant idiots who wanted their dressing room to be as stupid as a men's team'. I was told that's an exact quote."

While listening to Rodriguez, Choy had found the passage he was looking for in one of the files he had just read.

"This might just prove the plausibility of your theory about incel involvement," said Choy. "This is from one of the files my computer person sent me. It's on a semi-private page of the incel website. Anyone who passes their first level of screening can read this: 'There are ways of overcoming the humiliation of involuntary celibacy. Women are naturally attracted to self-assured men of power, which we know you are right now thinking 'that's not me'. But there is one sure-fire way to attract women who will desperately want to have sex with you. Have you ever heard that women can't resist a man in uniform? Well, it's true and you don't have to join the army or the police force to prove it. There are militia groups you can join that will instil in you the discipline and military bearing that you so desperately desire.' Then it goes on to describe how women's bodies are wired to have sex with strong, disciplined military men."

"You're kidding, right?" said Rodriguez who moved to a spot behind Choy, where she could read his laptop screen.

"Wish I was."

"Wow, this is amazing."

Choy stood up so that she could sit down and read.

"This is like a how-to manual written by a 14-year-old boy trying to impress his friends with everything he knows about sex."

She continued reading. "'When you're hard, take, don't ask. Women might pretend to resist, but the truth is they want to be taken. The proof is they will soon get wet once you enter them. Their body doesn't lie. Not like their *FeminNazi* influenced brain.' Oh my god! This is like instructions on how to rape."

"Now you know who we're dealing with," he said as she continued to read.

***

The smell inside the Olympic Oval was almost the same as that of Britannia arena and Eight Rinks in Burnaby where Choy had been learning to play goal over the past six months. While first used as the speedskating oval for the 1988 Calgary Winter Games and so a much more impressive building than the other two, the combination of ice-making and sweat produced an odor that he guessed was familiar to hockey players across the planet.

A secretary in the Athletics Department said that some members of the Dinos women's hockey team would be skating from 8:30 to 9:30 a.m. on one of the two hockey ice surfaces inside the huge speedskating oval. While he worried that he might be late when he left Rodriguez in the hotel room to get a little sleep, it turned out the walk to the rink was short and he made it in time to see the last five minutes of practice. Then he had 15 minutes on his phone to search for an apartment hotel, hopefully one with a two-bedroom suite that would offer a suitable level of privacy and comfort for him and his intern. At 10:20 he was sitting on a bench outside the Dinos dressing room with the two teammates who said they knew Emma best.

"She is very passionate," said Megan Blackhorse, who, according to the media guide was 20 and from the Kanai First Nation near Lethbridge. "About hockey, about acting, about environmentalism, about politics, about everything she does. And determined to do whatever she needs to succeed. That's why I know she'll recover from the coma."

"She's the kind of person who becomes friends with people who don't have any," said Charlene Wong, a 22-year old from Moose Jaw. "My first season here, before Emma came, I didn't hang out with anyone on the team. Everyone treated me like I was the 'Chinese girl' who only made the team because of political correctness or something. I almost transferred to the University of Saskatchewan, but then Emma came."

"The three of us became friends during our very first practice together and it was all because of Emma," said Blackhorse. "Charlene was in one corner, by herself and I was in the other when she skated onto the ice. She took one look at the two circles of girls, where everyone else was talking and laughing and skated straight to me, introduced herself and then dragged me over to Charlene."

"She's a natural leader," said Wong. "At first the rest of the girls treated us like outsiders, not really part of the team, but you can't do that with Emma. I mean, like, it's just not possible. She's so friendly, out-going and a nice to everyone."

"Plus she's our best player. She led the league with the lowest goals against average as a rookie."

"She's a fantastic skater. She could play any position. She understands the game better than anyone I've ever played with; she can explain everything, every position."

"And she helps everybody," said Blackhorse.

"With positive advice, never negative. And she's not a show off. Emma doesn't care if anyone knows she's helping you. She does it quietly and you get the feeling she's doing it because she cares, not because you're somebody to humiliate or impress."

"We vote on who is going to be captain before the season starts and I guarantee it will be Emma."

"If she gets better," said Wong.

"I guarantee she's going to get better."

"I hope so."

Choy thought this all sounded too much like deification of the dead or 'if you don't have something good to say about someone, don't say anything at all.' At a minimum it didn't square with what Caroline had told Rodriguez about her daughter's relationship with other team members.

"Do you guys know what Emma was doing the days before the assault?" asked Choy. "Who she was talking to or going to see?"

Both shook their heads.

"She didn't say anything about going to Vancouver or an incel chat room?"

"An incel chat room?" said Wong. "Like the guy who killed her grandmother?"

"She was pretending to be one of them so she could write a story."

"She didn't say anything to me," said Blackhorse, who then looked at her teammate.

"Me neither," answered Wong. "But I'm not surprised. Like Megan said, she's very passionate and only has one speed, full on."

"You didn't notice anything out of the ordinary the last couple of weeks?" said Choy.

"Other than her grandmother recently died and she went to Vancouver?" said Wong. "Which wasn't really out of the ordinary because she was visiting an aunt. Half the team is not around until August. The girls here need the money from working at the hockey school and that doesn't start for another ten days. Honestly, I thought Emma was here early only because she was fighting with her mother again."

"She told you that?" said Choy.

"Not this time, but she said stuff before."

"There was one unusual thing," said Blackhorse. "Looking back. She asked if I knew anyone in the environmental movement. An activist who was really serious."

"Did she say why?" asked Choy.

"No."

"She was always talking about the environment, global warming and the oil industry spewing carbon dioxide," said Wong. "A lot of girls have parents who work in the oil industry."

"Was anybody mad at her for what she said?"

"I don't think so," said Wong. "At least I never heard anybody say anything."

"So, what was unusual about her asking if you knew anybody?"

"First the fact she asked me when I thought she would have been the one who knew people like that," said Blackhorse. "I gave her the name of a guy, a grad student in sociology and a local lefty type I met at some Idle No More events. He's not Indigenous, but he was helpful and respectful when people I know asked to borrow a sound system for a rally after the verdict came down for the white farmer who shot Colten Boushie."

"What's Idle No More?" said Wong.

"It's like Black Lives Matter, only for Indians," said Blackhorse.

Wong's face suggested there was a lot she didn't know about her friend and teammate.

"His name is Billy Goodwin, but people call him Ginger," she continued. "I told her to go to the Student Union office or the Old Y on 11ᵗʰ Avenue and ask around; someone would know how to contact him."

"And did she?" asked Choy.

"Ya, that's the really unusual part. I asked her like a week later if she ever contacted him and she had. Said he was a great guy, very interesting and was spending a lot of time with him."

The two women looked like that was the strangest thing either had ever heard.

"Emma never hung around with guys," said Wong.

"Never," added her friend for emphasis.

"You know she is a lesbian?" said Wong.

Choy nodded. "First thing she told me when we met."

"She was like that with everyone," said Blackhorse. "Up front and matter of fact, like it's the most normal thing in the world."

"So, it was weird that she liked this Ginger guy and spent time with him?"

"Very weird," said Wong. "She didn't like most men. Said things."

"Like what?"

"Hardcore feminist stuff. She was always like 'women have to do everything on their own and not rely on men'."

"That's not really hardcore feminism," said Blackhorse. "That's common sense."

Wong looked annoyed.

"Well it isn't, especially when men take off soon as their baby is born. But I agree that Emma making friends with a guy was weird."

Next on Choy's agenda was finding this young man whose nickname came from a famous pre-First World War British Columbia labour leader whose murder sparked the first general strike in Canadian history and then more recent controversy over a stretch of Vancouver Island highway named after him.

But first he had to get back to the motel, pick up Rodriguez and take her to the new hotel where he had booked a two-bedroom apartment. It was not cheap, but it was less expensive than two rooms at the first motel.

***

Five minutes into a conversation with Billy Goodwin at a coffee shop on 10th Avenue Southwest, not far from their new hotel, Choy understood why he and Emma hit it off. People as alike as these two either became best friends or mortal enemies.

"She's like a really strong feminist, an environmentalist, not wired on making money and really likes to talk and think about everything," said Goodwin when asked why he thought they got along so well. "We're two peas from the same pod."

"She did tell you about being a lesbian?"

"Ya. So?"

"Just curious."

"You think a cisgendered male can't be friends with a lesbian?"

Rodriguez looked at Choy, then back at Goodwin.

It's got to the first time I ever heard someone actually use the word 'cisgendered'.

"It means having a gender that corresponds to your perceived body parts," Choy said to her, before continuing. "Some of my best friends over the years have been lesbians."

There were maybe ten minutes more of jargon-laced sentences before they finally arrived at useful conversation. The kid was some sort of anarchist-environmentalist missionary who felt compelled to proselytize everyone he met.

"It was the neo-Nazis who did this to her," said Goodwin, finally getting to the point of the interview. "She found out something and they tried to kill her."

"Which neo-Nazis?" asked Rodriguez.

"They change names like snakes shed their skins, but the ones who did it are probably associated with the so-called Three Percenters. They're most active right now, but it's really just a coalition of all sorts of smaller groups."

"I was told that Emma wanted information about environmentalism," said Choy.

"She wanted to trace the money that backs anti-environmental groups."

"Here in Calgary? Oil money?" said Choy, who glared at Rodriguez to prevent her from interfering with his line of questions.

Goodwin nodded.

"Why?"

"She had this theory that there's this like super-fascist, a rich oil man who is pouring money into all sorts of right wing causes, just like the Koch family in the United States. She thought tracing him through anti-environmental groups would be easiest because pro-environmental groups had probably already done the research."

A look from Choy caused Rodriguez to mime zipping her mouth.

"So she wanted you to tell her who to contact?"

"She wanted to be introduced to people," said Goodwin. "There's a lot of paranoia now because of right wing infiltrators, the so-called Not Fake Media who have been pretending to be environmentally sympathetic university students and then come out a month later with a made-up crazy expose of how some rich liberal American billionaire is trying to undermine the Canadian oil industry."

"There's a lot of that?"

"Enough to make people careful."

"Right wing reporters who try to infiltrate the environmental movement?" asked Rodriguez.

"They try to infiltrate everything that is even remotely 'left wing'." They've moved up from The Donald's America becoming great again along with the other neo-Nazis. Business is booming in Alberta for the right wing media. They have money from rich donors, so if you're like a young journalism grad who wants to earn a living, one way to make your name and get a job is by some bullshit hit job exposé of liberals, lefties or universities."

"I've heard about stuff like that in the States, but here?" said Choy, still not buying what this young man was selling.

"You think a rich oil man from Calgary is different from a rich oil man in Dallas or Houston? They've got the same self-interest. You think immigrant-bashing White supremacists only exist south of the border? We have them here too, I guarantee you. And right wing ideologues? The University of Calgary is a hotbed of Straussians."

"What's a Straussian?" asked Rodriguez, who again couldn't stop herself from jumping in.

"You haven't heard of the dead right wing German-American conservative philosopher Leo Strauss?" said Goodwin. "The guy who argued 'perpetual deception of the citizens by those in power is critical because they need to be led, and they need strong rulers to tell them what's good for them.' Surely you've heard of Ayn Rand?"

"Of course," said Rodriguez.

"What do you get when you cross Ayn Rand and Leo Strauss?" said Goodwin. "A Rebel Media reporter. Someone who has been taught that the best way to tell a lie is by claiming that they're exposing liberal liars."

"In my experience, most conservative reporters are unprincipled opportunists who suck up to power to get a column, and not really ideological at all," said Choy.

"Not these Rebel Media, Breitbart News types. The point of their job is to be ideological. They're selling an ideology, a narrow view of the world that some rich people think is in their self-interest or why else would they be paying for it."

"The mainstream media has always mostly sold the conservative viewpoints of its owners," said Choy, who knew this from personal experience.

"Of course. But the only way these right wing media types can fool ordinary people into supporting them is by pretending they are leading a rebellion against some liberal establishment that has never actually existed."

"Someone wrote a book about how conservatives have been selling themselves like that for over 200 years," said Choy, remembering a review he'd read. "'The Conservative Mind' it was called. Have you read it?"

This ideological version of male peacocks displaying their feathers to impress the female present continued for some time until Choy realized that, despite enjoying himself, the point of his interview was to generate leads. So, at the next possible segue point, he changed the subject. "Speaking of bad guys, and how to find them, who did you end up introducing Emma to?"

***

Tamara Lind's office was above a restaurant in a renovated two-story brick building on 11th Street, just a few blocks from their new hotel and 17th Avenue Southwest, the southern boundary of the old Calgary money neighbourhood of Mount Royal. Choy had told Rodriguez it was best if she not accompany him on the next two interviews to preserve her ability to go undercover in the milieus where the interviewees travelled. She did not object, in fact seemed pleased and decided to head back to the hospital to see Caroline.

"I'm an independent journalist working on a story that Emma Murphy asked me to look into," said Choy, as he glanced around at furnishings that spoke of expensive good taste. "Do you remember speaking to her?"

"Yes." She looked more suspicious than friendly.

"You heard what happened to her?"

"Emma? What happened?"

"She's been in a coma for almost a week after being hit across the head with a hockey stick," he answered. "The police and doctors don't know if she'll live or not."

Lind stood up, then sat down, then stood up again. "Sorry, but I'm confused. Was she playing hockey?"

"No, it happened in her apartment. It was on the TV and both newspapers had small stories. 'Woman attacked in Hillhurst Apartment'."

She shook her head. "I didn't see anything." She sat down once again behind her desk. "Do the police know who?"

"They haven't charged anybody. But I think whoever did it might somehow be connected to a name or names you gave Emma."

She stared at him intensely as if trying to make up her mind about something. "What did you say your name was when you called me?"

"Waylon Choy."

She shook her head. "And your real name is?"

"Waylon Choy," he answered, after stopping to return what now was Lind's glare. "You're really going to ask me to explain my name?"

"It's just …"

"My five times great grandfather came to the Cariboo during the gold rush and married a non-Chinese woman," he explained for at least the 500th time. "He was the last person of one hundred percent Chinese descent in my family. Really all I have from him is the name."

"I'm sorry," said Lind, who now looked embarrassed. "I didn't mean … I was confused. I am confused. Emma. What's your connection to her?"

"I'm a former *Vancouver Sun* reporter who now does freelance work," he said, handing her a card. "I write magazine articles and books. She contacted me and asked for my help with a story about an incel chatroom she had infiltrated. She had come to Vancouver, Abbotsford actually, because she discovered the identity of a guy in the chatroom who was threatening violence against women. She followed him and ended up overhearing a conversation with two other guys that sounded like they were planning an attack. A few days later an attack happened. Two young First Nations women were abducted and sexually assaulted."

"Oh my god."

"Then she came back to Calgary and continued to work on the story. I'm told she came to you for help with figuring out if a rich oil man who is funding anti-environmental groups might also be involved with these incels."

"Oh my god," Lind repeated as she stood up again and made a complete 360 degree circle around the large space. "Oh my god, oh my god, oh my god."

Choy, still standing in front of her desk, waited until she once again stood across from him.

"Emma never told me any of this. Never said a word about any stories she was working on with a journalist. She told me the information was for a class project about money and how it shapes politics."

"What did you tell her?"

"Not a lot," said Lind. "I gave her two names and explained their involvement in a network of anti-environmental, pro-oil propagandists. One calls himself a journalist, just like you, and the other is a very wealthy, but publicity shy, third generation oil multimillion, maybe billionaire."

"Did she tell you that her grandmother was one of the people killed when that guy in Toronto drove up onto the sidewalk?"

"Her grandmother? By that incel?"

"And Billy Goodwin never told you either?"

"He just phoned me up and asked if I would meet with this university student friend of his. I said yes. Emma showed up and I told her all about a project we funded in which a retired professor from the University of Alberta traced the funding and interconnections among a half dozen so-called think tanks and web-based media outlets that defend the oil industry and attack environmentalists."

"Did that project produce a report?"

"Of course."

"May I have a copy?"

"Sure," she said, turning to the bank of file cabinets behind her and pulling out a professionally produced printed report. "This got almost no mainstream media attention, even though we spent a lot of money making sure it looked important. And it is. Important."

Choy quickly looked over the slick booklet.

"A few days before it was to come out, Peter Baxter did this massive attack on us, claiming to prove American billionaires were secretly funding us to undermine the Canadian oil industry. The media went gaga over his hatchet job, which then gave them an excuse to ignore us."

"Who is Peter Baxter?"

"You haven't heard of him? He runs the fastest growing websites in Alberta. In three years his alt-right media empire has grown from just himself to 18 staff, pumping out 20 or 30 videos a week, which appear on three different websites, all of which he controls, even though you'd never know it if you were an ordinary viewer. He is best buddies with the guy who is grand pooh bah of the Three Percenters. You heard of them?"

Choy nodded.

"They claim to be training with guns to defend Canadian values or something like," said Lind. "I never really took them seriously, but maybe … You think one of them assaulted Emma?"

"Maybe, but I don't really know. That's why I'm trying to follow the same trail she did. I need to figure out where it led her."

"Aren't you worried the same thing might happen to you?"

"Of course," said Choy. "But I've been writing about these right wing crazies for a few years now and one thing I've learned, you can't let them scare you. Or at least you can't let them see you acting like they scare you. That's what they thrive on."

She nodded.

"What's the rich guy's name?"

"Allan Brinkman."

"Never heard of him," said Choy.

"Very few people have, but he controls one of the largest privately held oil companies in North America, very heavily involved in the tar sands," said Lind. "And I grew up with him. We were neighbours. My parents and his parents … We belonged to the same clubs. I even dated him a few times."

"And then you took different paths?"

"Something like that," she said. "He changed after his mother died."

Choy could tell there was more to the story. Events or actions that she didn't like talking about.

"Does he still live in Calgary?"

"Mostly. A house about ten blocks from here and an estate south of the city. Why? Are you planning to visit him?"

"Maybe."

"He's become more and more paranoid over the past couple of years, so that might not be possible or a good idea," she said. "He's hired some of those Three Percenters as bodyguards."

A rich guy with extreme right wing bodyguards who may or may not be killers. This sounds familiar.

"I'll keep that in mind," said Choy, who planned on talking with Baxter, the journalist, to start with anyway. "If I need to see him, but I probably don't."

"If you do, let me know," said Lind. "I find it hard to believe that Allan has actually become violent, but the people around him … They're taking advantage of someone who doesn't really know what he's doing anymore. It's like Allan is trapped in a cult and does whatever they tell him."

"Were you close friends at one point?" Choy said, even though he was pretty sure about the answer.

She nodded.

"Did you tell any of this stuff to Emma?" he asked, as a thought occurred to him.

"No, she was in a big hurry. She more or less just wanted the names. I assumed she wanted to confront them with a microphone. And was in a hurry to do it."

Choy thought about this. Had she gone straight to one of these men and said something that caused a goon to attack her? Had one of these men ordered the attack? Or perhaps a 'bodyguard' took it upon himself to silence a mouthy lesbian busybody?

"Do you think that's why someone attacked her?" asked Lind. "Because she, a young woman, embarrassed one of them in front of their macho, violent hangers-on?"

"Maybe."

"I should have told her about the bodyguards. I can't believe I didn't say anything."

"You didn't know what was going on."

"Will you keep me informed? I feel guilty about sending her into a ... Please?"

"I will," he nodded. "Can I ask you something else?"

She stared at him.

"Your family is in the oil business too?"

"Was."

"And was rich? Is rich?"

"Not as rich as Allan's."

"What makes one rich person become an environmentalist while another, who grew up in the same neighbourhood and was friends with the first, becomes the funder of extreme right wing, anti-immigrant, White nationalist, anti-environmental groups?"

"It's complicated," she said shrugging.

"Which one of you is closer to the norm, the average rich Calgary oil-money family?"

"I don't think it's fair to make generalizations about rich people," she answered, annoyed. "They, we, are not some mono-lithic group."

What would be the point of arguing about this with her?

"Generalizations are usually unfair," he answered. "I'm sorry if I offended you."

People with money are just like the rest of us. Except they can pay others enough to agree with them.

6.

After leaving Lind's office he called Rodriguez. She was at the university and said something interesting had come up but couldn't talk so he opened the Google Maps app on his phone to see where he needed to go next.

Baxter Media offices were in a south of the downtown railway tracks neighbourhood a few blocks from the Stampede Grounds and within walking distance of where he was. Getting there was a pleasant stroll through a residential part of the old Beltline neighbourhood during which he performed the glove save drills from Emma's training manual. The yoga-like repetitions helped him focus on the best approach to take with Peter Baxter. Walking along the tree-lined streets his left hand moved up, down and sideways as he picked off imaginary pucks until he reached the new 50-story tower that looked unfinished and almost abandoned, a result of the commercial real estate crash that followed the latest collapse in oil prices.

The receptionist at Baxter Media looked overwhelmed. She was unpacking a box while speaking on the phone and listening to a young male reporter who was demanding answers about some of his stuff that was missing as Choy entered the twelfth floor office. He watched her heroic efforts to cope for a few seconds, but when the distraction of talking to two people at the same time became too great and the box in her arms was about to slip out of her grasp, Choy took it from her and placed it on the floor. Her grateful smile was returned by his sympathetic one. Finally, after the aggressive, file-less reporter stormed out of the reception area, she spoke to him: "Thank you for helping me with the box. It's been crazy here, what with the move and all. All these reporters expect me to know where everything is, and as you can see that's impossible."

"Glad to be able to help."

Suddenly she looked sheepish. "But I'm the one who is supposed to help you. Can I help you?"

Is she flirting with me?

He liked the way she looked and noticed there was no ring on her relationship finger.

"My name is Waylon Choy. I'm a freelance writer from Vancouver. I'd like to speak with Mr. Baxter."

Her smile made him smile. Then as she demurely looked down, but immediately back up, their eyes momentarily connected and he felt a jolt of sexual energy.

She is flirting with me.

But he knew better than to trust his instincts when it came to such matters. He had always fallen for good looking women who were out of his league. Like his ex-wife, who was beautiful, smart and from an important, well-connected West Vancouver family, a combination that made her divorce from a mere reporter, whose father was a gambling addict living in the Downtown Eastside, all but inevitable. The receptionist was about to say something but was once more distracted by the beeping sounds that came from her phone. Her look spoke of an apology.

"There's no hurry. I can wait," Choy said before her words were formed.

"Catherine!" said another young male reporter who stormed into the reception area but stopped when he saw Choy standing in front of her desk. He shook his head and stomped out.

"Don't worry about me Catherine," said Choy, noticing her reaction to the disappearing reporter. "I'll just park myself over here until things settle down."

"I don't think he likes me," said Catherine, standing up and taking a few steps away from her desk. "Always on edge, blames other people when he makes a mistake. You know the type."

He nodded as they again made eye contact. He felt the same energy as before and suspected she did as well because of the way she kept looking up from her phone.

"It's not your fault if there's too much work for one person," said Choy. "Deal with the phone calls; the reporters and I can wait."

Her next smile looked like a thank you as she sat back down to deal with the calls. A late thirtyish, average looking man, of average height, average build, dirty blond hair and a general nondescript look but wearing expensive shoes, slacks, shirt and a bolo tie strode into the space. He looked at Catherine as if she was about to be the target of his attention but was distracted by Choy's presence.

"Hi there," he said. "I'm Peter Baxter. Can I help you?"

"Waylon Choy."

The two men shook hands.

"So, what brings you to the office of Baxter Media?" said Baxter.

"I'm a former *Vancouver Sun* reporter who took a buyout," said Choy.

"Sorry, we have a policy of not hiring anyone who worked for the dying, fake new outlets," he said, smiling. "Unless …"

"I'm not looking for a job," Choy interrupted him. "I'm enjoying life as a freelancer. I was visiting a friend here in Calgary and she told me that you guys were the fastest growing media outlet in Alberta and I thought to myself this is a story readers in Vancouver might be interested in. I know I am. As a journalist who has been living through the death by a thousand cuts last two decades of Canada's media I have to ask: What's your secret?"

The flattery seemed to work as Baxter's friendly smile grew slightly bigger.

"Well, why don't you come into my office, so you can sit down and I'll tell you all about it," said Baxter. "Please excuse the clutter, but we're moving into this new space. We hired six more journalists and the old offices couldn't fit us anymore. Here we have room to grow."

Baxter's glass desk would have been suitably impressive for the CEO of a mid-sized oil company, but seemed inappropriately grand for an online media company, even a successful one.

"The desk came with the sublease," said Baxter, picking up on Choy's reaction to the office furnishings. "A little over the top, don't you think?"

"Built to impress," said Choy, trying to keep his friendly voice and smile.

"You said your name was Choy," said Baxter, sitting down on an ergonomic chair that had at least a half dozen handles and adjustable knobs. "You don't look like a Choy."

"No."

"The name must have been handy when you worked for the *Vancouver Sun*."

"I got hired because of it 27 years ago," Choy said, his smile turning purposively impish, because he knew exactly what this guy meant by the statement.

"Is that true?"

"You betcha."

Baxter laughed as if this was one of the funniest things he'd ever heard. "Damn, that's a good one. You got the job because someone thought you were Chinese! Damn!"

Of course a right winger would find it amusing that a 'white person' would benefit from having a Chinese name. It plays into political tropes that appeal to many conservatives: a dislike of affirmative action programs, xenophobic nativism, fear of immigrants taking "our" jobs, but with a twist that the "white person" triumphs in the end.

While his plan had been to meet Baxter and simply see where the interview led, this friendly banter offered the possibility of an off-guard conversation that was every journalist's dream. Shared laughter could establish a bond that would allow his subject to believe the two men were friends, or at least fellow travellers, so Choy joined in.

"To the day I quit and took the company buyout, management was pretty much scared shitless to get rid of me because there were so few Chinese working in the newsroom," he said, provoking further guffaws from the man on the other side of the desk. "Everybody who read my byline thought I was one of only a handful of Asians. That's why I always preferred newspaper journalism. You don't need to reveal your face."

The two men laughed together for a few more seconds, then Baxter grew serious and looked carefully at Choy.

"So how did you get the name?"

"I was adopted by a fifth generation Chinese-Canadian family. They're very mainstream Canadians who mostly vote Conservative. My Mom and Dad hate all the immigrants flooding Vancouver from Hong Kong, Taiwan, Singapore, China — especially the rich ones buying up all the houses."

Baxter smiled tentatively. "You serious?" he asked.

"Yes," said Choy. "There's quite a bit of hostility in the old Chinese community against newcomers."

"I did not know that," he answered. "Interesting."

"My Dad thinks we should cut off all immigration until the price of housing drops 50 per cent," said Choy. "I guess house prices aren't a big issue in Alberta, but they sure are in B.C."

Baxter, suddenly looking serious, stared from across the desk, as if he were considering what to say next. After a few moments he said: "Are you an antifa?"

Caught off guard by the question, it wasn't difficult to appear confused. "I'm sorry?" said Choy. "Am I a what?"

"An antifa."

"An 'antifa' what? You mean like an anti-fascist supporter or member of some group?"

"Did you come here to interview me in order to get some juicy quote you think might expose me as the next Adolph Hitler?"

"No. And I'm not a member of any political group. I'm a journalist. I've never even spoke to an 'antifa' as far as I know, let alone engaged in some sort of conspiracy with one."

Baxter continued to give him a look that was clearly meant to intimidate.

"I thought we were having a friendly conversation as a prelude to me asking you about Baxter Media," said Choy. "Did I say some things because I thought a right wing media owner might appreciate them and loosen his guard? Yes. I'm guilty. But I try to do the same with everyone I interview. It's called putting people at ease."

The staring continued.

"Would I like you to say something outrageous or show me your SS tattoo? Of course, because it would make a good story, but that's not the reason I'm here."

"Why are you here?"

He stared at Baxter for a few seconds.

What the hell, go for it.

"Because there's a young woman in a coma fighting for her life, who came to see you a day or two before someone bashed her on the side of her head with a hockey stick and I wanted to check if that visit had anything to do with her attack."

Baxter's upper lip twitched, its first movement in a few minutes.

"And I am genuinely interested in how any media organization — left, right, centre — survives, let alone thrives in these dog days of journalism."

"Okay," Baxter finally said. "You seem honest, for a liberal media type. I'll talk to you."

Baxter was more or less cooperative and almost pleasant after expressing sympathy for Emma. He claimed that while she had called to make an appointment he was too busy to see her. They had talked for a few minutes on the phone; she asked him what he knew about four or five people and he answered her questions, even though she was rude and "unladylike" assertive. He said he found that many young women reporters thought rudeness was the best way to demonstrate their ability to compete with men, while in fact, a much better tactic was to use their natural "girly guile". After he spoke the words he paused and asked Choy if he thought the term "girly guile" demonstrated a sexist attitude.

"Probably, but that's kind of to be expected. I mean, you do run a far right website."

Baxter smiled. "I like your directness," he said. "But we don't consider ourselves either sexist or far right. Many people say we are, but our goals are simply to speak the truth as we see it, to provoke the cultural elites and have fun while doing it. Occasionally some people even find that a little left wing. Of course, most of the time we're seen as right wing, but we don't go out of our way to fit into a neat ideological niche. Biology, not ideology, dictates that women have babies, so they need to become experts at nurturing. I don't say this because I'm right wing or sexist, but because it is the truth. Women are physically weaker than men, another truth and that's why they use guile instead of force. It's a better survival strategy for their kind."

Choy let the man ramble about women's biological fate and the common sense underlying sexism, refusing to take the bait being placed in front of him. Not that he was uninterested in debate, but the strategy was transparent: Baxter was trying to avoid discussion about Emma by provoking an argument about the "proper" place of women in society. These "alt-right" types relished this sort of obfuscation by provocation.

Instead, at an appropriate moment, Choy changed the subject back to why Baxter Media was thriving while so many other news outlets were dying. This led to more banal claims of truth telling and a good sense of humour as the source of success, but after enduring a little more puffery they finally got to the topic of financial backers. According to Baxter, the investors in his media company, while ideologically supportive, expected to eventually earn a profit. "That's how capitalism works and they are most definitely enthusiastic capitalists," he said.

"Like Allan Brinkman?" said Choy. "Is he an enthusiastic capitalist who expects to earn a profit from all the money he's put into Baxter Media? I'm told he's your biggest single investor."

"Who told you this?"

"A friend of his."

"That's the exact same answer this Emma of yours gave me."

"To the exact same question?"

"And like her, I assume you too will refuse to name the 'friend' who provided this information?"

"The more important question is not who provided the information, but rather is it true?" said Choy, trying his best not to smirk. "You did say your organization is thriving because it tells the truth, didn't you?"

For a moment Baxter had that gopher-about-to-be-squished-between-car-tires-and-pavement-look, but then recovered sufficiently to produce a sort of half sneer. "We are a private company that has no legal obligation to reveal any information about our investors."

"That's how you answer my question? What would one of your reporters say on camera to a university president or a politician who responded like that?" Choy followed up his verbal challenge with his best steely glare.

After a few seconds of silence Baxter smiled, this time genuinely. "You're good. Sure you're not interested in a job?"

"Pretty sure I'm not ideological enough for you, even if I were," he answered, while keeping up the intensity of his frown. "But I'm not."

Surprisingly jovial, Baxter's smile grew. "Okay, I give up," he said. "Allan is our biggest investor. He believes in this business and I'm proud to call him a partner, as well as a friend."

"Did you tell Emma that as well?"

"You think Allan had her beaten up? Clearly you don't know the man. He's kind and gentle, meek and mild, one of the least violent people I know."

"Did you tell Emma he was your biggest investor?"

He nodded.

"Did you know that your gentle friend has hired Three Percenters as his bodyguards?" said Choy.

"And what's wrong with that?" said Baxter, aggressiveness back in his voice. "They're well-trained, former Canadian special forces and loyal. Oh, I know, they're not politically correct enough for you. They're not sensitive to the needs of every Jane and John who can't decide what gender they really are, not ashamed of the White English-speaking men who built this country, not pussy whipped enough …"

The emotion in his voice suggested a less friendly side than his smiley-face-used-car-salesman persona.

"My concern is that they're not unwilling to beat a woman to death with a hockey stick," Choy interrupted, "to prove exactly how tough and 'non-pussy whipped' they are."

The two men were back to a staring contest.

"You are way off base on this," Baxter finally said.

"Am I? Why don't you arrange an interview with Brinkman then, so I can see for myself what a nice guy he is. And while you're at it, get him to bring along his former special forces bodyguards, who will impress me with their loyalty and Canadian patriotism."

"You don't believe I'd do that. You think Allan and I have something to hide," he said. "Well, I tell you what. Give me your cell number and I'll arrange exactly the interviews you want. Any particular times work best for you tomorrow?"

"Whatever time and place suits them, I'll make myself available," Choy said, continuing to make eye contact.

"Good, I'll have Catherine phone you with the details," he answered, maintaining the stare down for a few more seconds before speaking again. "But now I'm afraid our news meeting beckons."

"Yes," answered Choy, turning away as he stood up. "Thank you for your time."

He made a point of giving Catherine a big smile as he walked into the reception area.

"I hope things settle down here and everything works out for you with this job, I mean if you really want it. Then he added quietly: "Don't take any bullshit. This place isn't worth it."

The secretary looked around to see if anyone was listening. Once she determined no one was, she returned Choy's smile.

She's definitely interested in me.

***

After a walk back to the hotel and some Google searches, he phoned the number he had for Frank Polansky. A woman answered.

"Is Frank around?"

A silence was followed by a nervous voice. "Who is this?"

"Waylon Choy, an old friend. I used to work at the *Vancouver Sun*. Frank and I … Is this Gwen?"

"Yes," she said. "Hello Waylon. You haven't heard?"

He's dead.

"Frank died four months ago," she continued. "He was riding his bike — Frank said you and he cycled together when he visited Vancouver — and a car hit him."

"I'm really sorry Gwen," said Choy. "I don't know what to say. Frank was one of the best journalists I ever met and a really good person."

The silence was full of pain, for both of them.

"The police don't know how it happened or who exactly hit him," said Gwen, sounding like she might be crying. "There was a chinook and he was riding home, 7 p.m. on a Thursday from downtown and someone, the police think maybe a delivery truck or van, knocked him off the bike and he fell between two parked cars. It was February and slippery. His forehead hit one of the cars and … He wasn't found until hours later. The police think the driver of the truck might not have even noticed. They say they are still investigating, but after all this time, I can't imagine …"

Bad luck, just like working for the Herald when the strike happened.

"Is there anything I can do?"

Choy couldn't read the silence.

"You mean like investigate what happened?" she said, after a few moments.

"Anything I can do to help," said Choy. "Do you need anything?"

"Frank had a good insurance policy," she answered. "He was always very diligent about things like that. And I don't think there is anything to investigate. I mean he was working on some stories about corporate fraud, but there's absolutely no indication that had anything to do with the accident. Frank's life was filled with bad luck. He must have told you that."

"He did."

Yet another silence. "Why did you call Waylon? Is there something I can help you with?"

"I thought Frank might have some ideas. about a story."

"I'm sure he would have," she said. "I'm sorry we didn't contact you about the funeral, but it was a small, family gathering."

"I understand."

The following silence was the most awkward of all.

"Good-bye Waylon," Gwen finally said.

"Good-bye Gwen.

Once she hung up Choy sat at the hotel room desk, staring out the window for a few minutes, contemplating the fragility of life.

Strange how often death surprises us even though it happens to every-one. Bad luck. Negative serendipity.

He'd long thought 'The Randomness of Life and Death" would be a great title for a novel. If only he had a story to go along with the title.

I should check out how much life insurance costs.

He thought about going to the nearest bar and having a drink to toast Frank's life but decided the best way to honour him was by continuing to work on the story. Get to the root of it, investigate, damn it, that's what Frank would have said.

A phone call to Rodriguez led him to walking to the nearest CTrain stop, a ride to the University of Calgary campus and Grace McHenry, a professor in the Department of Philosophy who taught a women's studies course titled A History of Misogyny: Law, Culture and Religion.

He didn't expect the conversation to be particularly useful, but Rodriguez said Emma's teammates and mother had mentioned McHenry as a prof she admired. In fact, Choy was expecting the only utility of the conversation would be in distracting him from thinking about Frank's death and tomorrow's interview with Allan Brinkman. That meeting would be key to making progress and he needed to be prepared.

Which persona to use? Assertive, macho tough guy pushing for answers? Amiable, but quietly persistent, upbeat good fellow? Deferential inquisitor, awed by being in the presence of such a rich and powerful person? Hard to know what might work best until the interview actually starts.

Rodriguez filled him in on what she had learned that day, then they met with the professor in her office. While Choy's body was present, very little of his attention was focused on the conversation between the two women. The words they were speaking entered his consciousness in fragments that interrupted his primary concern. Thankfully Rodriguez seemed enthusiastic about interviewing the prof.

"Yes, there were many societies that, as far as we can tell, were not misogynist. In fact, many of the earliest religions worshipped the mother, fecundity, and believed life itself was a gift given by women — a rather obvious conclusion given childbirth, one would think," said the professor.

If he's the one who ordered the beating of a woman to death — safest to assume that— what's the best way to approach him? If at all?

"We see the transition away from female gods the best in early Greek societies. The archeological record reveals the female idols giving way to male."

Why I am I doing this? Again. Guilt. Emma. Of course, I'm scared. Any sane person would be. Why do I do things that scare me? Don't think about it.

"So, what are the factors that have been linked to a rise in misogyny?" said Rodriguez.

"War, plunder, pillage, piracy, trade, capitalism — these are all associated with an increase in misogyny."

"Are you saying the rise in misogyny caused all these things or is a reflection of them?" the younger woman responded, obviously fascinated by the ideas the professor was raising.

While he again faded out of the conversation, further along in the professor's lecture she said something that stuck in his brain. "We look at misogyny from various points of view," she said. "How the dislike of women may manifest itself — violence, discrimination, belittling, objectification, exclusion, patriarchy, male privilege, etc. — how the idea of women's inferiority has evolved over time in religion, philosophy, culture and the more modern discourses of psychology and sociology, how the need to justify the exploitation of women has resulted in the various philosophies of sexism, and more. But what I try to do is connect the dots. Following upon something Marx wrote — to paraphrase — the point is not to describe the world, but rather to change it. My area of research is the conceptualization of ideas, practices and changes to societal structures that would challenge the grip misogyny has on our world."

It was then the thought arose, the culmination of almost random synaptic firing inside a brain that had recently registered the death of a friend and spent hours considering the hatred of women. At that precise moment it occurred to him that anything a Women Studies department could think of, so too could organized neo-Nazis. Or maybe one of them simply took a course?

"Do misogynists ever enroll in your program?" he asked and could immediately tell by the scrunched forehead, the flaring then twitching of a nose and quizzical eyes that the question surprised and perplexed McHenry. "Is there an organized right wing response to the kind of work you do? Is there a philosopher of misogyny that right wingers would read and I could take a look at?"

Both Rodriguez and the professor stared at him and shook their heads.

"What did I say?" he asked, seeing their annoyance.

"There are thousands of philosophers of misogyny — they wrote the Bible, the Koran, the Talmud, the American Constitution ..." said Rodriguez.

McHenry nodded vigorously.

"I understand, but I mean now. Is there someone writing this stuff now?"

"Open any newspaper, read a business column explaining why women are vastly under-represented on corporate boards ..." said the professor.

"Someone that's particularly popular on the extreme right?"

"Maybe Jordan Peterson, although to say he is a philosopher would be like saying a Tonka toy is a truck," McHenry answered.

"I guess what I'm asking is ... Are any of the right wing women haters smart enough to understand what you say and do in Women's Studies and actually use the research about the connection between capitalism and misogyny to make the argument for putting women in their place in order to defend capitalism?"

He could tell the professor was stumped, perhaps because she had, like him, always assumed right wingers, especially the extreme ones, were stupid.

"An interesting question," was all she said before continuing on with her speaking notes for Women's Studies 501.

Boring. Still, how often does an hour-long interview produce a revelation and force you to think about a story in a whole new way?

What if some right wingers are, in fact, clever? What if they purpose-fully appear to be stupid in order to appeal to a certain sort of voter? Like the politicians who wear cowboy hats in a transparent attempt to appeal to country folk, they put on an act to symbolically say to people who are stupid, 'I am one of you'. But of course these folks don't consider themselves stupid — very few people think that of themselves — but are rather people who gravitate to sim-ple, black and white explanations, like for example the readers of supermarket tabloids and consumers of right wing radio talk programs.

An assumption that right wingers are stupid would give them a tremendous advantage — it's always better to have an opponent who underestimates you. Like Trump as president — the assump-tion that he is stupid offers him endless opportunities to manipulate public debate. A stupid president cannot possibly be clever enough to do that. And assuming he is a few cards short of a full deck func-tions to excuse any mistakes he does make. After all, he is stupid.

What if there is some really clever, amoral, power hungry Hitler-in-waiting hiding in the background, manipulating events and people in an attempt to gain ultimate power? From his work about Vancouver's former police chief, he knew that people who admired Hitler and patterned their lives after him did exist. What if someone like that had decided to use misogyny as an organizing tool, a way to gather a lot of angry young men together into a personal army?

What if Allan Brinkman is that person?

7.

Rodriguez was pissed off, the depth of her disappointment demonstrated by a sullen silence beginning when Choy told her she couldn't come with him to interview Brinkman. He used the same excuse as before, 'it's to protect your identity in case we need you for some undercover work', but the real reason was to protect her.

I can't have her on my conscience. No way. Not another one. Another what? Another young woman. Is that sexist?

Thankfully, he was able to banish these thoughts in a swirling blizzard of questions and possible answers about the derivation of the word conscience. Did the fact that 'con' and 'science' were together have some significance? Then came memories of silly newsroom conversations about imaginary oddball origins of words. All this kept his foreboding feelings in the shadows at the back of his brain so that in the foreground he could prepare himself for an important interview as he drove in a topless convertible into the foothills of the Rocky Mountains southwest of Calgary. Choy went back and forth within himself over the best approach to take in interviewing a 40-something rich kid supporter of extreme right wing causes. Of course, there was only one possible answer to the question, the same one as always: Be prepared, but keep an open mind and react to the person; remember that an interview is a living creature, with its own needs, personality and lifespan.

Who told me that? Billy Ferguson, the old Scottish entertainment editor who retired six months after I started at the Sun. Funniest man I ever met. Should have been a comedian. When I told him that he said journalism was a hell of a lot easier and provided a steady income with about the same access to decent whiskey.

The entrance to Brinkman's property was marked by an eight-foot-high gate across a well-groomed gravel road about three kilometres south off the highway into Kananaskis country. A big, muscular, soldierly looking guy wearing cowboy boots, blue jeans and a shirt that would have been appropriate at the Stampede Parade came out of a small guardhouse as Choy drove up.

"I have an appointment to see Mr. Brinkman," Choy said, smiling at the scowling guard. "Waylon Choy is the name."

Reacting to the name, his tough guy scowl turned into an angry glare. Choy offered an ironic cheerful smile when the guard made eye contact before disappearing inside the guardhouse. Then the wait began. After a few annoying minutes he looked through his cassettes, pulling one out from the carefully catalogued collection, opened the case and put it into the mint condition 50-year-old player that he had found in a going-out-of-business sale at one of the oldest pawn shops in the Downtown Eastside, yet another victim of the yuppification of his neighbourhood. He turned the volume up to the highest setting and couldn't help the grin growing on his face as he waited for the Bhangra's greatest hits compilation to begin playing. If there was one thing western White Canadian racists disliked more than Chinese it was south Asians. Within ten seconds of 'Beware of the Boys' blaring from his top-of-the-line Kicker door speakers, the guard once again appeared, glared one last time at Choy, then opened the gate.

The road to Brinkman's house was uphill through a long stretch of pasture where cattle of a breed that Choy did not recognize grazed.

"Mr. Choy?" said a slight, well-tanned, blonde haired, 40-ish but looked younger, medium height man wearing jeans, shirt and cowboy boots — a style similar to the security guard outside the gate — who was standing in front of the huge log structure that seemed to be at least 100 metres across. "I'm Allan Brinkman."

"Hi, good to meet you and thanks for doing this," said Choy.

"I'm flattered that a journalist as prominent as you would be interested in talking to me," he said, obviously trying to ingratiate himself.

"Hardly prominent," he answered, unable to stop himself from appearing flattered.

"I read your entire series of articles about the Committee of One Thousand — very informative and fair, I thought — and then that book, "Drugged and Dying", well that is simply a masterpiece of contemporary journalism. The story of that young woman is absolutely tragic. You capture the dilemma of contemporary drug policy — what is the best way forward — and I do believe that your book convinced me to take a serious look at the decriminalization of all substances people use to get themselves high."

"Thank you," were the only words that Choy could think of.

"What did you think of the cattle on your drive from the gate? They're my proudest achievement."

"I didn't recognize the breed," said Choy, relieved to change the subject. "And I do know a little about the business because I did a feature about 15 years ago on a Pemberton area rancher who back then was considered one of the best cattle breeders in the country."

"Pemberton? Was the man's name Alf Strand?" asked Brinkman, looking excited.

"You heard of him?"

"Oh my Lord," he said, appearing genuinely thrilled. "You interviewed Alf Strand? He's the reason I got into cattle breeding. He's like the Wayne Gretzky of our industry."

"Is he still active?" said Choy. "He must have been at least 70-years-old when I sat at his kitchen table."

"He died a few years back, but there's now an award named after him for Canadian breeder of the year," said Brinkman, shaking his head. "I can't believe you interviewed Alf Strand. Now I'm even more honoured that you're going to interview me."

Choy looked at his feet, embarrassed at how easily he had fallen prey to the oldest of all interview tricks, softening up the interviewer with praise. "So what breed is it in the pasture beside the road?" he asked, needing to create some space to get the discussion back on his track.

"Doesn't have a name yet," he said. "They're a cross between Argentine Criolla and Ankole."

Choy lifted his shoulders to indicate he had heard of neither breed.

"As the name indicates, the Criolla is from South America, Argentina, the Pampas, and are descendants of the cattle brought to the Americas by the conquistadores, adapted for 500 years to those grasslands. The Ankole are from Africa, around the Great Lakes region — got my bull from Uganda — and have existed in that part of the world for thousands of years. Both are good for meat and milk. Both are tremendously well adapted to their environment, with extremely stable genetics, so I'm hoping their offspring will be the sort of low maintenance, versatile, but relatively high productivity creatures that will be necessary as we adapt to climate change."

An extreme right wing oilman who acknowledges global warming?

"There's already a growing demand for sustainable products from animals that integrate well into their environment. The milk from this cross has a very high butter fat content and makes an extremely tasty grass-fed steak, all on less pasture land than any other widely raised breed, and with those massive horns they can defend themselves against most predators, so they can be safely left out on the range for much greater periods of time as wolves reclaim their rightful place as top predator on the land."

An extreme right wing oilman environmentalist?

"I'm impressed."

"By what?" asked Brinkman. "The cattle or …"

"Never ran into a funder of extreme right wing causes who acknowledges global warming and talks like an environmentalist." Choy said calculating that a turn back to the subject of politics would allow him to regain control of the interview.

"You're impressed by a right winger who actually acknowledges the reality of the world we live in?"

"Something like that."

"Or is it that you are impressed when a conservative doesn't fit the stereotype the liberal media has created for us?"

"Also possible," answered Choy.

"What if I told you that it's simply good business to make preparations just in case your enemies are right? That I don't believe in global warming at all, but am hedging my investments?"

"I'd say that was a more believable explanation than the alternative."

Brinkman smiled and turned to the stairs that led up to a wrap-around verandah. "Please join me for a lemonade or iced tea and we can get this interview underway."

"Sounds wonderful."

Choy started with questions about his family background and sources of wealth. The answers seemed honest and complete, even if they were tinged with a hint of resentment over the intrusion into his private affairs.

"I'm told you were actually quite liberal, maybe even left wing in your youth."

"It's true."

"What happened to change your mind?"

"Life," Brinkman answered. "Growing up. Reading. Thinking."

"Tamara Lind told me you changed after your mother died."

"Tamara has always insisted on psychological explanations for everything that happens in life," he said, looking somewhat nostalgic at the mention of her name. "It's true that in my youth I re-acted very badly to my mother and father's view of the world. I was rebellious, mostly as a matter of principle. They were prominent Conservatives, so I decided to be a socialist. My father died when I was 14, which only reinforced my leaning to the left. He was one of the pioneers of the oil sands and Tamara showed me pictures of a moon-like landscape, to which I reacted very badly, becoming a so-called environmentalist. To borrow from Tamara's psychological jargon, I was mad at my father for abandoning me, i.e. dying, and becoming a socialist environmentalist was my way of expressing that anger. It wasn't until after my mother died six years ago, that I was forced to grow up, become responsible, run my companies, see the world for how it actually is instead of what some people want it to be."

"What do some people want it to be?"

"Fair, kind, gentle, loving, logical."

"And it is none of those things?"

"If you have ever tried running a business you will know the answer to that question."

"So, in reality the world is … what?" said Choy, finally feeling more in control.

"A competition in which the strong survive and sometimes prosper. You may wish it wasn't so, but that's how it is."

"Are you another rich guy Ayn Rander?"

"I have read and enjoyed Ayn Rand's books, but I'm afraid her view of the world is as idealistic as the worst socialists. There's no pure capitalism; never has been and never will be. Smart or hard working people are not necessarily rewarded. We live in a fundamentally unequal society and all these utopian ideologies — capitalism, socialism, anarchism, communism — fail to understand and accommodate that reality."

"What do you mean by a 'fundamentally unequal society'," said Choy, whose goal was now to keep Brinkman talking.

"People are not created equal," he answered. "Why does that sound so shocking when we all know it's true? Some of us are smart, some of us are dumb and most of us are somewhere in the middle. A few of us are gifted physically, some are disabled and most of us are somewhere in the middle. Some of us are wealthy and most of us are poor. As a result there never was and never will be equality of opportunity, let alone equality of performance. If you base the premise of your philosophy on anything other than this reality, you are building a structure that is bound to collapse, killing millions, as we have seen when communists or other idealists have actually gained power."

"So you don't believe in idealism. What is the alternative?"

"Realism, of course. We accept the world the way it is, not expect it to become something wished for."

"But what does realism mean? People see such different things when looking at the same picture, so how can there be only one reality? And isn't arguing that we should accept 'the world the way it is' awfully self-serving for someone as rich and powerful as you obviously are?"

Brinkman smiled and said: "We are all self-serving, that is a reality everybody must understand."

Choy thought of challenging this assertion by saying something about raising children or anthropological evidence that cooperation, not competition, was the key to human survival and evolution, but didn't. While argument can be a useful interview technique, in his experience most people reveal their innermost thoughts only when speaking to people they think might agree with them. While not true for those who think they are smarter than everyone and try to prove it through debate, most people become guarded when challenged, so the safest approach is to simply ask questions that draw people out.

"So how does realism and an understanding that we are all self-serving lead you to provide funding for Baxter Media and anti-environmental groups and a right wing militia group like the Three Percenters?"

"While we almost certainly wouldn't agree with each other regarding the characterization of the politics of these groups, your question is how my general philosophical views have become translated into actual political activity? Is that correct?"

"Yes."

He remained silent for a half minute. "Perhaps the best way to answer your question is by telling a story about cattle breeding."

Choy tried to smile, but the thought of this rich 'kid', barely past 40, telling a story to illustrate a political lesson like some father-of-Canadian-Medicare Tommy Douglas or Honest Abe Lincoln wannabe, kept a frown on his face.

"Cattle will breed perfectly fine on their own with no human intervention," Brinkman continued, ignoring Choy's obvious displeasure. "Bulls will mount any cow and a cow in heat will accept any bull. Over the medium and long run that will inevitably lead to, if you let nature take its course, a diffusion of special characteristics, a mongrelisation that is the triumph of the mediocre, the average, the ordinary, over the extraordinary. On the other hand, with the intervention of an intelligent breeder, we have created special animals that gain weight much quicker than average, produce more milk than normal, have a much higher butterfat content to their milk than the run of the mill cow, tolerate certain types of feed much better than an ordinary animal — the miracle of selective breeding has resulted in an abundance of reasonably priced dairy and beef products, to the general benefit of humankind."

Is this story headed where I think it is?

"Nature taking its course is like the demands for equality, which only leads to mongrelisation and the triumph of the mediocre."

"Are you saying we need the selective breeding of human beings?" The tone of Choy's voice was critical, tending towards sarcastic, despite his best effort to remain a neutral interviewer.

"In certain circumstances that might not be a bad idea, but that's not what I'm talking about at all," answered Brinkman. "You're missing my point."

"Which is?"

"My point is that the economy and human society in general, need the interventions of intelligent human beings to maximize our potential. The randomness of nature, the effect of 'equality for all' is mediocrity and stagnation."

"So you'd prefer to replace equality for all with an oligarchy?"

"Come now, you don't really believe we live in a society with equality for all?" Brinkmann said, sneering. "Or is that your idealism speaking? We have an economic and political system dominated by the interests of a relatively small number of wealthy people, that's reality. And it has worked out very well for most of us in this country over the past 150 years. We have one of the world's highest standards of living, our life expectancy and general health is top notch — sure we have our problems, but they won't be solved by more equality and socialism. Rather, we need to understand what has worked well for us in the past and learn from that in order to build a better future."

As often happened when Choy took notes and tried to follow someone's argument, he was a few sentences behind in his reaction. "So you're saying the system in Canada, the USA, the so-called western liberal democracies, has never been real democracy? It's always been more of an oligarchy?"

"What is it with you people in the media always needing labels? I never used the words 'oligarchy' or 'democracy' and I'm not sure I even know what they mean. You use these words to scare people, but I'm not playing along with your game."

This was the first time Brinkman raised his voice, which worried Choy because he had not even gotten to the subject he most wanted to discuss. He decided to back off, rather than to press ahead. "I'm just trying to clarify what you meant, but if you'd rather not use those words, I can respect that. I'm really not here to do a hatchet job. I want my readers to understand what you say, what you do and what you believe."

"Do you find with many people that believing, saying and doing are different?" said Brinkmann, appearing intrigued by this question. "Words, actions and ideas that are at odds with each other?"

"Honestly? Yes. Especially with people involved in politics. They often say one thing and do something very different, which leads one to understand their ideas are at odds with their words."

This explanation brought a smile to Brinkman's face and he offered a friendly pat on the arm to demonstrate his approval. "Of course you are right, but you don't have to worry about that with me. I rejected Leo Strauss and esoteric writing years ago, although if I were still a Straussian, it might suit me to deny it."

He watched as the guy's smile grew into a grin; apparently Brinkman thought himself clever to say, 'careful, I might be a liar' without really saying it. But rather than confront him, for the sake of the interview, Choy changed the subject.

"I'd really like to get a sense of what you believe, especially as it relates to the groups you choose to fund. For instance, the

Three Percenters seem to promote a very male-centred point of view. And Baxter Media often attacks feminists and LGBT activists. Would you describe yourself as a traditionalist when it comes to sexuality and gender roles?"

"The life expectancy of White males has been dropping in this country because men have been taught to be embarrassed about who they are. Do I think that is a problem? I certainly do."

"I think you are quoting American statistics," said Choy. "I've never read anywhere that life expectancy for White Canadian males has fallen."

"What happens in America, always eventually happens here as well," he answered, annoyed at the challenge to his 'facts'. "The suicide rate for males in Canada has gone up, that I'm certain of, and it is because we are constantly told being a man is a problem. Radical Feminazis have undermined the very fabric of family life and left our society adrift. That's why we have such high rates of drug use, divorce, abortion and mental illness."

"That's all the fault of radical feminists?"

"Men and women have lost their way because the glue that held our families together has been weakened by the socialists and communists and Marxists who have taken over the so-called women's movement, infiltrated our universities and have long been trying to destroy our way of life, including the family. Don't believe me? Read their own literature. They proclaim loudly and clearly their aim is to destroy the family. You ask me if I am a traditionalist when it comes to gender roles and the family? You might as well ask me if I'm a traditionalist when it comes to oxygen. If it disappeared can you imagine the trouble the world would be in? Life itself would disappear. Well, the same is true of the family. So-called traditional values are the oxygen that allows the family to breathe and live."

"Okay," said Choy, making a show of writing in his notebook. 'Traditional values are the oxygen that allows the family to breathe and live.' But now I'd like to turn to what you do. I'm curious about the utility of using what some call misogyny as an organizing tool. Has it been a conscious decision on your part to direct your funding to groups that seem to focus on attracting men? Especially young ones?"

"I hadn't really thought of that before," he answered. "But now that you put it this way, yes, I can see it is true. So, the answer is no, it was not a conscious decision, but it is a good thing. Young men have energy, commitment and stamina. They make the best cowboys and the best soldiers. I like to think I am playing a small part in building a movement based on the values of cowboys and soldiers. Order, respect, honour, hard work, a willingness to sacrifice — these are the building blocks of a healthy society."

"Cowboys and soldiers?" repeated Choy. "Can you see how some people might be made a little nervous when someone from the far right talks about building a movement based on the values of cowboys and soldiers? That they might see images of stormtroopers in brown uniforms?"

"I don't care what the degenerate lying liberal media says about us, calling us neo-Nazis and other names. Fighting for freedom and truth has always meant being called names by the rich and powerful."

Choy couldn't help his response; the question just popped out. "Aren't you rich and powerful?"

His glare was brief and then turned into a smug smile. He looked like he was considering a response, then changed his mind. A frown momentarily appeared, but finally the smile returned.

"The government could pass a law tomorrow that destroys my business and confiscates all my wealth," he answered. "Compared to that how powerful am I?"

Except that you've already admitted rich people own the government, thought Choy, but didn't say it. Brinkmann was not the first rich person he had interviewed who enjoyed playing David up against some mythical Goliath government. In his experience they did not react well to reasoned challenge. If he wanted the interview to continue, it was best to ignore the obvious huge hole in the rich guy's argument.

So Choy returned the smile, as if he agreed with the point made, because he wanted to continue asking questions, hopefully revealing some nugget of information that would lead to the 5Ws of what happened to Emma Murphy. But despite his effort, or lack thereof, the next hour of his life was filled with shallow alt-right pontification on subjects ranging from how the environmental movement was a communist conspiracy to undermine capitalism all the way to how evolution was just a theory, an opinion no more believable than the Book of Genesis in the Bible, a position argued even though Brinkmann claimed he was not particularly religious. In other words, the man was a stereotype of the extreme right, a not-so-bright rich guy who thinks he is extremely clever and acts as a money bag, buying defenders of wealth and privilege who are even less bright because they believe themselves to be fighting against 'the system' and cannot see how they are being used by those who actually run it. Except for marvelling how this 200-year-old right wing scam continued to work so well, Choy felt like he had learned nothing useful. His mood was sour and his expectations low when he thanked Brinkmann for his time and asked if he could now speak to the Three Percenter head of his security team, as Baxter had promised.

"Yes of course, Mike has been waiting for us to finish," he answered, standing up. "He has listened to the entire interview I'm sure, so you won't need to go over anything we have already covered."

He continued with his rich person's good manners smile for a few seconds.

"He'll be here any second now. His office is not far away."

A few moments later Michael Turner, the "friend" of Brian Grayson and Barry Archibald back in Abbotsford came out of the house.

"Michael Turner meet Waylon Choy," said Brinkman.

8.

"Brinkman's got a half decent head and his heart is in the right place, but sometimes he needs a push to get him going in the right direction," said Turner, all chummy as the two of them walked back towards Choy's car. "I do love your ride. Had my eye on it since back in Mission. You do the restoration yourself?"

"I've got to confess, the thought of being friendly with a prime suspect in the abduction and sexual assault of two women makes me shiver," said Choy, walking a few feet behind, because being near this guy gave him the creeps.

Turner looked back and shrugged. "You're the one who wanted to interview me."

"Why did you and your two buddies do it?" said Choy as he touched Turner's arm and stopped walking to make him turn around. "Was it some kind of gang initiation rite? Those two pathetic losers wanted into your secret neo-Nazi inner circle and you made them kidnap and rape women to prove their unquestioning loyalty? Did you videotape what they did so you can always keep them in line?"

He hoped this was the verbal equivalent of a left-right to the head. Turner made eye contact, but was emotionless for a few seconds, before his annoying smugness returned, the evidence of which was a slight, crooked smile.

"Does Brinkman know about your trip to Vancouver? About your extracurricular activities? I'll bet he wouldn't be too pleased about that kind of publicity."

A boxer never knows exactly which blow is going to cause the most damage. You just keep punching.

"Or is he behind it all? You're just following orders from the new Fuhrer?"

The smugness turned to anger.

"You know nothing at all about me."

"True, but you wouldn't believe how many sources of information you develop over the course of 30 years as a journalist. And with the way people use the Internet nowadays — especially your alt-right, let's announce to the world how tough we are, little kiddies hiding in their parents basements wannabe thugs — it's amazing what my friendly neighbourhood computer geek can find for me." Choy smiled and tried his best to manifest the sort of smugness that spills out of your brain and reveals itself in all corners of your body.

"You don't want to tangle with me," Turner said, his voice menacingly low, while maintaining eye contact.

"You're right," Choy answered quickly. "I don't want to have anything to do with you. Talking with a chickenshit scum rapist like you is the last thing on earth I would choose to do, but c'est la vie, that's the life of a journalist."

The two men stood, eyes fixed on each other, only a few metres from the convertible.

"And yes, I did restore the car myself," said Choy. "I'd offer you a ride, but that car, like Woodie Guthrie's guitar, hates fascists."

He was proud of himself for remembering the story about the great American songwriter's musical instrument of choice. Choy held his smug look for as long as he could then turned and walked to his vehicle. Driving away without looking back at the neo-Nazi almost felt good.

***

"Have you found out anything more about Michael Turner?" Choy said after pulling into a strip mall parking lot in a 1960s neighbourhood of southwest Calgary after his cellphone demanded attention. On the screen he could see the image of Allison Bouchard, sitting in her car.

"What happened?" she responded. "What did you find out?"

"He's the head of security for one of the major funders of extreme right wing causes in Alberta."

"Seriously?" she said, her face scrunched like when he made a play at bridge that surprised her.

He nodded as if she were in front of him instead of a thousand kilometres away. Facetime and other programs like it miraculously transformed a phone conversation into something more like being in the same room with the person you are talking to, although there was still the tangible reality of presence missing.

"Wow," she responded. "You think the rich guy knows what his employee is up to?"

"Hard to believe he doesn't. Did you find out anything more about him?"

"He's definitely well known in Fraser Valley extreme right, White nationalist circles. He started at least two groups over the past few years here in the Valley and I'm told he has connections to some of the biggest, scariest militia groups that try to recruit law enforcement and military south of the border. I've been shown some pretty shocking photos and video."

"Can you send them to me?"

"He's a full-on, hardcore, unapologetic Nazi who is apparently very smart. And did you know he was in the army and the RCMP? Kicked out of the latter."

"Has anyone written about him before?"

"A woman from the University of Toronto who did her psychology PhD thesis last year on three neo-Nazis," answered Bouchard. "The section on Turner is an interesting look at his childhood — grew up in a military family with an alcoholic mother and a father who was a very strict disciplinarian, kind of sad really — but filled with all kinds of psychological theories that I just can't buy into."

"You have a digital copy of that too?"

"Yes and I'll send it as soon as I get off the phone," she answered. "I'm heading to a rendezvous with an Abbotsford cop who I've promised not to name, not even to you. It's taken me over a week to get him to talk and he's extremely paranoid. We're meeting in downtown Vancouver, well, Commercial Drive. Said he doesn't feel safe in the Valley."

"What do you think he's got for you?"

"I'd rather not talk about it on the phone."

"I'm told Facetime is pretty secure," said Choy.

"Maybe on a computer, but I don't trust cellphones."

"Okay."

Better safe than sorry.

"I'm not kidding, or exaggerating, about this Michael Turner," said Bouchard. "The videos he's made, his history, the PhD thesis, all paint a picture of someone who glorifies violence. 'It washes us clean,' I believe is an exact quote. You better be careful."

"You too," he responded quickly.

"My kids are grown up," she said just as quickly.

"Are you saying grandmothers aren't important?"

The two journalists shared a smile on their small screens and a few moments of silence.

"You sure you're comfortable being involved in this?" Choy asked, breaking the thoughtful moment. "Are you sorry you agreed to help?"

"I'm scared," she said, "I'd be lying if I said anything different. But this is also the most exciting story I've worked on in a decade. The last few years at the *Times*, I was mostly rewriting press releases from car dealerships or the Rotary Club or the local MP. This feels like real journalism, something that could make a difference. Expose some very bad people and maybe make where I live a better place. Kind of what I thought journalists were supposed to do. So, no, I am not sorry I agreed to help. It's the best decision I've made in years."

"Good, I'm glad."

"Let's go get these bastards," she said, then pressed the red button on her screen.

Despite the bravado Choy had put on display for Bouchard, he was uncertain about once again confronting angry, violent extreme right wingers. He was scared.

I can't think that way.

He opened the car door and stood in the parking lot.

Chest save drills.

Any passerby would have seen a middle aged man performing a strange dance beside a cool old car and wondered if this was another crazy street person. But one again Choy found the puck choreography strangely settling and invigorating at the same time.

***

As he sat at the desk in the hotel living room reading the PhD thesis emailed to him, his cellphone vibrated. An unknown number.

"Hello, Mr. Choy," said a woman's voice.

"Yes."

"This is Catherine. You might not remember me …"

"The receptionist at Baxter Media?"

"I quit my job today. I just couldn't stand those people anymore."

"I understand. You seemed like the only sane person there."

"Thank you," she said and paused as if she were thinking about how to say something. "It was actually you that made me realize a job wasn't worth the stress I was feeling."

"Oh dear."

"I called to say thank you."

"Well, then you're welcome."

He could sense she had something else to say, but the silence lasted at least ten seconds, which, given the context, was a very long time.

"Would it be possible to meet with you?" she finally said and Choy immediately knew she had some important information for him. Clerical workers and other 'invisible' people are always the best sources for leaks.

"Sure," he answered. "When?"

"Well …"

"Now?"

"That would be best, if you are free."

"I'll make myself free. Where?"

"Do you have a car? Could you pick me up? In front of the old library at 12th and 2nd Street Southwest."

"I know where that is. I can be there in ten minutes."

"Thank you."

"See you soon."

Given that his new hotel was at 8th Street and 14th Avenue Southwest, and traffic was light, Choy pulled up behind the old sandstone library building exactly when he said he would. Within seconds Catherine opened the passenger door to the topless convertible.

"It's a very old car," she said. "But in very good condition."

"A 1965 AMC Ambassador 990. I rebuilt it myself."

"My father worked on a 1953 Chevy for at least ten years, but it's nowhere close to being finished."

"My marriage was breaking up and I had a lot of time on my hands," he answered, then realized he was sending a signal that he was no longer married. "I'm kind of compulsive when it comes to doing stuff or learning a new hobby. This took over my life and I couldn't stop or really focus on anything else until it was done. Probably one of the reasons my wife left me."

Why am I telling her the intimate details of my life?

He knew the answer. He wanted her sympathy.

"Wish I could focus on one thing for more than a couple of days at a time," she answered. "My problem is never finishing what I start. My father is going to tell me that again when he learns I quit my job."

"You live with your father?"

She nodded, obviously embarrassed. "My mother died when I was 14 and my father developed MS when I was 18, so … that's why he never finished restoring the car."

"How long have you been looking after him?"

"A dozen years."

"That must be very hard. How is he doing?"

"Not well. Not well at all. He went into the hospital six weeks ago. That's when I took the job. I don't know if he will ever return home."

"I'm sorry to hear that."

"He's suffered a lot and doesn't want to continue. He's asked me …" her sentence broke off as she looked at Choy. "I don't know why I'm telling you all this, but you seem a sympathetic listener. I could tell when I first met you. You seemed interested in me."

"I try to be a good journalist and a decent human being."

"I haven't seen many of those lately. Good journalists or decent human beings. That office, the reporters, Mr. Baxter, they're all stabbing each other in the back."

Choy looked at her carefully, sensed her uncertainty, then smiled gently, before speaking. "Would you like me to drive somewhere? Take you home? Or we could go for coffee. Something to eat?"

"I am hungry," she answered. "I didn't bring a lunch because I decided last night that it was time to quit. I feel like a hamburger and milkshake."

"Where's your favourite place?"

"Peter's Drive-In," she said quickly, smiling for the first time. "Have you been? The best burger in town. About 50 years ago it won a magazine award as best burger in Canada, my father told me."

"Sounds perfect. Tell me which way to drive."

Ten minutes later they were in a drive-through line and five minutes after that they were parked on a street on the crest of a hill overlooking the oil company towers of downtown Calgary.

"This burger is great," said Choy after biting into the double burger Catherine recommended he order.

"Try the milkshake," she said.

"I've never had banana butterscotch before," he said, then sucked hard to draw up the thick liquid. "Wow, that is good."

"Taste my maple walnut," she said handing him her shake.

They exchanged drinks and as he tasted hers, he smiled again and nodded. "Not sure which I like better."

"We can share."

"Okay."

Choy was feeling good. She seemed to like him and she was nice. A woman who looked after her sick father. How could anyone not be attracted to such a person?

"I've never done anything like this before," she said suddenly looking scared and serious again.

For a moment Choy thought she might be referring to sharing a milkshake with a stranger.

"The jobs before, although always temporary, I've been a good and loyal employee, so it feels sort of strange to do this, but I heard something … I've got to tell someone."

"What did you hear?"

"Someone is planning to plant a bomb."

"Who?"

"I'm not sure, but Mr. Baxter knows. I heard him talking. I was in the big closet inside his office, unpacking his books and the door was mostly closed so he didn't see me when he came back to his desk. He put his cell on speakerphone and that's when I heard the voice talking about an explosion at the Stampede chuckwagon races."

"Someone is going to plant a bomb at the chuckwagon races?"

"I think so."

"Did you recognize the voice?"

She shook her head. "The cellphone speaker is tinny and I was inside the closet, trying not to let on I was there."

"Was it a man?"

"I think so."

"What exactly did he say?"

"I couldn't hear it all, but it was definitely about a bomb at the chuckwagon races. I was going to call the police, but it wasn't a hundred percent clear. Maybe it's some sort of story Mr. Baxter is working on. I don't think so, but …" She let the thought disappear into her self-doubt. "Then I thought of you and you were nice to me and you're a real journalist, so … You seemed trustworthy. What should I do?"

"You did the right thing by calling me," said Choy even though he was unsure what to do with the information.

Does it make sense to involve the police?

"I hope so."

He held out his hand and she grabbed it.

"I won't lie to you and I'll be transparent, tell you anything I decide to do before I do it, okay?"

She nodded.

"This could get complicated because, like you said, it might be a legitimate story Baxter is working on, or at least he could claim that, so we need to be very careful."

She nodded again.

"The first thing to do is record exactly what you remember. You need to think carefully about what you heard and recreate it the best you can. Okay? I have a digital recorder program here on my phone. Can you spend a few minutes gathering your thoughts and putting yourself back in that closet?"

"Okay."

"When you're ready, I'll start asking questions and recording."

One more nod.

***

"Why did you ask to meet me again?" said 'Ginger' Goodwin. "You've found out something important, haven't you?"

"Maybe, but I mostly want to ask your advice," said Choy, as the two men and Rodriguez sat in a Thai restaurant up the hill on 17th Avenue that Goodwin said was good.

"What did you find out?"

"I can't tell you now, maybe later. Right now I need your help."

Goodwin looked at him, obviously annoyed, but still sympathetic and flattered to be asked for assistance.

"Is there a bar or some other place where the Three Percenters hang out?" asked Rodriguez.

"They're planning something, aren't they?" said Goodwin.

"Why do you ask that?" said Choy.

"I've heard some stuff," said Goodwin, once again excited and showing it. "You think you're the only person asking around about who attacked Emma Murphy?"

He smiled at Rodriguez.

"What did you hear?" said Choy.

"I can't tell you now, maybe later."

"This is how you're going to play this? As a competition?"

"You started it."

"No, I simply told you the truth. I heard something from somebody and that person has been promised discretion. A journalist lives or dies depending on how well he protects his contacts."

"Well I heard something from somebody too and that person has also been promised discretion. An Antifa lives or dies depending on how well he protects his contacts."

Choy sighed.

"I saw you in the student union building today," he said to Rodriguez.

The kid has a point, but there's no way I can trust him. His lips are as loose as Mick Jagger's singing onstage in front of a hundred thousand concert goers.

He looked down at his plate and then up at Goodwin. "Okay, you've made your point, but how do we help each other?"

The kid just stared at him with a silly but self-confident half grin glued to his face.

"I'm told there's someone planning an action that involves an explosive device," Choy finally said in a low voice, as he leaned forward across the table.

"A neo-Nazi?" whispered Goodwin.

A quick, almost imperceptible nod was the only response.

"Holy shit!" he mouthed and then looked around the restaurant as if worried someone was listening.

"Your turn," said Choy.

"Nothing near as good as that." He looked around the room once more before continuing. "The fascists have infiltrated our anti-TransMountain Pipeline coalition again. The third time in the past year."

"How do you know?" asked Rodriguez, always eager to participate, despite being told to back off by Choy a half dozen times.

"Let's just say I have sources of information."

"If you have someone inside you need to tell us," said Choy. "It's important."

"You really think you're the only ones who need to keep secrets?"

"Who is the infiltrator?" asked Rodriguez.

"A guy from Vancouver who claims to have a background in animal rights campaigning. My guess is he was an infiltrator there too but was never discovered and did some good work for the coalition there to make it seem he was legit. I'm guessing it was all part of a plan to gain cred before moving here."

"So it had to have been planned for some time?" said Rodriguez.

"They are getting more and more sophisticated. Friends of mine south of the border tell me this sort of thing has been going on down there for a few years and has really ramped up with Trump in power. Rich neo-Nazis hire private security firms to infiltrate environmental groups."

"What are you going to do?" said Rodriguez.

"Expose him as soon as someone from Vancouver uncovers who he really is."

"You sure exposing him is the way to go?" Choy said as an idea floated into his thoughts.

"You think we should play him and see what he does?" said Goodwin.

"Maybe," said Choy. "Isn't it worth considering? Does anyone other than you and your source of information know about him?"

"No. Just learned about it this afternoon and then you called."

Like going from a few chords and a chorus to an entire song, the thought that entered Choy's consciousness had blossomed into an entire opera.

What if a bomb at the Stampede and an animal rights activist infiltrating an anti-pipeline coalition were connected? What if Baxter Media, the Three Percenters and Allan Brinkman had concocted a false flag operation designed to make pipeline opponents look bad? All three would benefit — Baxter out in front of the story, oil companies' opponents made to look bad and the Three Percenters would look justified in preparing for war. It was a certainly a plausible enough theory to exert some effort testing it.

"Why don't you hold off on talking about this with anyone else and I'll get a reporter working with me who knows a lot about right wing groups in B.C. to look into his background?"

"What do you think he's up to?" said Goodwin, who as he spoke thought of something else. "Say you don't think …"

He leaned across the table before continuing. "You don't think the explosive device and the infiltrator could be connected?" he said in a whisper.

The kid is smart, I'll give him that.

Choy shrugged. Rodriguez looked confused.

"Holy shit! That is what you think."

"The infiltrator will be the bomber so that the blame will fall on environmentalists?" Rodriguez asked. "Is that what you think?"

Goodwin nodded and when Rodriguez looked at Choy, his eyes told her that's what he believed as well.

"This is incredible," she said.

"Incredible but maybe true," said Goodwin, putting his hand over hers.

He is definitely flirting with my intern.

"We've got to keep calm and be very careful," said Choy, trying to ignore the romance budding in front of him. "I've dealt with these sorts of people before and close friends have been killed. Journalists have been killed. Innocent people."

"I can't believe it!" she said, both thrilled and scared, while looking intensely at Goodwin.

***

Choy was certain it was a date even though that's not what Goodwin called it. He asked Rodriguez if she was interested in coming with him to meet some people at a bar where his source might be. It was too tempting for Rodriguez to say no. Choy was old enough to be Bal's father, but was not her father or even really her employer. Still, he had to stop himself from asking what time she would be home.

On his walk back to the hotel, in the summer's late evening light, Choy tried to gather his thoughts. How could they monitor this infiltrator? Should they contact the police? If they did, which ones, city or RCMP?

As he walked along a Beltline side street past apartment towers and the occasional old brick or sandstone house, a whitish 'fluff', sort of like an unrefined cotton, covered the sidewalks and swirled in a light breeze. He looked carefully at the old trees lining the street. Cottonwood poplars. He'd written a story about them a long time ago. Cities had once planted the hardy, popular poplars, but they'd gone out of fashion because the 'fluff' they produced as part of their reproductive process was blamed for allergies and some people even claimed it was a fire hazard.

The legacy of decades as a journalist: a head full of moderately interesting, but ultimately useless, factoids.

It was too early to sleep, but too late to visit Emma in the hospital, and Rodriguez had already done that twice today, so he decided to continue walking along 15th Avenue eastward, parallel to the busy commercial strip along 17th Avenue.

How should we deal with the information gathered today?

Reporting what he knew to the police would earn him Brownie points at best and what if the cops had been infiltrated by the Three Percenters? But if he didn't go to the police and tried to deal with this himself? There's no way they could keep a close watch on the infiltrator. Even more important was the morality of allowing someone to potentially plant a bomb; Choy was not prepared to live with that possibility.

On balance, he was leaning towards calling the Calgary cop he had spoken to previously, perhaps feeling him out before actually telling him what they knew. The tricky part would be keeping Catherine out of it. If he didn't offer her up, why would the cops take his story seriously?

When he was less than a block away from his hotel Choy's phone vibrated. It was Goodwin.

"You know how Bal asked me if there was a bar or someplace else the neo-Nazis get together at?" he said, sounding winded.

"Ya?"

"We're at one of those places right now. You care to join us?"

9.

"All of them are Nazis?" said Choy, scanning the other side of the large, crowded poolroom on Edmonton Trail.

Choy had met Rodriguez and Goodwin in the parking lot outside the bar. Both men agreed it would be better if Rodriguez didn't go inside because she would lose her ability to go undercover, which might be very useful, very soon. She was once again displeased and this time resisted, but lost the argument when Choy flagged down a taxi passing by and asked the driver how much the fare would be to their hotel and gave him ten dollars more.

Are we trying to protect her from danger? Of course. Is that sexist? Maybe. Probably.

Neither man spoke about it after she left.

"These ones call themselves Proud Boys, just like the violent assholes in the States they are copying," Goodwin said as they sat and watched.

"Do they hang out here regularly?"

"We have people monitoring their chat room and I got an email while Bal and I were waiting for some people at another bar," said Goodwin. "That's all I know."

"Are they all members?"

"Doubt it. Probably only one or two are actual neo-Nazis. The rest are hangers-on or wannabes."

It was a group of about 20 people, of which only one looked to be a woman. The typical age seemed to be between 30 and 40, but a few were older and younger. They had four pool tables in a corner and the same number of bar tables nearby. From looking at them you wouldn't guess they were neo-Nazis, although some of the men had that brush-cut military look favoured by many on the extreme right.

"Not many women," said Choy.

"Most of these guys are probably incels or serious misogynists, who both hate and are scared of women."

"How do you know that?"

"We read what they write in their chatrooms."

"Were you the one who showed Emma how to get into their chatroom?"

He shook his head. "She figured that out on her own."

"Who is 'we'?"

"The Calgary Anti-Fascist Alliance. We're dedicated to defeating the rise of fascism in this city. We do whatever it takes to make sure these guys don't get a platform to spread their racist, homophobic, anti-trans, anti-Semitic, anti-socialist propaganda."

"'Whatever it takes'. What does that mean?"

"Identifying them, exposing them to the community." He stood. "Can we switch chairs?"

As Choy went along with the request, his tablemate opened a backpack, pulling out a camera.

"A lot of these guys' employers don't know they're neo-Nazis. Same with their landlords and neighbours. So we let people know."

Goodwin began taking photos, which, if anyone was watching, would have appeared to be of the guy across the table from him. "Misogyny is like the gateway drug to the harder stuff, which is fascism," he said, while continuing to shoot. "What you have to understand is that their attraction to the right is all about order and what these guys perceive as the loss of their rights, which are really their privileges — male privilege, cisgender privilege and White privilege. Their road to fascism almost always starts with what they perceive as a disruption to the proper position of males in society. Feminism and LGBTQ rights threaten male privilege, by questioning why the father should be head of a family, by pointing out that gender is not binary and maybe not fixed at all, or by arguing that there may be better alternatives to the nuclear family. This enrages a certain kind of man and if the organized right gets its hands on them while they are feeling that anger — it's not hard to turn male rage into White male rage."

"Blame the immigrants for the fact my father had a better job than I do?" said Choy.

"Something like that. The neo-Nazis offer simple explanations. We say capitalists have gotten greedier and greedier, turned to neoliberalism, drove down wages here by crushing the union movement, destroyed the agricultural economy over there, which, along with climate change, is causing mass migration, and you are living the result. They say it's all the immigrants fault."

"So what do you do to counteract their message?" said Choy. "What do you actually do to combat them?"

Goodwin put his camera back in his backpack, then smiled. "I'll show you."

He stood up, strapped his pack onto his back and started walking towards the other side of the pool hall.

"What are you doing?" said Choy, scared that his companion was about to confront 20 neo-Nazis. "Ginger!"

"Are you coming?" he answered, looking back for a moment.

"Wait," Choy said, trying to catch up. "This is not a good idea. What are you going to do? I'm a journalist. I can't get involved; we don't take sides."

Goodwin, stopped, turned, stared, then sneered. A few moments later he once again walked towards the neo-Nazis. Choy was left standing by himself, trying to decide what to do.

***

"Have you done that many times before?" said Choy as the two men sat in the front seat of his car outside Goodwin's apartment building in Sunnyside, across the Bow River from downtown.

"Ya," he said, nodding and then smiling. "It was fun, wasn't it?"

Choy couldn't help but join in, unable to deny the thrill of 'taking a side' this time. "My heart is still beating faster than normal. Twenty minutes after the confrontation is over and I'll bet it is still 115 beats per second. I must have gotten up to 160 or 170."

"You were running awfully fast," said Goodwin. "You may have broken the world record for the 50-metre-sprint-with-a-half-dozen-Nazis-on-your-tail."

"Well you ran 100 metres in the same time span, what with them chasing you to the other side of the parking lot and then back to my car."

"Fascists give me wings!"

Choy laughed at this twist on the Red Bull energy drink commercials. "The best part was when you stood there yelling at them, calling them 'women-hating, immigrant bashing, Adolph Hitler wannabe, racist fascists who pick on people who can't defend themselves' and all those other people were watching. Then when you say, 'looks to me like everyone in this pool hall is the descendent of an immigrant, even you assholes' and those two women hollered, 'right on', that was the layer of melted chocolate on top of the Nanaimo bar."

"You were pretty good yourself when that big twit with the prison tattoos starts walking towards me saying, 'you're pretty brave for one guy up against all of us' and you step forward, like you're just part of the crowd saying 'my grandfather fought a war to defeat fascist, racist Nazis like you and so did the grandfathers of most people in this room, so he isn't one guy against all of you — he's got the backing of all of us' and like 30 people start cheering."

"It just came out in the heat of the moment," Choy said, proud of himself. "But it worked out well, especially when the manager comes up and tells them he doesn't want their kind in his pool room anymore."

"Too bad he didn't kick them out of his parking lot as well," said Goodwin smiling.

"They would have kicked our asses if that cop car hadn't showed up and scared them off."

"Don't tell anyone else that!"

"It does kind of ruin the ending of a story about two brave Antifas triumphing over dastardly fascists, doesn't it?"

"Let's say 20 of them were waiting outside for us, but we did our best Bruce Lee impersonations and then when that didn't work we outran the bastards to your car," said Goodwin, still enjoying himself. "But we'll say our car was electric or a hybrid at least, not a 1965 gas guzzler extreme planet destroyer."

"You sound like my daughter."

"Your daughter understands the need to sharply reduce the use of private automobiles if we are to ever save the planet?"

"Something like that," said Choy. "Or she just loves to give her old man the gears."

"Either way, if you have a daughter like her, I should take back all the bad things I said about you."

"What bad things?"

"I forget the exact wording of a very long list, but there was some pretty nasty stuff."

After the two men enjoyed a few seconds of laughter, silence erupted under the star-lit sky.

"I had a good time," said Choy. "But in my experience there's not a lot of happy endings when dealing with these sorts of people."

"Emma is proof of that."

"We need to talk tomorrow to decide what to do with our information."

Goodwin answered with a vague nod that turned into a scrunch of his nose and lips.

"Can you meet me for breakfast?"

"I've got an early class, but I'll be free by about 11, so an early lunch, if you're buying?"

"Sure," said Choy. "I had my first Peter's Drive-In burger today and I'm thinking about a repeat performance tomorrow, or later today, whatever the case may be. Can I pick you up?"

"Mostly I don't eat meat," he answered. "But I do like their shakes and onion rings, so it's a date. Pick me up here at 11:30."

"I'll bring Bal, unless she has something else planned."

"That would be perfect," he said, smiling.

***

Choy and Rodriguez parked in front of Goodwin's apartment building at 11:20, waited fifteen minutes and then phoned him, but the call was not picked up. Buzzing his apartment produced no response. After another half hour of waiting, more calls and messages, Rodriguez phoned the Department of Sociology.

"He was supposed to lead a seminar this morning, but didn't show up," said the department secretary. "It's not like him at all. He's certainly never missed a class before and I haven't been able to reach him."

As they digested the news, Choy realized what needed to be done. He searched his contacts list for Peter Sullivan, the Calgary police detective who first called him about Emma.

The cop looked exactly as imagined, 50ish, overweight, a reluctant wearer of suits who had a permanently dour visage. The frown on his face grew as he listened to the story about Goodwin's disappearance, the confrontation with neo-Nazis the previous night, a warning about a bomb attack on the Stampede and how it was all connected to Emma Murphy's attack.

"Well, you have an active imagination, I'll give you that," Sullivan said when Choy and Rodriguez ran out of things to say. "And you sure as hell don't look Chinese. Or you Mexican/Indian."

The cop stared at them from across the hotel suite's living room.

"That's all you have to say?" said Rodriguez.

"No, but it will do for now," he answered, obviously seeing himself as a Humphrey-Bogart-type, tough guy wit.

"You're not going to do anything?" she said.

"About?"

"A graduate student missing after a confrontation with neo-Nazis," she said. "A possible conspiracy to plant a bomb at the Stampede. The beating, almost to death, of Emma Murphy by the same crowd of people a week ago."

"For all we know this graduate student, who you admit was the instigator of the confrontation with your so-called neo-Nazis, may have met a girlfriend and they are shacked up in a love nest somewhere."

Choy noticed Rodriguez's reaction to this, confirmation that she was interested in Goodwin.

"If you're any kind of a journalist you know we don't act on missing persons reports for at least three days unless there's a damn good reason. And, who is to say this 'possible conspiracy to plant a bomb' isn't just a way for you guys to get the police to hassle some people you disagree with politically? You offer no proof other than a supposed statement by some unknown person who you say is well connected. As for the assault on Emma Murphy, I have spent many hours investigating that crime and resent you implying I have done nothing."

"That's how you're going to play this?" said Choy.

"I never play."

The two men stared at each other.

"I never said I was Chinese," said Choy after a few seconds of silence. "You made an assumption based on incomplete and obviously insufficient information."

"Exactly what you're asking me to do with this missing person and so-called bomb."

More staring.

Perhaps the cop has a point.

"And my grandfather was Chilean and my mother Irish but loved Bollywood movies," said Rodriguez. "I got the first name from her favourite actress."

Choy decided to back down again because they needed this cop on their side. "I understand why you thought I was Chinese and why you can't actually do anything based on the information I have given you, given the circumstances," he said. "I know you guys have rules and procedures that need to be followed."

The staring stopped as both men instead looked at their feet for a few seconds.

"Does it annoy you I thought you were Chinese?" Sullivan finally said.

"I'm proud of that part of my heritage, but my whole life people have tried to define me by my name."

"Kind of like me being a cop and people assuming that makes me a certain kind of person. I've always been annoyed by that."

Choy had to admit, to himself at least, that he was guilty as charged. He did stereotype cops and had done so with this one in particular.

This guy is smarter than I assumed. Maybe even nicer.

"So, what should we do?" Choy finally asked, trying to sound contrite and forthright. "Ginger can be annoyingly earnest, like he has all the answers to solve every problem in the world, but the Sociology Department secretary says he has never missed teaching a class before and as for this bomb thing, I only told you because it seemed the right thing to do. We could try to expose these assholes ourselves, but we don't have the police's resources and I'd feel terrible if they actually blew something up and people were hurt."

Sullivan nodded.

"What's your advice?" Choy asked a second time.

The wait for his answer was short. "Talk to whoever your source is about the bomb and convince them to talk to me. If there is a credible threat of course we'll … And I'll check around about Goodwin, see if there were any reports of suspicious behaviour this morning near his apartment or the university. Does he take the C-Train?"

"I don't know, but he doesn't have a car."

"I'll check into the Sunnyside station. We have a new facial recognition program."

"Do you need a picture of him?"

"We've got lots of those," said Sullivan, winking.

What does he mean?

"What do you mean?" Rodriguez verbalized.

"Let's just say he's known to us and is not the most popular guy in certain circles."

"You got a file on him but not the right wingers?" said Rodriguez indignantly.

"I never said that," he answered quickly, but then after a moment added, "Like I told Choy the first time we spoke, I'm a guy who leans to the right politically, but that doesn't interfere with my duty to uphold the law. I can't say that's true of everyone in the department."

Choy, based on experience, understood what he was saying. Some cops were sympathetic to the extreme right.

***

When Choy phoned the number Catherine had given him she didn't answer so he left a message that it was important they talk. Rodriguez had gone for a walk 'across the river,' which he assumed meant looking for Goodwin. He decided that a walk to clear his head was not a bad idea. After 15 minutes he found himself near the building where Baxter Media was located. On a whim he decided to see if Baxter was there. The pretext for the visit could be to thank him for arranging the interview with Brinkman and that might morph into chitchat about the Three Percenters and the Proud Boys. Perhaps he could ask if there was any connection between the two groups. Ask for expert help on understanding the nuances of various alt-right groups. Maybe offer to buy him coffee or a late lunch. One never knew when some crumbs of useful information might fall from a Tim Hortons table.

When he got to the receptionist's desk, the older woman sitting there smiled and said: "How may I help you?"

"Is Peter in?" Choy asked.

"I'm afraid he's gone for the day. Can I take a message?"

"Could you tell him that Waylon Choy dropped by to say hello."

"Waylon Choy?" she repeated.

"Tell him I just wanted to chat, nothing important."

She looked up at him and then down at her notepad as if wishing he would go away.

"You just start working here this week?" he said, trying to be friendly.

"I've worked for Baxter Media since it began three years ago," she answered. "Mr. Baxter and I are the original team."

What does this mean?

"I was in here a few days ago and Catherine was working here," said Choy.

"Kate? Peter's wife, she was helping out with the move. I had a terrible cold so I missed a few days. Poor dear was a lifesaver. She took time off from her own job and absolutely rescued us."

"Great to have a job where you can do that," said Choy, probing further.

"Well, she owns her own public relations firm, works mostly for oil companies and you know how our horrible socialist provincial government has undermined industry confidence, so she hasn't been that busy lately."

He nodded as if agreeing.

"She said something about her father's health," he added.

"Yes, he has deteriorating multiple sclerosis. An awful disease. She's a saint the way she looks after him."

Saints don't lie and try to set up people.

"I had a good friend whose father had MS and all the time she spent with him was very hard on her marriage," said Choy, who felt like truth was an object of derision in this office. "I hope Catherine and Peter aren't going through anything similar."

"Those two lovebirds? You don't have to worry about them. They see eye to eye on absolutely everything. I've never met a couple who complement each other more than them."

"I am so relieved to hear that," said Choy. "Well, it has been nice chatting with you and once again tell Peter I dropped by to say hello."

"I will," she said smiling.

"Thanks and nice meeting you," he said, holding his hand out.

"Denise, Denise Tomkins," she answered, shaking his hand.

"Hopefully I'll see you soon Denise."

"That would be nice," she answered as he opened the door into the hallway.

Damn, piss, shit, he said to himself, hopefully not audible to others. He repeated the curses, while shaking his head as he waited for the elevator.

They played me for a sucker and I swallowed the bait so hard the hook came out through my gills.

Then he had a further revelation of possible sucker-hood. What if Goodwin was the real right wing infiltrator into the left and environmental movements in Calgary? What if everything Ginger and Catherine said and did was part of a plan to make him look like a crazy person to the police? If it was their plan, it had certainly worked.

What the hell do I do now?

***

"I checked with an old friend of mine who works intelligence for the RCMP in Vancouver and he says you're not crazy," said Detective Sullivan. "You're a journalist who doesn't much trust cops, but you're not crazy. He also says you've done some good work in recent years uncovering information about corruption and illegal activities in both American and Canadian police forces, so I guess you have good reason not to trust us."

"Honestly, I'm getting to the point where I don't trust anyone," said Choy. "And I tell you it's not a good place to be." He was mostly just grateful this cop had not laughed when he told him the story of being set up. "I can't believe I fell for their story."

"You did the right thing by calling me immediately," said Sullivan. "Most people would be more concerned with looking like a fool to the police than telling the truth."

"That was my first reaction, but then I asked myself what a good journalist would do. And the answer was make a timely correction. We all make mistakes, but what sets off the good journalist from the bad or mediocre is being more concerned with the truth than how you might look."

"You just made that up, those thoughts never entered your mind before you called me, did they?" said Sullivan, smiling.

"No," answered Choy feeling like a cat with the canary's tail feather sticking out of its mouth, "but they should have."

"Life is one long line of should haves," the detective said, back to being serious.

"Shouldn't there be less of them as you get older. Don't we learn from our mistakes?"

Sullivan frowned and shook his head.

"Me neither," said Choy.

"I have four daughters and I'm making the same mistakes with the last one as I did with the first."

"Four? Geez, one is tough enough. My daughter is great, but I really don't understand her. My son makes a whole helluva lot more sense to me."

"Wish I had a son."

"Would you trade one of your daughters for a son?"

The grizzled old cop thought about this for a few seconds and then shook his head. "No, I would not and the idea of having another baby around the house scares the bejesus out of me, so I guess that means I'm satisfied with what we've got."

The two men smiled at each other again.

"Four daughters," said Choy, thinking about a cop as a father rather than just a symbol of authority. "Must be hard to work on a case like Emma's."

Sullivan nodded. "I hate anything bad involving young women. You realize how many shithole men there are in the world. Sometimes I think maybe a young woman like Emma, you know, a lesbian, has made a smarter choice. Be safe, stay away from men."

"I hear you."

Not that this strategy worked for Emma.

The silence was broken by the detective's guffaw before he spoke. "Listen to us, two cuddly papa bears. Holy shit, what's this job doing to me? Thirty-one years as this goddamn city has gotten bigger and bigger and meaner and meaner."

"Retire like me, take whatever money they offer you and run straight to doing whatever you want, whenever you want."

"With four daughters and a wife who has never worked outside the home? No way. I got to keep bringing in a paycheque until my youngest is finished school. That's what you sign on for when you stick your dick in without protection, as my old man would often say."

This is a good guy. Maybe I should have talked like this with cops before.

"Besides, I only figured out how to do this job right a few years ago," Sullivan continued. "Now that I have enough experience, there's an obligation to use it, don't you think?"

"Sort of why I continue to stick my nose into places where people don't want it. Only in my case it's a lot easier to do the job right when I don't have a boss, or a paycheque."

"You're financially independent?"

"Only if I don't think about it," he answered. "But I know my kids will be well looked after because their mother is a successful lawyer."

"Jesus H. Christ, I take back all the nice things I said about you. A fucking reporter married to a fucking lawyer. There's no fucking way I can be friends with you."

"We're divorced. And you're only called a reporter when you work for someone else. I work for myself, so I'm an independent journalist, just another name for an unpaid snoop."

"And you got kids?"

"Sixteen year-old girl and a 13-year-old boy."

"Okay then, I won't hold an ex-lawyer against you. If you got some alcohol. It's past quitting time and I could really use a drink."

"There's beer in the fridge. Help yourself."

"Don't mind if I do."

The hotel suite had a small kitchen a few steps from the detective's chair.

"Do you want one?"

"Why not."

"Oh, I can give you a hundred reasons to say no," came the response, along with two beers. "But that would be coming from a guy whose family is riddled with drunks."

"Gambling is the addiction of choice in my family," said Choy, reaching for a can.

"I respect a gambler. Take a risk to win something. At least a gambler has the possibility of doing well, making a big score. What good ever comes from being a drunk?"

"No good ultimately comes from being a gambler either, trust me on that one."

"You're a gambler too though, aren't you? You risk your life by writing about these Nazis. When you investigate them, you don't have the protection of a badge and you're not carrying a gun. Or are you?"

Chow shook his head. "The only firearm I ever touched was a pellet gun when I was 10 and visited my cousin in Moose Jaw. But you're right about the gambler part, risking my life to write a story. I've thought a lot about that in the past few years. It is a rush, probably very similar to what my father gets when he bets a grand on a hockey game."

The detective took a long guzzle of beer and then looked straight ahead, as if he were embarrassed for his partner in discussion. Then he lifted his can to make a toast. "To fathers who shape us, even if we swear we're never going to turn out like them."

"To fathers."

"You want to know the real reason I can't retire?" said Sullivan. "Because I'm afraid with nothing to do I'll be hoisting beers like this by noon every day, just like my old man."

Choy looked at the cop he had considered an enemy a short while before, nodded and offered a sympathetic smile.

After a few moments of silence, Sullivan said, "Piss on it, I'm going to do it. And not because we've become all buddy buddy, but because you might be able to help me."

"You're going to do what?"

"I'm going to tell you what my investigation has uncovered in the matter of the assault on Emma Murphy and certain other matters."

Is this what comes from treating a cop like a fellow human being?

10.

After calling Rodriguez, who was at the university, to tell her what he had learned from Sullivan, Choy's laptop began ringing, a notification that someone was calling on Facetime. It was Bouchard.

"You won't believe what I just learned," he said, upon seeing her face on the screen.

"Me too," she responded, staring back at him. "But you go first."

"You feel comfortable now on Facetime between two laptops?" said Choy.

"I'm told it is as secure as you can get, which might not be saying much, but what choice do we have?"

"The Calgary cop, Detective Sullivan opened up to me."

"Opened up?"

"We're friends now and I'm not just saying that. I like the guy. He is down to earth and takes his job seriously. He's funny and entertaining. He's got four daughters and he's really bothered by how women are treated in this world."

"Never thought I'd hear Waylon Choy talk like that about a cop. Please tell me the guy is also an evangelical Christian. That would be absolutely perfect."

"No, just a good Irish Catholic."

"Close enough! Waylon Choy is friends with a church-going cop! Amen to that!"

"Now that you've had your fun can I tell you what I learned?"

"I'm listening."

"The guy Sullivan thinks beat Emma with a hockey stick is named Charles Dobson. He was posting in the incel chatroom that Emma infiltrated, telling the guys how he gets girls by using date rape drugs and being a real man; he attends the University of

Calgary; he's president of some far right political club there and, get this, he worked on the leadership campaign for the current head of the opposition in Alberta."

"Simon Henry? The former federal cabinet minister?"

"The very one."

"Why did this detective let you in on this?"

"Sullivan thinks his investigation is being obstructed. Pressure from on high."

"So he spills some of the story your way because he wants a reporter poking his nose into this Charles Dobson to stir things up, make the people blocking the investigation back off?"

"Exactly."

"So, your new best buddy, the cop, is using you and that's okay?"

"I'm using him, he's using me, you know the drill, that's how it works," said Choy, who could see from Bouchard's face on the laptop screen that she was upset. "If he gives me what I came to Calgary for, does the price I pay ultimately matter?"

"A cop trying to manoeuvre around his superiors, using you as bait to expose some extreme right wing thug connected to a politician who everyone says will be the next Premier of Alberta? And you add in what I learned from the only cop with a conscience in Abbotsford."

"Which is?"

"My source tells me there's a strong probability that the leader of the extreme right in the Fraser Valley is, in fact, working for the RCMP, which in itself might be good news, except for the fact I'm told he has gone rogue."

"Turner?"

"I wasn't told that directly, but who else can it be?"

"What does it mean that he's gone rogue?"

"What I was told is he was always a serious right winger and he joined the RCMP because he wanted to recruit inside Canada's most important police force, but the Mounties never picked up on this, or didn't care even though he openly tried to get other recruits to join the Three Percenters. The brass knew exactly what he was doing. They knew he was a hardcore right-wing White nationalist but thought they could control and use him to gain intelligence on the extreme right on both sides of the border. My source doesn't know for sure but thinks CSIS and maybe even the FBI are involved as well. Anyway, Turner is now acting way too independently for some, but there's a battle inside the Mounties, with some bigwigs supporting him and others who see the need to go into damage-control mode by disowning the whole operation. And if that isn't a big enough mess, turning this into a cluster bleep of epic proportions is the fact that a certain high ranking Abbotsford city police officer's nephew was sent in undercover to check out Turner, before they knew he was RCMP."

"Barry Archibald is a plant by the cops?"

"A spectacularly stupid one, according to my source."

"What on earth have we stumbled into?" said Choy. "This could be the police fuck-up exposé of the century."

"And a sure fire way of getting us both get killed," answered Bouchard. "Can you think of something to investigate that would put a bigger red target on both our backs? Plus the guys mad at us have guns and the means to cover up their crimes."

"I've been lied to and set up by these people; they've abducted and sexually assaulted two women that we know about; they almost certainly beat another young woman so badly she may never regain consciousness; and now we learn there may be cops involved. How the hell can we not write about this?"

Bouchard looked both frightened and embarrassed. "I'm not saying we drop the story. But we've got to be careful. I've always had friendly relations with the police and now ..."

"I understand. I do. I've been through this before. Cops and violent neo-Nazis, who just might be one and the same. It destroys your illusion of who to call when you're in danger. Worse maybe, it destroys your ability to believe 'the authorities' are telling the truth. If they can lie about a few things, why not everything? Trust me, I hope none of what we've been told about this is true, but what if it is? Don't we have an obligation to find out?"

"I wondered why you seemed so worried about my commitment to chasing this story," said Bouchard. "I thought you were questioning my commitment to journalism, but now it's obvious you somehow knew we would get to this point."

"I didn't know, but it doesn't surprise me either."

"You were questioning my commitment to risking my or my family's lives."

"You can't think that way."

"But I am and how do you put that cat back in the suitcase?"

Two friends staring at each other via computer screens a thousand kilometres away from the other, each needing to decide how important a good story was to them.

"I won't be upset if you decide to back away," said Choy, offering an easy way out. "If you want, you can help in the background. I've got an intern now and she's good. Impulsive, but a real go-getter. Ironic, eh, me complaining about an intern being impulsive?"

Bouchard did not react to his words, not a smile, nothing. He knew what she was going to say next.

"Maybe backing off would be best," she said. "I'm … it's just that … but …"

"Don't worry about it. You've done amazing work."

"I'm sorry."

He sat at the desk for half a minute after her face disappeared from his screen. Then he stood up and began doing the butterfly slide drills on the hotel living room carpet, his feet pressed together at the right corner of his imaginary net. Down onto his knees, feet pointing perpendicular to his body. Push to his left along the carpet. Up onto his feet. Move to the left and down to his knees again. Slide to the left corner of his net. Up onto his feet. Repeat moving right.

Maintain your focus even when the puck is in the other team's end.

***

With Bouchard out and Polansky dead he only had one co-investigator and she was an amateur, not even a rookie pro. Choy briefly considered looking for someone else, but he didn't know anyone else in Calgary and had no time to ask around. He would have to rely on himself, plus the information TwoSpiritPhoenix could gather, and hope that Rodriguez was helpful and that 'showing her the ropes' — must be derived from sailor talk — was not too distracting. He decided to call her.

"Bal," he said, "what are you up to?"

"I'm still at the university. There's an event taking place this evening on campus where I'm almost certain to meet this Charles Dobson. It's a social put on by the conservative club he belongs to."

"Good work," he said, but then thought about Bouchard's concern for safety. "Listen, don't stick your head up too much, okay? If what Sullivan says about him is true, this guy is dangerous."

"He's a spoiled rich kid and a bully."

"With ties to undercover cops and neo-Nazis. I just got off the phone with Bouchard who is backing off from the story because she thinks working on it is too risky."

"That's too bad," Rodriguez answered. "But the key to uncovering the rest of the story is here in Calgary, not back in the Lower Mainland."

She's definitely smart and has good instincts.

"I agree, but Bouchard is right about the danger."

"I've worked lots of shifts in the VGH emergency room," she answered. "You learn pretty quickly not to be intimidated by violent people or you find another place to work."

"Be careful, that's all I'm saying."

"Thanks to you and Ginger, none of these Nazis know who I am. They'll treat me like any girl who comes to a party."

"Exactly what I'm afraid of."

"I can handle myself."

"What's your plan?"

"Go to the event, tell people I'm enrolled as a graduate student next semester and am in town looking for a place to stay. I saw the poster and decided to go. Try to meet this Charles character, then see what happens."

"Remember this is a kid who discusses the use of date rape drugs on the Internet and counsels incels to 'be a man and take what they want' when it comes to women."

"I'll be careful father."

"I'm serious," said Choy "and I'm not being sexist or ageist or treating you like my daughter. We both signed a contract. One of my responsibilities is to keep you safe and one of your responsibilities it to follow my instructions."

"How about we say the working day is done and I'm going to a party on my own time?"

"Bal, don't …"

"I appreciate your concern, but I can and will look after myself."

"Bal …"

"You can give me instruction about writing, interviewing, research methods or anything else that pertains to being an investigative journalist, but you cannot decide for me who I can talk to or what is too dangerous. I understand you have a daughter who is only a few years younger than me and when you look at me you see her, but that is your problem, not mine."

What can I say?

"These people scare you because stuff happened in the past, but they don't scare me. There have been bullies in my life going all the way back to Grade 1. They sense fear and prey on it. I am not and never have been a victim."

Silence.

"Don't wait up for me. I'll call if I discover something incredible. Otherwise I'll talk to you in the morning."

When she ended the call, Choy was left frustrated and angry, mostly with himself. He should have realized that giving her orders would never work. While he had more experience and hence more insight about these neo-Nazis, he also had lived through the futility of bossing around intelligent, headstrong young women.

From which, apparently, I've learned nothing at all.

Of course, which experiences one chooses to learn from was a topic with a significant psychological literature. He knew this because he wrote a story a decade earlier. A UBC psychologist conducted an experiment that showed experiences which confirmed pre-existing beliefs were much more powerful than ones that went against what a person already believed.

I just confirmed to Bal that men always try to boss her around.

***

Just after 6 a.m. Choy was woken by persistent knocking on the door to the hotel suite. After stumbling out of bed, into the hallway where Bal's bedroom door was closed, he hesitated in front of the exit then pressed his right eye against the peephole. It was Goodwin. He opened the door wide enough to engage the safety latch.

"Waylon, let me in."

"It's 6 a.m. What do you want?"

"Please."

He closed the door in order to remove the chain from the latch holder, then opened it again. Goodwin stood in front of him, unshaven, his jeans covered with dirt, his white shirt from two nights earlier stained purple in spots, his hair matted and sticky.

"Why are you looking at me like you don't want me here?" said Goodwin.

"What happened?"

"They knocked on my apartment door and barged in."

"Who? What are you talking about?"

"The Nazis from the pool hall, about an hour after you dropped me off, they woke me up with their knocking — I thought maybe it was you and something had happened — then pushed me into the living room. There were a half dozen of them, laughing and telling me I'm a commie bastard who is going to pay the price, all kinds of shit and they made me drink something. Next thing I remember clearly I'm somewhere else."

"Jesus," said Choy, motioning for him to enter and directing him to the living room because Bal was still sleeping.

"I think I was tied up inside a car, everything was all out of focus," said Goodwin as he sat on the living room couch. "They took me somewhere, a park, maybe by the zoo, they were laughing. My bum is sore. They stuck a dildo in my ass, I think, or maybe that was a dream."

"We've got to call the police," said Choy.

"No police. I don't believe in the state or police or … The cops wouldn't believe me anyway … I've tried that route before … They're more likely to arrest me than … Pretty sure they injected me with something."

He rolled up his left sleeve to reveal two needle marks.

"No police," Goodwin repeated. "They said I was a commie faggot junkie and the cops were watching me. Said the police were going to find me and my drugs. They put something in my pocket. Everything was kind of in and out of focus or maybe consciousness. How long did they have me?"

"You tell me."

"How long has it been?"

Choy said nothing as he wondered if this might be part of an elaborate set-up.

Seems unlikely. What would be the purpose?

"Was it this morning that you were supposed to pick me up?"

"Yesterday."

"But I wasn't there?"

"You don't sound all here now."

"They drove me in another car. We were in a big room. Then it was dark again and they dropped me in an alley. I must have fallen asleep and then I woke up and there was a couple kissing and when they noticed me started laughing. Then I was walking, a 7-11 and I tried to buy some coffee but there was no money in my pockets, only some drug wrapped in tinfoil. Back on the street, a young woman, on her way to work, gave me her coffee and I drank it. My mind started to clear and I remembered you told me about this hotel and I didn't want to go back to my apartment alone, so I walked here but the desk clerk wouldn't tell me your room number. I argued with him for 20 minutes at the front desk, told him what happened, told him your name and Bal's name and finally he let me come up."

"It may have been your smell," said Choy. "You know what street people who never shower get like? That's you."

Goodwin looked at himself, and then, disoriented and helpless, at Choy.

"You want to take a shower?"

"Maybe it will help me wake up."

"But keep the noise down," said Choy. "I didn't hear Bal come in so it must have been very late. I've got some gym clothes that will fit you and I was going to take a load to the laundromat on the main floor anyway, so give me what you've got on."

As Choy waited for the filthy clothes to be passed to him from inside the bathroom, he wondered what to believe.

Could this guy be a right wing infiltrator? Seems unlikely, but …

There was no actual proof, so why had the notion even entered his brain? A reaction to learning about Baxter's wife. Still, gut feelings are sometimes right.

And sometimes wrong.

How do you know who is telling the truth? These right wingers keep on repeating their lies, over and over again, until some people believe them.

Lessons learned from Donald Trump and the extreme right.

But it can't be just any lie. It has to be plausible. It has to be prepared for. First you build doubt and then you play on that doubt — I know Baxter's wife is not who she said she was, so maybe there are more people like her. So maybe Goodwin is a spy. It's like the alt-right and their conspiracy theories. They build on doubt about official stories — the Kennedy assassination, 9-11. They build on the distrust of government — which people have good reasons for, like starting wars based on lies — then build conspiracy theories on top of conspiracy theories on top of conspiracy theories.

What's my point?

If people don't know what the truth is you are able to define it for them. To create the ability to manufacture truth, you first have to create doubt. It's the necessary first step to building absolute faith about whatever you say. The Adolph Hitler school of creating storm troopers and loyal party members.

They lied to me a few times and now I think everything is a lie.

There was no way Goodwin could be a right wing infiltrator. He knew it because the kid was a believer and didn't just spout rhetoric that could be learned.

"Waylon," shouted Goodwin over the sound of aerated water spraying against a shower curtain. "I'm sorry, I forgot and just climbed into the shower. I left my clothes on the floor."

Choy opened the door and grabbed the stinky pile

"Waylon," said Goodwin, before the door closed again.

"Ya?"

"Are you mad about something? The way you looked at me and didn't want to let me in."

"No, you woke me up, that's all. And I had one helluva day yesterday. There's a lot to tell you. When your mind has cleared up I'll fill you in."

***

After setting up Goodwin in his bedroom, going to the laundromat and then for breakfast, Rodriguez was still sleeping so Choy dove into printed copies of the *Globe and Mail* and *Calgary Herald*. He needed to clear cobwebs spun by dangerous spiders that would devour anyone who tried to shine a light on their activities. Then figure out what to do next.

So far, working on this story was like picking on a frayed thread on your sleeve only to discover that for each one you pull out, two more come loose. What were the questions he was trying to answer? Who beat Emma with a hockey stick and why? Who abducted and assaulted two women in Abbotsford? What exactly is the relationship between Baxter Media, Allan Brinkman and Michael Turner? Why would Baxter and his wife try to send him on a wild bomb chase? To divert his attention. From what? Had the RCMP infiltrated the extreme right or had the extreme right infiltrated the RCMP? Other police forces? Was Sullivan, the police detective, to be trusted? Was Bouchard right? Was pursuing this story life threatening? If so, from whom? Was Bal right to dismiss his concerns over dangers lurking in alt-right shadows? And the original question that Emma had come to him with: Who are these incels, what are they up to and what is their connection to the wider alt-right? Were these all part of a single puzzle or had pieces from a few boxes somehow gotten mixed together?

The way forward? Same as most of the time, talk to people.

He took his cellphone from his shirt pocket and tapped the number that TwoSpiritPhoenix had given him in case of an emergency. When the call went to voicemail he said the words that were supposed to result in a soon-as-possible Skype discussion: "Hey, the band has a gig coming up and we need a bass player. Are you in?" About a minute later, he took the voice-only return call on his laptop.

"What's wrong?" ze said.

"The story just gets more and more complicated and I need help."

"I sent what you asked for."

"And that helped a bit, but I asked for the wrong thing, or at least it's not what I need right now. The story has morphed into something much bigger."

"What do you need?"

"Any communication you can find amongst a number of people."

"What number?"

"Four at least, maybe five or six."

"Communication that involves all of them or any subset or two, three, four, or five?"

"Any subset. It would be great if you could get the actual contents of all the communication, but even aggregate numbers would be helpful — who is talking to whom and how often. Basically any internal communication they have would be prefect. I'm assuming they have some sort of encrypted, private way of discussing important stuff amongst themselves."

"You're sure they don't just get together somewhere private and talk?"

"I have no clue what they do, but I'm hoping like young people everywhere they use computers when they communicate."

"That's it?" ze asked, after a slight pause.

"Some of the people involved might be cops," Choy said. "Or maybe even CSIS."

"That's good to know."

"Anything you can give me that confirms communications with the police would help."

"For the entire list?"

"Yes.

"What have you gotten yourself into?"

"That's the question I'm hoping you can help me answer."

After a little more discussion — ze had made it clear from the beginning of their relationship that five minutes was zir conversation limit, which ze claimed was due to security concerns, but Choy guessed was also due to the stress ze felt when talking to other people — came the by now seemingly normal request for him to send zir all the details in a coded message.

While it was difficult, since their first conversation Choy had made a serious effort to think of TwoSpiritPhoenix and always refer to zir using zir choice of pronouns. It had been extremely jarring at first, especially to someone who had spent hours most days of his life writing, but the task had become easier over time. Apparently some multi or non-gendered people preferred other pronouns, but TwoSpiritPhoenix instructed him to use ze and zir. This change in the English language, or perhaps it was the more fundamental change in a way of thinking, bothered some people. Right wingers used this annoyance, which they tried to turn into anger, as a means to build support for various political movements. The fear of change and desire to keep things the way they are, were longstanding themes in conservative movements going back at least a few hundred years, so they were obviously effective, but why? Change was a constant part of life, so why do some people have such a hard time accepting it? Because change is threatening? But what is threatening about using gender neutral pronouns? Because it questions a Manichean, binary view of the world? If gender is more complicated than man/woman, then maybe philosophy or religion must also be about more than good/evil or god/devil.

Maybe it is simply that some people have such a hard time figuring out how the world works that once they think they have mastered it, any change to the status quo threatens their sense of accomplishment.

To write the best version of this story, Choy understood it was necessary to get into the minds of incels, neo-Nazis and alt-righters. Why do they think and act the way they think and act? Was this a simple matter of asking them?

***

After an hour of planning his next moves and still no stirring from Rodriguez's bedroom, Choy woke up Goodwin and drove him back to his apartment. The two men entered the place together, finding the contents of his four rooms strewn on the floor and a swastika drawn with a green marker on his bathroom mirror. Choy again wanted to call the police, but Goodwin insisted he didn't want them involved and said he would be okay if left alone, so Choy departed to the Foothills Hospital.

When he arrived at Emma's room, her mother was still there, sitting on a chair, just as she was days earlier.

"Has there been any change?" asked Choy.

She shook her head.

"How long are you going to stay in Calgary?"

"Until … something happens," she said. "I have almost 16 weeks of banked vacation and if that runs out I can take unpaid leave. I can afford not to work for half a year."

"I hope it doesn't come to that."

She shrugged, then looked at Emma. "She could wake up ten minutes from now. Or … They're planning surgery again tomorrow and then the prognosis is likely to be clearer."

"Are they hopeful?"

"Have you learned anything about who did this?"

"That's one of the reasons I came today," Choy answered.

"Who was it?" she said, interrupting him.

"There's a suspect, but the police don't have enough proof yet."

"Have they told you his name?"

"They can't, but there may be a way to find out."

"How?"

"I need your permission to look through some of Emma's stuff at her apartment."

She stared at him for a moment.

"You want to look at the crime scene, don't you? For whatever it is you're writing. You want pictures so you can sell your book or magazine article or …"

"That's not it at all," he said. "Please believe me."

"Why should I?"

"I've been told something in confidence, by someone who could get into big trouble. They want to help. If I go to the apartment and look through her stuff, there will be something pointing in the right direction."

Her stern look softened, then changed completely. "Okay, but I want to go with you."

"Of course, if you're up to it."

"The police gave me the key yesterday. They said the crime scene investigation was complete, so I could sleep there, rather than sit in this chair, but I haven't been able to."

"I understand."

"If we went together … maybe …"

"Of course. Do you want to go now?"

Her blank stare was slowly displaced by a nod, slight at first, but then more vigorous. As Choy walked over to her and offered his hand, he noticed the smell of her clothes that had not been changed for a week.

What shape would I be in if something like this happened to Samantha?

"Do you have a suitcase?" he asked.

She nodded again.

"Do you want to bring it with us?"

Another nod. "The nursing station," she said.

"I'll go get it and let the nurses know we're leaving."

"Thank you," she said, crying while looking at her daughter.

It was a small one-bedroom basement apartment about 20 blocks from the campus in a neighbourhood with houses built in the 1940s and 50s. After taking a quick look in each room to get an idea of the general layout, it became clear that Detective Sullivan had arranged with someone to clean and straighten up. There was no sign of the attack or of the investigation.

"They did a good job cleaning up," said Choy. "Making it ready for you to stay. Are you comfortable with doing that?"

She nodded tentatively. "I think so."

"Do you want me to do a load of wash for you?" he said, trying to be helpful.

"Do I smell that bad?" she said.

He tried to control it, but Choy's embarrassment was almost certainly vividly evident. "I didn't mean … I just want to help you settle in. If there's anything …"

"Where do you need to look?"

"On Emma's desk," he said turning to the table on the other side of the living room.

"If you find what you need quickly I can be left alone to have my first bath in 10 days, then perhaps even get some sleep without nurses waking me up every hour," she said. "And while the offer is much appreciated I've been doing my own laundry since I was 10."

"Of course."

Choy went to the table, finding Emma's daily agenda exactly where Sullivan had told him it would be. He opened it and flipped through its pages until he came to the entry for two weeks earlier. Written in pencil was the name Charles Dobson, 4 pm, La Taqueria, MacHall. Now, Choy could honestly say he learned of the name Charles Dobson when he looked through Emma's agenda.

"Did you find what you need?"

He nodded.

"Is there anything else?"

He shook his head and she used the fingers of her right hand to mime walking, a message that while apparently asking him to leave, was really telling him not to worry.

Driving back to the hotel, all he could think about were Caroline's sad eyes that revealed the depth of her pain. Then when he went up to his suite Bal's bedroom door was still closed. He knocked. Again. And again. Then he opened it. She was not there and the bed had not been slept on.

11.

Even Choy had to admit the possibility that Rodriguez had spent the night somewhere else, and not called, to prove a point. Still, he was worried. What if something had happened? What if someone at the party had dropped a date rape drug into her drink? What if she had been assaulted? He would be responsible for anything bad that happened to her. Should he call the police?

Instead of Sullivan he phoned Goodwin, who was obviously still sleeping off his experience with the neo-Nazis because it took three successive calls before he finally answered.

"She's at Dobson's party?" he finally said after listening to Choy's worries for more than a minute. "What's she wearing? I'll go and say hi."

Is he still asleep?

"Ginger? Are you okay?"

"I like her, but I don't know if she likes me," he said, ignoring the question.

Choy's ex-wife often talked in her sleep, sometimes even getting out of bed. Once, a few days after watching the German film Das Boot on TV, he had found her in the basement, obviously dreaming about being on a submarine that was about to sink. The trick was to fit into what the person was dreaming, go along with it, but direct them somewhere safe. So that's what he tried with Goodwin.

"I'm not sure what she's wearing, but I could find out. You want me to find out?"

"Yes."

"Did you give Bal the name of someone at the university to talk to? Maybe that person knows what she's wearing."

"Merilee. Merilee Watson at the student union office."

"Okay, I'll go talk to Merilee and then find Bal. I'll tell her to meet you at your bed."

"At my bed?"

"Yes. Go back to your bed and she'll meet you there."

"Okay."

Less than a half hour later Choy was in the student union building asking for Ginger Goodwin's friend Merilee Watson, the office coordinator.

"Ginger told me he gave your name to Bal Rodriguez."

"And?"

"I'm Waylon Choy. Bal is working for me as an intern. I'm an investigative journalist."

"You're Choy?" Watson said, a glare proving she didn't believe him.

"I got the name from a five 'greats' grandfather, who was the last completely Chinese person in my family."

"You don't need to explain your genealogy to me."

"Based on your disbelieving look it appeared I did."

"Hey, I'm sorry," she answered, wearing her embarrassment like a white shirt stained by spilled wine. "Older man asking about a young woman and I get defensive, especially with all the dangerous creeps we've had around here lately."

"We're working on a story about one of them," said Choy. "The creep who hit Emma Murphy across the side of the head with a goalie stick."

He held out his hand and Watson shook it, rather reluctantly it seemed.

"I know, Bal told me," she said. "You want to see the same footage I showed Emma and the police?"

"Footage?"

"From the food court?"

What did Goodwin tell the girl he was trying to impress that he didn't tell me?

"Right," said Choy. "The footage, yes of course. That's what I came to see."

She took him to a tiny security office filled with monitors and pressed a few buttons below a blank screen. The five-minute long recording was of a half full food court, with some people coming and going, some people sitting alone, while others were in groups. Nothing remarkable is happening until Emma can be seen standing up, obviously angry. The man across the table from her remains seated until Emma, standing, picks up a cup of some liquid and splashes it on him. He then stands, grabs her arm, and looks set to throw a punch with his right arm. As everyone in the foot court has turned to watch this scene the man relaxes, scans the people around him, then looks intensely at Emma before walking away.

"That's it?"

Watson nodded and held out a USB drive. "You want a copy?"

"Sure," said Choy, taking the thumb sized device. "Do you know what they were arguing about?"

"A friend was walking through the food court just as this was going down. She told me that when Emma stood up, she yelled, 'Shut the fuck up, you sick freak!'"

"Like the guy had said something sexually inappropriate?"

She nodded. "Everyone knows he's a rich prick who thinks every woman on campus is dying to pull his penis out of his pants and blow him."

Choy's reaction must have been more visible than he intended.

"You think I'm crude?" Watson said, agitated. "Emma said he offered her $500 to dress up in her hockey gear, then take it off piece by piece as he watched and masturbated."

"That's when she stood up and threw the drink?"

"That's what I was told."

"What's this guy's name?"

"Everyone I know calls him Chucky but his real name is Charles Dobson."

"That's Dobson? Now it all makes sense."

"His father is a Texas oil multi-millionaire who has a building on campus named after him and his mother was a Brinkman."

"Allan Brinkman's sister?"

"I don't know who that is, but if he's rich he's probably related," she answered. "Chucky is also president of the Edmund Burke Society on campus."

Reading Choy's lack of recognition, she continued, "It's like a really old student conservative group that goes all the way back to the early 1970s. It supposedly was very mainstream, but in the past few years it's moved further and further to the right. It's also tied in closely with the new provincial opposition party."

"So Chucky is well connected?"

"Asshole to asshole, rich people stick together like maggots feeding off a dead cow."

Watson clearly had a colourful way with words.

"A few women have lodged formal complaints about him, but it's always her word against his and guess who they believe? The guy with a building named after his dad. Then in response he and his Edmund Burke friends bring some American alt-right supposed 'free speech' advocate to talk about how feminists, gay rights advocates and the left are trying to silence everyone in the name of political correctness."

"Did you tell all this to Bal?"

"And a lot more too," she answered. "She wanted to know everything about the crazy right wingers on campus. They're extremely well organized here. They get money from rich assholes' foundations, which means their parties usually have free booze, or whatever else you're into. So, you can imagine the kind of people they attract."

"You told Bal about one such party last night?"

She shook her head. "She already knew about it. There were posters everywhere."

"I don't suppose you know anybody else who might have gone?"

"Why?"

"She didn't come back to her hotel room last night and she's not answering her phone."

"That doesn't necessarily mean anything," she said, but a concerned look belied her words.

"I agree, it's probably nothing," he said.

"Maybe she met somebody. Stranger things have happened."

"Exactly," said Choy. "But, just to be safe, you don't happen to know someone else who might have been there?"

"Definitely not my crowd."

"Do you know where Charles, Chucky, hangs out at this time of day?"

"Weirdly enough, I do. Follow the smell of testosterone and sweaty hard drives, which will lead you to The Dungeon."

Choy didn't have a clue what she was talking about.

"It's what we call the video games room. In the basement, where sane women fear to tread."

As he headed to the basement Choy had to decide whether to ask about Bal directly. If he did, that would blow any cover she might have established for herself. And if something had happened to her at the party Dobson would not admit it anyway. So, even though his fatherly protective urge made it difficult, he decided to act tactically.

When he saw him, Choy couldn't figure out if Chucky better fit the stereotype of a conservative student club president or the nerdy gamer constantly hanging out with other guys who shared his love for digital killing, fighting evil and stopping the alien hordes from entering your castle. While his clothes were expensive — an almost corporate, button-down blue shirt, a narrow tie, blazer and pressed trousers — his physical appearance was not at all private school rowing club and rugby athletic. Rather, he was skinny with pasty skin and possessed a distinct lack of any discernible muscle mass.

"I'm writing a book about the new right in Canada and I'm told you're the president of the Edmund Burke Society at the university," said Choy, not exactly lying, but staying far enough away from the truth that 'Chucky' might agree to an interview. "I understand it is one of the oldest student political groups in the country, not directly connected to a party, that promotes right wing ideology and I'd like to ask a few questions about that."

"I wouldn't use the term 'ideology'," answered Dobson, impressed with himself and the notion that a journalist was interested in interviewing him. "That sounds like we're promoting some totalitarian, communist, wildly out there way of thinking, but we're really just all about common sense. We promote ideas and ways of doing things that have been tested and clearly work. We are against moral relativism and cultural experimentation because history tells us these inevitably lead to authoritarianism. We are today's version of old time conservatives."

He was articulate and talkative — even though his words sometimes sounded like he was reading from a script — so, after introductions, and Dobson's inquiry into Choy's name, the two men left The Dungeon to conduct an interview in the same food court where 10 days earlier Emma had thrown iced tea over a similar blazer.

At first he took it easy on 'Chucky' throwing him easy-to-hit underhand lobs that were mostly answered with right wing formulaic efficiency, but as the questions became more difficult Dobson soon showed signs of frustration.

"You say Steve Bannon and Jordan Peterson are two of your heroes, but some critics would say both are anti-woman, homophobic, anti-transsexual and gateways, at a minimum, to the extreme right, including White nationalism. How do you respond to these critics?"

"I generally don't respond to liberal purveyors of victimhood, I ridicule them," he said quickly. "But, if I were to engage them in debate, I'd say our society, the most successful in human history, has had cultural and social norms that have served us well for hundreds of years. Men and women have been encouraged and expected to act in certain ways, to take on certain roles. Those who attack these cultural and social norms talk like there are no negative consequences from the disruption they cause, but is it just coincidence that along with women's and homosexual's so-called liberation we see these deadly social ills creeping into our communities? What has caused the breakdown of the family, a jump in crime, drug addiction, homelessness, abortion? People have lost their sense of right and wrong because moral relativists who do not believe in natural law have been put in charge by the liberal elites."

"So you're an opponent of women's, gay and transgender rights?"

"I'm in favour of everyone's rights, except for their right to make others conform to their agenda," he said with a forced smile.

At that moment Choy decided to increase the pressure, to see how resilient this guy's self-satisfied smugness really was. "What does that mean?" he asked, his tone changing from neutral acceptance to aggression. "Conform to their agenda? Who is asking you to conform to what agenda?"

"The gays, feminists and transsexuals, they want everyone to accept their sick morals as perfectly normal, encouraging little children to think and act like them."

"What on earth are you talking about?"

"They encourage children who were born girls or boys to tell their parents that they no longer accept the vagina or penis they were born with. They want to switch sides and not only is society supposed to accept this, we are also supposed to pay for it!" Dobson's voice rose an octave between the beginning and end of his two sentences.

"What's your problem with transsexuals?"

"They want to destroy our society, to infect us with their sickness."

"Their sickness? But if they are sick shouldn't we treat them? Just like any other sick person living in our society?"

"They don't want to be made well; they want us to accept their sickness as normal."

"Do you believe God created 'normal' people but not trans-sexuals or gays or feminists?"

"I never said that!"

"No, but it's the logical conclusion from other things you have said. You cite 'natural law' which is generally defined as the belief that God gave us a set of rules, the ones outlined in the Bible, so you're some sort of Christian fundamentalist. You've said feminists are 'out to destroy Judeo-Christian values'. You've said 'gay people are godless and an affront to those of us who believe in a normal family'. And you've said feminists, gays and transsexuals 'want everyone else to conform to their agenda'. They're all, to you, obviously very bad people. So, did God, or the Devil, create these people?"

Dobson's anger and frustration were obvious. "I'm not stupid. You're trying to get me to say something that you can use in a story to make me look bad."

"Are you actually even religious?" Choy continued on the attack. "Or are you one of those alt-right types who are pretend religious, because of all the conservative evangelicals?"

"I'm a Christian."

"Are you sure about that?"

Dobson looked at him like he knew what was coming.

"Would a Christian ask a woman to dress up in hockey equipment and then do a striptease for him?" said Choy. "A woman who was not his wife, or his girlfriend, or even a heterosexual? Would a Christian sexually harass numerous women both on and off campus?"

"None of that has been proven. The women who made complaints are communists and blackmailers who know my family is wealthy."

"Would a Christian smash a woman in the head with a hockey stick, sending her into a coma that she may never come out of?"

Dobson smiled. Choy thought of an interview he had done with a psychiatrist who wrote a book about psychopaths called *In the Absence of Empathy*. To feel guilt one must identify with others. Completely self-centered people don't care about anyone else.

"You think I don't know who you are?" Dobson said. "You think you fooled me with a story about writing a book about Canada's right? You're that journalist from Vancouver snooping into the same stuff that got a certain hockey-playing dyke sent to hospital. You think you're playing me, but I was playing you all along."

His 'I am in charge even though you think you are' was yet another indication of his psychopathy. These people always believe they are running the show.

"Why did you do it?" said Choy. "Emma refused to sleep with you? She laughed at you? Because she's stronger than you, an athlete? And you can't stand the thought of a woman being better than you at anything? You wanted to humiliate her, but she refused to be humiliated. You were going to hit her, right here in the food court, but other people were around and you know there is closed circuit video, so you waited a few days, followed her home one night, grabbed her goalie stick and smashed it across her head. That's what a bitch like her deserves, right Chucky?"

"Don't call me that!"

"Does it bother you when people call you Chucky to your face, like they do all the time behind your back? Did Emma call you Chucky that night when you hit her?"

He raged in silence.

"Did she call you Chucky and laugh at you? She did, didn't she? So you shut her up and you're not one bit sorry, are you?"

He tried not to react but his upper lip betrayed his anger.

"All the women like her should be shut up, right? They deserve to have their heads bashed in because they do not accept the superiority of men. They refuse your sexual advances and sleep in sin with other women. But that last part you could accept, so long as she made it part of your sexual fantasy, right. You could accept a woman lying with another woman so long as you were lying there with them, right? I know exactly how your pathetic, juvenile, misogynist mind works."

"You know nothing at all about me."

"I know you were there that night when Emma was assaulted. I know you did it. And I know the police are close to proving it."

"I was at a meeting with Peter Baxter and my uncle the night she was assaulted. The police already checked my alibi and both my uncle and Mr. Baxter confirmed I was with them."

Sullivan didn't tell me this bit of important information.

"But we both know that's not true, don't we?" Choy said, pretending he already knew about the alibi. "I've already talked to your uncle and to Baxter and I passed on certain information to the police. You just might find, sooner rather than later, that your alibi is not as strong as you think."

As the two men glared at each, Choy smiled, then stood up.

"You reek of misogyny," he said. "The stench of your woman hatred, or is it your juvenile fear that the 'weaker sex' is actually stronger than you, is making me nauseous. I need to go back to my hotel and take a shower. See you around Chucky."

Three women at a nearby table giggled, as if they had heard Choy's words. He guessed it was simply fortuitous timing, but couldn't help his smile. Despite walking away and not looking back, he could feel Dobson's rage. A guy like this, an anger like that; this would not be the last time they confronted each other.

***

As soon as he got onto the C-Train, he called Bal's cell, but once again there was no answer.

If something has happened to her. What? What will I do if something has happened to her?

The dread of once again having to speak to the parents of someone killed because of him was overwhelming so he immediately did his best to convince himself nothing bad had happened.

She's not dead. She's not dead. There's no reason to think she's dead or even harmed in any way.

But there's always a reason to think she might be dead if you are creative enough.

You're being absurd. Think about something you have control over.

Why are Baxter and Brinkman giving Chucky an alibi? What's in it for them? Brinkman could simply be doing it to protect his sister, but what about Baxter? Is he blackmailing Brinkman? Or simply stockpiling favours from the rich patron of his booming media empire? It hardly seemed likely to be the other way around. That

Chucky had something on Baxter and Brinkman. He didn't seem clever enough. On the other hand, he should not assume just because someone acted stupid and sounded stupid that he was, in fact, stupid. The entire world had watched as that mistake was made in the world's most powerful country. While Trump had once seemed as bright as a bulb with the dimmer turned low, he had proven that the truly stupid were people who had underestimated him. Underestimation is the great weakness of everyone who thinks they are smarter than others. Better to always assume your adversary is worthy of your respect, at least until proven otherwise.

Focus. Why might Brinkman and Baxter give Chucky an alibi? Baxter is the key.

Or maybe keeping pressure on Chucky is the way to go.

Sullivan certainly promoted the idea of pressure. Get Chucky angry and maybe he'll do something stupid.

Why not do both?

The best strategy is to try uncovering the reasons for the phony alibi while keeping pressure on Chucky. Two prongs of the same fork used to lift up and turn over the bloody steak that was the story of who assaulted Emma Murphy.

He needed a better understanding of who was who in the hierarchy of these alt-right groups. People with such conservative views always believed in hierarchy. One of them was almost certainly running the show. Brinkman was the obvious candidate because of his money, but he just didn't seem clever enough. Turner, on the other hand … Wouldn't that be something if an undercover cop turned out to be the behind-the-scenes leader.

As the train crossed the Bow River into downtown, Choy stood up to get off at the next stop. Walking under train tracks above the Eighth Street underpass, his phone vibrated. He looked at the screen, which read: 'Bal calling'.

"Where are you?" he said immediately after touching the talk icon.

"Back at the hotel."

"I've been calling for the past five hours."

"I see that."

"Where were you?"

"You think it's a good idea to talk on the phone?" said Rodriguez. "You said it was never a good idea to do that, especially if the conversation was important."

I did say that.

"I'll be at the hotel in five or ten minutes."

"Okay, talk to you then."

***

"You'll never guess what I found out," Rodriguez said, a bubbling excitement in her voice, as soon as Choy walked through the door. "Charles Dobson had a public fight with Emma two days before she was assaulted."

"I know," said Choy.

"People at the university call him Chucky."

"I know."

Choy walked slowly into the living room, then sat on the couch, pouting with a simmering glare. She noticed his look but kept talking regardless.

"Chucky thinks Michael Turner might be an undercover cop. They don't get along at all."

If true this is an important piece of information.

"Chucky tells his friends at the university that he's the leader of the far right in Alberta and maybe all of Canada. Chucky also tells them he's got connections all the way back to Donald Trump's inner circle."

It was difficult to maintain the pout when excited by the information she had uncovered.

"Apparently three or four of the local far-right groups actually share the same leadership and are fed potential members from the incel chatroom, which is also run by the same people. Chucky brags about bringing in recruits for alt-right groups all across North America and says linking up with the incels was his idea."

Choy's scowl was replaced by questions dying to get out.

"It sounds like, whoever's idea it really was, there's a lot of resources being put into this, with some serious money behind it. I'm told, from someone who knows computers, that they've got state of the art servers and software, plus people who know how to run them. Apparently they have equipment in the Ukraine, Hungary, Canada and the USA to avoid being shut down by legal action in any one country. My guy doesn't know exactly how much all this costs, but he thinks it must be millions."

"Who is your guy?"

"A source on the inside," she said, smiling proudly.

"Someone close to Chucky?

She nodded.

"He just spilled the beans to you?"

She shook her head.

"How did you get him to talk?"

"I spent the night with him."

Her tone was casual, but Choy thought he detected a note of nervousness as he stared at her.

"You slept with a guy?"

"I slept in his bed."

"What's that supposed to mean?"

"Exactly what it sounds like," she answered defensively. "I slept in his bed."

"In his bed? One of Chucky's friends?"

"Garth Jones. A very shy guy I met at the Edmund Burke Society party. Cute. He was standing there, drinking all by himself. Painfully shy, said maybe three words until I got him talking when we were back in his room. Actually smart, gentle, and surprisingly nice. He was recruited from an incel chatroom, grew up in southwestern Ontario and moved to Calgary because of Chucky. Apparently the incels, especially the ones attracted to White nationalism, think Chucky is a brilliant leader and very charismatic."

Choy was having a hard time processing anything other than his intern's information-gathering tactics. "You had sex with this guy in order to get him to talk?"

"That's none of your business! You're not my father or my priest."

"But I am your journalism mentor. I have a duty to discuss your information gathering techniques."

When she momentarily made eye contact it was hard to tell if her look was one of guilt or anger.

"If you gave a source money for information, would I be able to ask about that? Of course. We'd talk about the ethics and potential downsides to purchasing material. How is having sex with a source any different?"

"'Having sex.' You make it sound so sordid. I never said I had sex with him."

"Did you?"

Choy knew this probably sounded creepy coming from a man twice her age, but there was an important journalistic point to be made.

"Depends what your definition of sex is," she said, a hint of amusement in her voice.

"What's that supposed to mean?"

"It really is none of your business, but it means we never had intercourse."

Choy shook his head in disbelief. "Bill Clinton bullshit aside, you provided some sort of sexual favour to get information for a story. Where do you think that leads?"

"It obviously led to getting some important information."

Choy simply stared, not believing her words and attitude.

"Mostly I was just nice to him, which apparently no woman, including his mother, has ever been before."

"Mostly?"

"I let him touch my breasts and we slept naked together."

"You're right, I don't need to know the details," Choy said, then stood up and walked out of the living room, into his bedroom, back into the hallway and through the tiny kitchen before returning to the couch.

"I'm not your father and I'm not your employer, so I have no right to judge your moral compass or lay any trips on you about … whatever you do in your private life, but I am supposed to be mentoring you about journalism, so … How shall I put this? There's a problem with getting too close to your sources. There's also a problem with giving something in return for information, because it can affect the credibility of that information."

"What are you implying?"

"I'm not implying anything."

"Yes, you are," she said, anger rising in her voice. "You're implying that a woman journalist being nice to a man, becoming friends with a source is somehow a commodity, a 'favour' that is worth something. If I were a male reporter and just told you about all the great information I got would you have been all, like, how did you get it? I don't think so. And if a male journalist told you he slept with someone to get a story, you'd be like all, 'lucky you, you got the story and got laid'. Tell me I'm wrong! You won't, because I'm right. You're implying there's some sort of necessary double standard when it comes to male and female journalists. If female journalists use their sexuality that's wrong, but if a male does it, good for him!"

"I never said any of that," Choy said quietly, chastened because he realized there was some truth to what she said.

"But you were sure as hell thinking it!"

"You have no way to know what I was thinking."

"I've had enough discussions with the men in my life to know how you think."

"You feel confident that your sample size is large enough to make accurate generalizations about all men?" he answered, even though a part of him knew he should simply apologize and move on.

"If a male reporter slept with a politician or with someone's secretary to get a story, I'd have ethical questions about that too."

Rodriguez shook her head before continuing, then locked her eyes on his. "Look at me and tell me I'm wrong. Tell me you don't have a double standard when it comes to sex and gender."

If one of those right wing assholes had fed Bal drugs at the party and shoved a dildo … but I barely argued when Goodwin said he didn't want to involve the cops over similar behaviour.

"Okay, I have a double standard," he said. "But a helluva lot more women get raped than men."

She glared at him for a moment then contorted her face to show how stupid she thought his words were.

"What are you saying? That women have to be careful about using their sexuality because it's more dangerous for us?"

He nodded. "You disagree?"

"So a double standard is okay because men are trying to protect us?"

"I'm saying the dangers facing women are different, that's all."

"So who is raping all those women? The same men who want to protect us."

Choy didn't think he was wrong, but the words to express a convincing counter argument failed him. It was dangerous for women to use their sexuality to get what they wanted from men and the reverse was not necessarily true. But how could he explain that and not come across as a sexist pig?

Why are all the women in my life better at arguing than me?

She possessed a Star Wars like tractor-beam that locked his eyes to hers.

Time to give up. Admit defeat and move on. Change the subject.

"You're right, I'm wrong," he said quickly and not very loudly.

"I'm sorry, I didn't hear you," she said.

"You're right, I expressed a double standard when it comes to sexuality as a tool used by male and female journalists."

"Is this simply a problem with what you said, or what you believe?"

I still believe there are dangers women face that men don't. And that's a reality that doesn't go away just because you call it a double standard.

He shrugged because he wanted to change the subject. He did his best to look contrite.

Do I feel contrite? No.

She was smiling now. "At least you're honest."

I'm not. I'm a chickenshit liar.

"We're unlikely to make a significant dent in the scourge of sexism over the course of this conversation, right?" he said. "But we might go a long way to solving the mystery of who beat up Emma and why."

Her smile grew larger.

"Tell me everything that happened and what you learned," he said. "It sounds pretty amazing."

"It was," she answered, obviously dying to tell him all about it. "I can't believe I actually did it."

12.

After a two-hour epic tale voiced primarily by Rodriguez, with a few intruding queries from Choy, the two journalists were giddy with an excitement germinated from significant progress in uncovering the truth. Bubbly and talkative, they planned how to divide up the work that needed to be done next, then the male of the species '*diurnarius*' said: "I do have one question that's been bugging me. Would you have slept with him if you didn't kind of like him?"

"What do you mean?"

When he saw the sudden change in her mood Choy realized he was swimming into waters where riptides could pull him under, but he kept going regardless.

"I don't think I could do it with a woman I disliked."

She stared at him as if considering how to respond.

"You mean mechanically speaking?"

Her tone was flat so he couldn't read what effect his change of subject was having, but he suspected it was not positive. He suspected she suspected he was criticizing her again.

"Partly, I guess," he said hesitantly.

"Maybe it's easier for a woman, faking it, I mean."

"Exactly what every man fears. Lurking somewhere in the corner of our brains is the phobia of inadequacy," he said, relieved that she had kind of changed the subject. "These incels just have the worst cases."

"Are we talking about erections?" she said.

"I don't know, I guess so, sort of," he said, embarrassed by her pointing out what now seemed obvious.

"You know, I think this conversation is becoming inappropriate," she said, a serious look on her face. "It's making me uncomfortable."

Jesus, what did I say? What an idiot!

As Choy became serious, she smiled.

"Just kidding. You should see the look on your face."

"That's not funny."

"Oh yes it is. You look just like an old boyfriend I caught with his pants down ogling porn on his iPad."

"Accusations of inappropriate conduct by an older man with his young intern is pretty damn serious," he said, suddenly realizing that he never should have agreed to let Bal come with him on this trip. "It's not a joke."

Her sigh passed for an acknowledgement of the upset she had caused.

"We were joking around," she said. "Both of us."

"Until you made me realize what a precarious position I put myself in."

"What are you talking about?"

"'A middle-aged journalist, alone with his intern on a job, has been accused of making inappropriate sexual comments in the hotel suite they shared together.' What would you make of such a sentence if you read it in a newspaper?"

"I told you, I was joking."

"But what if you weren't? What if you didn't like me for some reason or wanted to get even with me for rejecting you or giving you a lousy grade, or were just plain crazy? What if you went back to Vancouver and took a complaint like that to your school's administration? That's why if I had thought things through I never would have agreed to this internship."

"Are you serious?"

"Is the Me Too Movement serious?"

"Most women are not crazy or vindictive or into blackmailing men."

"Most men are not rapists."

They looked at each other for a few moments.

"I'm not saying you ..." Choy began.

"I'm sorry, it was a stupid thing for me to say, not funny at all," Rodriguez interrupted. "I get why good men might be sensitive."

"Don't get me wrong, I support the Me Too Movement," he said. "Exposing these predators is necessary and important. It's just that it makes you think twice about putting yourself in a position ..."

"You have gone out of your way to accommodate and make me feel safe. This hotel suite, I know it costs a lot more than if you were staying by yourself. The meals. You've treated me like your own daughter, which I find irritating at times, but is understandable for someone, what, 25 years older than me."

More or less correct.

"You do remind me of Samantha the way you clobber me in arguments."

They smiled at each other. Both took deep breaths.

"Are we good?"

"We need to get back to work, right?" she said nodding to his question. "I'm going to the hospital."

"Sounds like a plan."

***

After Rodriguez left, Choy sat at the living room desk to begin writing the parts of the story they both agreed were ready, but then noticed a blinking red light on the phone indicating a message waiting. It was the hotel manager, letting him know that since the Stampede was starting in less than a week the room rate would be going up substantially and that the hotel was fully booked beginning on opening day. During the ten days of the so-called Greatest Outdoor Show on Earth all hotels within 20 kilometres of the Stampede Grounds would be fully booked and if he needed to stay in the city past July 6, a reservation at some more distant establishment would need to be made immediately.

Distracted by this news, and uncertain how much longer they needed to stay in Calgary, Choy checked a couple of hotel websites for reservations once the Stampede started. Available rooms were extremely expensive and required payment in full or were on the outskirts of the sprawling city and still outrageously priced. While he was considering how to proceed, his cellphone vibrated.

"Choy," said Detective Sullivan. "What did you say to the little weasel that got him so riled up? Apparently the deputy police chief got a call."

"How are you doing Detective Sullivan? Good to hear from you. I'm doing fine, thanks for asking."

"Ya, ya."

"And don't worry, your name never came up," said Choy. "I was very careful about that. I discovered the meeting Emma had with him, his name and where he was hanging out, all on my own, through independent verifiable sources."

"I appreciate that, but I really did call to find out what you said to him. I'm curious how you got him going."

"I told him anyone who watched the video could see he wanted to hit her right there in the food court, but he was smart enough to wait until they were alone. I called him Chucky and said everyone called him that behind his back. I told him he stunk of woman hatred and a juvenile fear of the 'weaker sex' and that sooner rather than later his alibi was going to collapse because of information I had given to the police."

"What information?"

"I never told him that."

"And you never told me either."

"Just like you never told me about Chucky's alibi," Choy answered.

"Better that you independently learned about that as well."

"Right."

Sullivan ignored the jibe. "You did well. You accomplished what we wanted to accomplish."

"What you wanted me to accomplish."

"Are you feeling used?"

"I wouldn't feel that way, except for a distinct impression that you are withholding information from me and I don't just mean the supposed alibi."

"I'm a cop and you're a journalist. We withhold information from each other. It's who we are and what we do."

He has a point.

"Besides, you did a good job with the information I gave you. You didn't need more."

"Thank you, I think."

"The kid is panicking."

"He's a psychopath, so I wouldn't bet on it," said Choy.

"I'll leave his diagnosis up to the experts, doctors and reporters. But a phone call to the assistant chief that quickly smells of panic."

"Maybe it was his uncle or Baxter."

"Then he called them. Same story."

"True."

"These guys think they're smart, but, like most shitheads, they will do something stupid."

Just as Choy heard these words someone knocked on the hotel room door.

"Hold on, someone's knocking."

He put the phone onto the coffee table and walked to the door.

"Michael Turner," said Choy, to his guest and to the detective hopefully still listening on the phone. "Did Brinkman send you? Or was it Baxter and Brinkman? Or the RCMP? Who is it exactly you are working for?"

Turner tried to hide it, but Choy's knowledge of his police status surprised him. He didn't respond at first, but then said: "We need to talk."

"About?"

"Charles Dobson, among other matters," he said. "It's important."

"You want an invitation into my hotel room? For me to trust you?"

"If I intended you harm, it certainly wouldn't be happening here."

Choy glanced at the cellphone on the coffee table and then motioned for Turner to enter. On his way back to sit on the couch he picked up the still transmitting cellphone and put it in his shirt pocket. His guest looked around.

"You have a whole suite? Nice."

"The place is a little run down, but we can't complain," said Choy, as he led Turner into the living room.

"We?" said Turner, smiling.

Choy returned the man-to-man smile with a self-confident shrug.

"Value for money, until the Stampede starts. The suite triples in price three days from now, so I've got to make sure my investigation is complete by then."

"How exactly is that going?"

"Great, we've uncovered some amazing stuff — a few holes for now, but the big picture is one of those stories a journalist is willing to die for," he said, intending to send a message. "Incel cha-troom, sexual assault, maybe murder, rich kid psychopath, nephew of rich guy funder of neo-Nazis, competing gangs of White nation-alist fascists, owner of far-right media outlet trying to set up a jour-nalist, and undercover police agents in the middle of it all. I mean it's pure left-liberal journo heaven, don't you think?"

"Who told you I was RCMP?"

"That's why you came to my hotel room? To ask me that? Who told you I knew?"

"Who told you about me?" Turner repeated.

"Maybe it was your boss," answered Choy. "Whoever that might be. Brinkman? Baxter? Someone at RCMP headquarters in Ot-tawa? Some right wing nutbar in the USA? All of the above? Or none of the above? I'm pretty sure it is none of the above. Even though you do take cash from all of the above, I'll bet you work only for yourself."

"Don't we all?" Turner answered. "Who told you?"

"Maybe it was the nephew of an Abbotsford cop who you convinced to participate in an abduction and sexual assault."

"Barry Archibald doesn't tie his shoelaces unless I tell him to."

"See, there's where you and your command-and-control military types get it all wrong. The very qualities that make your followers seem so loyal are exactly the qualities that make them so easy to turn against you. Weak will, not really any will of his own, the IQ of a strutting rooster, and scared of his own shadow. Sound familiar? Do you really think you're the only one who can manipu-late such people?"

"Who told you?"

"If you don't like my answers go find someone else to ques-tion."

"It's a crime to expose an undercover police agent," said Turner, pacing back and forth in front of the exterior window.

"Not when the agent directed the abduction and assault of two women, not when the undercover cop has gone rogue, when he's more of a far-right infiltrator into Canada's national police force, than vice versa, not when he shows up at my hotel room trying to prevent me from exposing the rich kid psychopath who smashed a hockey stick across the head of a young woman. While the RCMP might try to keep everything about you quiet, I'm pretty sure that when this story comes out, you'll find there's not much interest in prosecuting a journalist who revealed the sordid story."

"You really don't have a clue what you're dealing with."

Choy smiled again, while maintaining his relaxed-guy-watching-sports-on-TV-position on the couch. "So tell me your version of the truth. Us journalists love stories."

Turner stopped pacing, but remained silent, as if he were thinking.

"Sit down, I'll get us each a beer and you can fill me in on what it is I don't have a clue about," said Choy, standing and heading for the kitchen. When he returned with two cans, Turner was sitting, but his bum barely touched the edge of the chair across from the couch.

"Let me see your cellphone," said Turner, as Choy handed him a beer.

"My cellphone?"

"Ya, the one you didn't hang up and then put in your shirt pocket so whoever is on the other end can hear everything.

Choy didn't want the conversation's momentum shifting away, so he lifted the phone from his pocket as he held down the shut-off button until the Apple icon came onto the screen, then used his thumb to move the slider from left to right while keeping the screen where Turner could see it.

"Satisfied?" he said, as the screen went to black. Then he put his feet up on the couch. "Talk to me Mike."

"Michael."

"Talk to me Mike," Choy repeated, calculating that trash talk might throw this guy, another control freak, off his game enough to gain a small advantage.

Turner took a small sip of beer, then put the can on the coffee table. He looked down at the well-worn carpet and then up at Choy.

He's going to make 'the between two professionals just doing their job' argument.

"There's always a danger, when you're doing a job like mine, that people think you've gone over to the other side. Sometimes that's what we want certain people to think. To be effective, you have to do things to gain the trust of bad people. So, it's easy to understand why you'd think what you think. In many respects, the best proof that I'm effective is that you think I've turned. If I acted like an undercover police agent, how well would I be doing my job?"

Choy continued to listen without reacting.

"It's not that different than a journalist, sometimes you have to do things as a means to an important end. In what I do it's the same."

Bingo: two professionals.

"If you expose me … you'll ruin years of work, make keeping track of some very dangerous people more difficult … quite honestly it will be a disaster."

"Gee, Mike, Michael, I'd love to believe you, but all the evidence points in another direction," he said, doing his best to refrain from smiling.

"What about if I tell you something that will help with your story?" Turner said, changing tack to get the wind behind him. "Would that make it easier to believe me?"

"Perhaps."

This is going exactly where I hoped it would lead.

"Maybe if you tell me something I don't know," said Choy as he pulled on his end of the ocular tug-of-war he and Turner were now engaged in, "it would convince me that you're still a good guy. But it would have to be something that would get you into serious trouble with your right wing asshole buddies, if they found out you were the leak."

"You tell me who told you I'm RCMP, and I'll give you something good."

"Oh please, you first," said Choy, making a show of his faux politeness. "Really, I insist, you first."

Turner looked as if he wanted to slug his tormentor. "Why should I trust you?"

"You shouldn't, just like I shouldn't trust you and I don't. I've run into your type before, lying so often, playing off so many people against each that you don't know who you are and certainly not who you work for anymore. A specialist in telling people exactly what they need to hear so they trust you and then you betray that trust as often and as easily as you take a piss. Quite frankly, there really isn't anything you could tell me that would make me believe anything you say."

"Brinkman and Baxter are planning to take over the next Alberta provincial government," said Turner.

"I'm listening," said Choy, trying not to sound excited.

"They've got hundreds of supporters who have infiltrated pretty much every constituency association and the party head office of Conservatives United."

"There's no guarantee CU wins the next election."

"The polls have them at almost 60 percent."

"Wouldn't be the first time polls were wrong. And besides, even if they win the election, what does it mean to have supporters everywhere in the party? Do they have the leader?"

"No, not exactly."

"So he gains power and purges the extremists in the party, or at least shuts them up. It's an old story, played out federally and provincially time and time again across the country."

"They have a plan to prevent that," said Turner. "They've got connections down south with people in the Republican Party, alt-right Donald Trump supporters."

"So?"

"Their plan is to get CU elected, but a few weeks later to assassinate the leader, make it look like a crazed environmentalist-socialist did it, then have Brinkman or Baxter take over the leadership of the party. They'll have support from Trump and the right-wing American media for doing pretty much whatever they want."

"But they won't have the federal government, so ..."

"That's the next part of their plan. They have people close enough to Trump to believe he'd put the entire might of the Republican machine, not to mention whatever parts of the American government he controls in the service of making sure the right people are elected federally north of the border. They'll make Russian hacking and trolling look like amateur hour."

"This is all a little far-fetched and fantastic, kind of like something a police undercover cop caught with his pants down might conjure up to keep his bosses onside, but I'm not buying," said Choy. "And even if it were true, so what? I mean what politicians don't have a plan to take over the government? That's what they do. And when has the American government not interfered in the politics of other countries? Canada wouldn't even be the first place where the right wing nationalists who support Trump have helped like-minded nationalists win an election. I pitch this story to editors and they either say I'm crazy or yawn me out of their offices." He tilted his head slightly and spread his hands as if to ask, 'you got anything better?'

Turner again went into his 'look at me, I'm thinking' mode.

"Like I said before," Choy continued. "I need something that could get you in trouble to prove you're telling the truth."

"Spilling the beans about a planned assassination attempt doesn't qualify as something that could get me in trouble?"

"Do you have planning documents? The names of the people involved? Exactly how they're going to do it? Anything concrete?"

There was no response.

"You're all talk. And it doesn't implicate you in anything. How about you tell me what you did to make these guys trust you?"

Again he remained silent.

"Tell me who hit Emma Murphy on the side of the head with a hockey stick. And some information that would lead to the arrest and conviction of Brian Grayson and Barry Archibald for the abduction and assault of two women. That might prove you were a cop dedicated to serving justice."

After a moment of silence, Turner spoke slowly and seriously. "It was me who hit Emma Murphy. That's what I did to gain their confidence. But I was only supposed to scare her. It was an accident. She picked up the stick as a weapon, started swinging it at me, telling me to get out of her apartment. We started fighting over possession of it and one thing led to another. She was stronger than I thought and somehow, it really was an accident, her head and the end of the blade collided. It smacked her right in the temple and she fell down like a meteorite falling from the sky. It was a mess; she was bleeding and unconscious. I ... it really was an accident."

Why would this guy tell me he was the one who hit Emma if it wasn't true?

Despite this confession Choy remained certain that Dobson was the guilty party.

"I'm really sorry, and if my superior officers find out, they'll pull me out. How could they not? The entire operation will be shut down. Everything that's been accomplished so far will be for nothing. It's too bad, don't you think? I mean Emma was out to expose those guys in the incel chatroom, right? Shine some light on the dark corners of the neo-Nazi world and that's really what our operation is doing as well. Getting the necessary intel to keep both Canada and the USA safe. Make sure we stop these crazies before they do something completely over the top. Remember the Oklahoma City bombing? That's what guys like these are capable of."

"This is your play?" said Choy, amazed at Turner's audacity. "You're claiming to be continuing Emma's work? And she wouldn't want me to disrupt your operation."

"It's the truth."

"I think you were sent here to protect Dobson, by whatever lies necessary."

Turner's demeanour turned from solicitous to aggressive in an instant.

"What if I was sent here to shut you up, by whatever means necessary," he said, finally making himself comfortable. "What if those were my orders?"

"Meaning?"

"I do believe you are smart enough to figure that out," said Turner, again talking like he was in charge. "So what's it going to be?"

"Meaning I play along with the fiction that you're a RCMP undercover cop dedicated to monitoring the neo-Nazi world who Emma would think was one of the good guys? Or else something very bad will happen to me."

"Something like that."

Choy was more tired of these people's threats than fearful. He'd survived worse.

13.

Whether or not Turner was working for the RCMP was irrelevant. Even whether or not he was the one who assaulted Emma was irrelevant. Everything that Emma had stumbled into — the incels, abduction, assaults, her assault, the violence-spouting alt right, police involvement and whatever other conspiracies were planned — had to be exposed. People needed to know. Plus Choy and Rodriguez were already too far down the path of confrontation with these neo-Nazis whose violent rhetoric, he hoped, was matched by their fake bravado. He had already begun writing the story. While Choy was scared of them, that was not enough to make him back off.

His first call was to Detective Sullivan, asking to meet. Ten minutes later sitting in his car in the hotel parking lot Sullivan listened to the account of Turner's visit.

"The guy who just admitted to being the one who put Emma Murphy into a coma is an undercover RCMP agent? And you knew this for how long?"

"A few days. But he's lying about being the one who assaulted Emma."

"A few days and you never thought to tell me until now?"

"It wasn't relevant until now. Turner's name never came up in any of our discussions."

"He's the head of security for Allan Brinkman, the rich uncle of Charles Dobson and a known associate of Three Percenters, Odin Militia, Proud Boys and the U.S.-based Committee of One Thousand, all potentially violent extremist groups that Emma had been looking into."

"You never told me that Emma was looking into these groups," said Choy. "What was she doing and how long have you known that?"

"Since we got into her laptop hard drive and discovered some information that had been emailed to her from a university account she set up. She was breaking into these right wing web sites from public computers at the university library. Apparently she was a pretty good hacker. Which means the right wingers must have someone even better."

"That would have been helpful to know days ago," said Choy.

"The fucking RCMP," said Sullivan. "And he actually confessed?"

"He'll almost certainly deny it."

"But you say you have a reliable source who tells you Turner has gone rogue and is actually functioning as a neo-Nazi mole inside the RCMP?"

"That's what I'm told."

"How reliable is that source?"

"Very, but if I told you why, it could put that person in danger."

"Another cop told you, I can smell it."

"I never said that."

"This fucks up everything! Damn it! God damn it all to hell! Fuck!"

"He's not the only supposedly undercover agent I've run into investigating what happened to Emma," said Choy. "There's another one in the Fraser Valley, nephew of a municipal cop, who is also 'investigating' the Three Percenters and is good buddies with Turner."

"Jesus fucking Christ!"

"Hey, it's not as bad as it sounds, because I'm 99 per cent sure Turner didn't do it. He's covering for Dobson to gain leverage on Brinkman and Baxter."

"What's Baxter's connection to all this?"

"Not sure exactly, but there is one. He arranged my meeting with Brinkman for a reason. Baxter got his wife to convince me he was part of some conspiracy to bomb the Stampede and pin it on left-wing environmentalists for a reason."

"Why would he want to implicate himself?" said Sullivan. "That's been bugging me since you told me about it."

"It's got to be drawing our attention away from something he doesn't want us to see. Or maybe to something he does want us to notice. Maybe Turner's story about these guys planning to assassinate the new right wing premier, once he's elected, has some truth to it. Maybe they want the cops to find out about a fake story now because they figure if you investigate and there's nothing to it, you'll be skeptical a few months from now if you hear something similar."

"Sounds way too clever."

"Turner is not stupid and neither is Baxter. And maybe the others are smarter than we think."

"In 30 years of doing this job, I've learned that the simplest explanation is almost always the most accurate," said Sullivan.

"Okay, how about this? Maybe the point of their stories was to undermine my credibility in case I went to the cops."

"It did accomplish that," said Sullivan, who after a short silence changed the subject. "Is there anything else you're not telling me?"

"I could ask you the same question and remember, I'm a journalist and you're a cop. Keeping secrets from each other is what we do."

"Fuck. What do I tell the captain? He gets a phone call every day from Emma's mother and a few minutes after he does, I get a visit or a call from him."

"Pretend he's a journalist and keep stuff from him," said Choy, who thought Sullivan might respond with a laugh.

"That's actually not a bad idea," he said, not laughing at all.

"What did I say?" said Choy.

"I got to go," said Sullivan.

What did I say?

Choy got out of the car and as he walked into the hotel lobby Catherine Baxter was talking to the front desk clerk. He tried to sneak past her to the elevator, but she turned towards him and smiled.

"Mr. Choy, you're here. Please I need to speak with you."

"Mrs. Baxter, what do you want today? Got another story for me?"

"Could we talk in private?"

Choy frowned and shook his head.

She looked at him carefully as if plotting her next move.

"I'm sorry for what happened …"

"How did you find my hotel?"

"You told me on the phone when I called."

"What do you want?"

"My husband. He told me. He asked me to come here and … I really am sorry for pretending to be someone else. I'd like to make it up to you. I have some information."

Choy pointed to the couch in the middle of the hotel lobby. They sat about two feet apart.

She looked embarrassed.

"Your husband, he asked you to come here and what?"

"Told me to come here and … another story he wants me to tell you. At least I think it's a made-up story. I don't really know anymore; it is so hard to tell whether he's telling the truth or not."

She seemed genuinely confused and upset, but that was probably more related to her acting ability than to the truth.

"I understand if you don't want to see me or hear what I have to say," she continued. "Just tell me to go and I will."

Those same cat-like, but vulnerable, big green eyes that Choy had noticed the first time he saw her at the Baxter Media office stared at him again.

"I told him I didn't want to, but … he threatened me. If I don't do what he tells me …"

"What does he do?" challenged Choy, not wanting to be played by this woman again.

"I suffer from depression and go to a doctor for medication and if I don't do what he wants I'll be sent to an institution," she whispered. "He has powerful friends and they've done worse before."

He stared at her.

"I know you don't trust me, but can we please go somewhere more private? I'll answer any question you have."

The desire to unravel a complicated story into each strand of truth was a reporter's kryptonite.

He stood and pointed to the elevator. They entered with two other hotel guests. Choy had thought that when challenged she would offer up some vague general threat, but this was quite specific and exactly the sort of thing someone like Baxter, who believed the man was head of his family, might do. It was probably acting, but there was at least some possibility she was telling the truth. And he certainly wasn't scared of her. Not in a hotel suite with a separate living room, anyway.

"Come in," he said after unlocking the door with his pass card. She followed him into the living room where he motioned for her to sit on the sofa.

"He is very abusive," she immediately said, looking down.

"The real secretary at Baxter Media told me you and Peter have an ideal marriage. 'The best one' she knows, were her exact words."

"It's what everyone thinks. It's the image Peter insists on presenting to the world. If I say or do anything, if I don't smile and hold his hand wherever we go in public, if I don't tell absolutely everyone I meet about what a wonderful, absolutely brilliant man he is … Have you ever known someone who is kind, gentle, friendly and a wonderful human being in public, but the exact opposite in private? He's mean, threatening, domineering and an absolute tyrant when it's just the two of us."

He was prepared to believe this. Peter Baxter had certainly given off bad vibes and who knows what that sort of man was like in private with his wife. Or maybe Choy wanted to believe her story because of how much he disliked her husband.

"He told me to be prepared to sleep with you, that I should do it if necessary" she said and burst out crying. "His exact words were: 'Be prepared to fuck him.' What kind of man says that to his wife?"

"A pimp," Choy said, as if he were thinking out loud.

She looked straight into his eyes as tears rolled down her cheeks in a steady drip much like the result of a badly worn washer at the bottom of an old faucet stem in one of his house's two bathrooms. "A pimp," she repeated, nodding slightly. "Which means he thinks I am his whore."

"His property," he corrected her, reminded of a year-old conversation with an old J-school friend who worked in public relations for over 20 years and told him his brain was the 'property' of his boss while at work.

"He told me exactly that one time. 'A woman is the property of her husband.' He said Judaism, Christianity and Islam all agreed on that. 'That was the point of marriage', he said."

"He didn't strike me as a religious man," said Choy.

"He's not," she answered. "But he uses anything that might be to his benefit. He's the most selfish person I've ever known. He thinks everyone else is stupid. He's the only smart person in the entire world."

Another psychopath. Dobson, Turner and Baxter. A meeting with all three present must be quite the scene.

"I really am sorry for what I did before," she said, her tears returning. "I feel terrible."

Choy sat on the couch beside her, even though he knew it was a mistake. As soon as he did she began to sob and he moved closer to comfort her. She grabbed onto him, throwing her arms around him. "I've been such a fool. I've known for years it was time to leave, but … I'm scared. You don't know what he's capable of."

While a certain part of his brain was urging him to return her embrace, the rational thing to do remained clear.

Get up and move to another chair.

"Catherine," he said, pulling away and standing up. "I want to trust you … but it's going to take more than a few tears and a story about how terrible your husband is."

"I'm sorry," she said. "I understand. I just don't know where to turn. My family, they are Christians and think Peter is the perfect husband."

She gave him another look of desperation and abject hopelessness.

"What can I do to convince you I'm not a bad person?"

"I don't know you well enough to answer that question," he said, trying to keep his distance.

"You must have lost all respect for me … Do you hate me?"

"I don't trust you, that's all I know. I don't know you well enough to like or hate you."

"I like you. I liked you the moment you paid attention to me. I could see you are kind."

"What did your husband tell you to say to me?"

"I'm embarrassed."

"Why?"

"He told me to get close to you, to make you desire me. And I have. Even though I want to leave him, even though I hate him, I still do what he tells me. How crazy is that?"

What is she saying?

"What are you saying?" said a confused Choy. "That you have no free will? That what you've said to me in the last ten minutes has been an act? That none of it is true?"

"Everything I told you about my husband is true."

"Then what exactly are you saying?"

"He told me that a woman's power comes from her sexuality. He told me I am nothing without that. He told me to use it to make you trust me."

"And his telling you this made you angry?"

"As you said, he thinks I am his property, his whore, nothing but a means to get what he wants."

"But even though he made you angry, you went ahead and did his bidding?"

She shook her head. "No, you don't understand. I was determined not to do what he told me, to tell you the truth instead and I did. But you didn't believe me, not really. I could see it. Not until I flirted, stared into your eyes, offered myself … then you believed me. So Peter was right: A woman's power comes from her sexuality."

"Sexuality is powerful but that doesn't mean it's your only power. You run your own public relations company."

She hung her head. "I tried, but we've been losing money for two years. Peter told me that's what would happen and he was right."

"Every business catering to the oil industry has been losing money," said Choy. "Everyone says so."

"It doesn't matter why," she answered. "I failed, that's the truth and the bottom line. That's the power of capitalism, it separates winners from losers. And I am a loser."

"Capitalism makes most of us losers."

She looked stunned by his words. "Are you a communist?" she said, not sounding accusatory, but rather inquisitive.

"That's an extremely imprecise word that has many different meanings, depending on who is using it."

"But you don't believe in capitalism?"

"I don't believe in any 'ism' except for journalism, which means I question everything, including journalism."

"I've lived my entire life with people who believe in capitalism and hate communism, but I'm not sure what either really mean. The truth is I'm not sure about anything."

"Why did you come here?"

"I told you, my husband sent me."

"Why? What are you supposed to tell me?" Choy said, the sternness in his voice a result of his frustration at her avoiding the subject.

"I'm supposed to make you believe me again."

"By any means?"

She nodded.

"Including telling me a story about how he is an abusive husband who has threatened to have you institutionalized?"

"Yes."

"Including having sex with me?"

She gave him a look he didn't recognize. "That was my idea. But he didn't object. He never objects."

"You've done it before?"

"Do you think it improper when men use their bodies to become multimillionaires?"

"You mean like athletes?"

"Who keep scorecards about how many women they sleep with. These are men's heroes. But if a woman uses her body to get ahead …"

"Why did your husband send you, if he sent you?"

"Do you know what the Proud Boys call their organization for women?" she said sounding upset. "'Proud Boys' Girls'. Peter wants me to join."

For a moment she looked angry, but that passed quickly.

"Peter thinks he is smarter than me, and I let him, but the truth is …"

"Do you even know what truth is?" Choy said, interrupting her.

"The truth is," she continued, "nothing happens in our family except what I want to happen. Men are so predictable and easy to manipulate, you, Peter, all of you. You believed me when I was crying, didn't you?"

Choy shook his head in disbelief about what she was saying rather than answer her question.

All of these people are crazy, her and her husband, Brinkman, Turner, Dobson, all of them are off.

"I studied acting in the theatre program at the University of Calgary," she continued, "so you shouldn't feel bad by how easily fooled you were."

"Why did you come here?"

"To confuse you," she answered after a few moments, a smile forming.

"Well, you've succeeded at that."

"To make you think we're all crazy."

"You can check that box as well."

"To make you underestimate us. People who think there's only one reality and use it to judge everyone else, always underestimate the power of a reality created by others."

"That sounds like your husband talking."

"Is it so hard to believe that he was repeating something I told him?"

"You create your own reality?" he asked.

"Through the power of our will, yes," she said, looking momentarily serious.

"Why did you come here?" said Choy, tired of her games.

She smiled again. "It is simple really. When it comes time for you to write our story, I want it to be clear who is really in charge. The others, they will all make their claim and because they are men you will believe them."

What is she talking about?

"But you need to ask yourself why was she the first one? Why was she the one who told you the others would make the same claim? And the answer is because it was her idea. They all copied her. They all learned from her. So she must be the one."

"I really don't have a clue what you are going on about," said Choy. "And I'm tired of this conversation. Could you please take your own private reality somewhere else."

As Choy stood he held out his left arm and pointed to the exit.

She is completely bonkers.

"Please," he said.

As she stared at him, there was a knock at his hotel door.

"Please," he repeated to Catherine. "I have another guest."

As she continued to sit and stare, he moved to the door and looked in the peephole. It was Ginger Goodwin again.

"I wanted to drop by to say thank you for helping me," said Goodwin. "I thought of phoning, but those neo-Nazis have made me a little paranoid."

"Bal is not here," Choy said and Goodwin looked embarrassed.

As his newest guest followed Choy into the living room, Catherine Baxter stood up.

"Hey, I'm sorry, I didn't know you had someone here," said Goodwin.

"She's on her way out," said Choy, giving Baxter the evil eye.

Goodwin stared at Choy and then at Catherine, obviously wondering about the dynamic between them.

"This is Peter Baxter's wife Catherine … Baxter," said Choy, in a way that made the fact she kept the guy's last name significant. "And this is your local Calgary neighbourhood anarchist, Ginger."

"Hey," said Goodwin.

"Pleased to meet you," said Catherine, holding out her hand.

After the two shook hands there was an awkward few moments before she began walking away from the couch. Before reaching the hallway into the entrance area she turned. "Remember what I told you. They'll say it was them, but it was really my idea. All of it. I'm the one who thinks of everything."

As she opened the door and walked out of the suite, Goodwin looked perplexed. "What was that all about? I sure as hell hope you don't have a thing going with Baxter's wife."

"Did it look like we have a thing going?"

His response was a shrug.

"She showed up here and first claimed her husband is abusing her and then says she is actually the brains of the entire operation, or at least that's what I think she said. She didn't make a lot of sense. Of course, there's always the possibility she's crazy like a fox."

"Baxter, Brinkman, the Three-Percenters, Proud Boys, Odin Militia, there's something going down," said Goodwin. "My contact says there's a lot of chatter about 'being ready' and 'shit could hit the fan'."

"A few days ago you thought that meant planning the Stampede bombing."

"Do you really know it isn't?" he answered.

An interesting question.

"If Catherine Baxter really is crazy as a fox, she sets us up, knowing we'll discover the set-up," said Choy. "Which makes us think the entire story is bogus, so we don't investigate that possibility anymore."

Goodwin nodded.

"I guess that's plausible, if you're a conspiracy nut," said Choy.

"And what are these extreme right, White nationalist, neo-Nazis known for?"

"Their conspiracy theory explanations of everything," Choy answered.

"Exactly."

"But they're crazy and we're sane. If we start thinking like them … they win and we lose."

"I agree it's not pleasant, but we do need to think like them every so often in order to figure out what they're planning."

"I've reported what we were told to the police, I don't know what else we can do," he said.

"Well, at a minimum we can keep our eyes and ears open and don't make assumptions."

As Goodwin spoke, Choy's phone began to vibrate. It was from a blocked number, but he had a feeling the caller had important information. "I need to take this call," he said.

"Can I use your bathroom?" asked Goodwin.

Choy held his hand out as an invitation to use the facilities then used one finger on the end of it to answer the call.

"I have what you asked for," said the voice on the cellphone. "The encryption key is 915621*&/azrb. You got that?"

"Give me a moment," said Choy as he pulled a pen from his shirt pocket and wrote on a hotel pad on the desk in the corner. "9915621*&/azrb?"

"Correct."

"Thank you."

TwoSpiritPhoenix had given Choy a link, username and password to a secure encryption key website. Once logged in, he punched in the numbers and letters that ze had given him, which generated an encryption key, that he then used after opening the encrypted Word file downloaded from a secure server. Ze had told Choy that the file was erased from the server immediately after download. Ze had also told him that the safest way to keep any information ze sent was by printing it, then immediately put the Word file into the 'incinerate trash' icon that ze had put onto his laptop. "Paper really confuses anyone under the age of 40 and that's most hackers," ze had told him.

But since there was no printer in the room, Choy saved a pdf of the downloaded file onto a USB thumb drive, then incinerated the Word file. As he stood up to take the memory stick downstairs to the business centre, Goodwin was staring at him from the other side of the living room.

"I really think we need to consider the possibility that Catherine Baxter is not crazy," he said. "Something is going on, I know it, and we may have a way of finding out what."

"I've got to print something," said Choy, as he headed to the exit. "I'll be back in five minutes, or better yet, come with me downstairs and we can talk on the way."

Why do I trust this guy?

"Okay, sure," said Goodwin.

Because he's so earnest, so young, so believable. He'd be a lousy liar.

"Before we go out into the hallway," he said, tagging at Choy's shoulder from behind. "I got some more information from my contact."

"The same one who helped Catherine Baxter set us up?"

"Maybe he did, maybe he didn't."

"What did he say this time?"

"They're meeting tomorrow at 7 a.m."

"Who?"

"All the important guys from the extreme right in southern Alberta — Proud Boys, Three-Percenters, Odin Militia and somebody from the USA."

"Like an outsider who is brokering a deal amongst the groups up here?"

"I was told who, when and where, but not exactly what or why."

"Could we get a look, take some pictures?" said Choy, thinking that photos were the one key element they were missing for a story.

"Exactly what I was thinking and yes we might be able to. It's a park on the south side of the Bow River, just west of Crowchild Trail. They're meeting at the launch site for canoes and dinghies. I've been there dozens of times, to put my inner tube into the river and float down to Prince's Island. There are trees very close to the water's edge where we could hide, but I've got an even better idea. Sometimes when we ride the tubes, guys put on wet suits and goggles — the water is very cold, even this time of year. We can take a couple of tubes, wetsuits and snorkel masks and watch them from a small island about thirty feet from the boat launch. If they see us, we just hop onto the tubes and float down the river. I even know a guy who has an underwater camera."

Choy nodded. It sounded like a decent plan.

"But we need to get there very early. And afterwards, if it all works out, we'll really float down the river. It's a lot of fun."

It sounded like it might be.

"Okay. Why not?"

It was worth the risk to get some visual evidence of the guys they would be writing about.

***

Less than two weeks into official summer, the sun rose only a few hours after it set, but because of Calgary's elevation even the very short 51-degree latitude nights and early mornings were quite cool, so Choy was happy to be wearing the wet suit with running shoes on his feet to stay warm and better navigate the slippery gravel bottom of the Bow River. They arrived at 5 a.m., twenty minutes before sunrise, unloaded the car then inflated the tractor tire inner tubes with a portable compressor and instructed Goodwin's friend Margaret to meet them in four or five hours at the Prince's Island boat landing. When the car left and the two men had a careful look around to make sure no one was watching, Goodwin pulled a half dozen miniature microphones and a small receiver from his backpack.

"Margaret is an environmental biologist. She uses these for studying the vocalizations of Black Tailed Prairie Dogs. I borrowed six of them, but it's better if she doesn't know. They transmit to a range of about a hundred metres, so if we hide them in the right places, we should be able to listen in from over there."

After scattering the microphones over an area they hoped would give them the best opportunity to monitor conversations, they carefully made their way across the rocky bottomed, shallow river channel to the small island where trees and tall grass would give them decent cover. They placed the tire tubes on a gravel beach on the far side of the island ready to push off if they were spotted. Then they laid down in some tall grass where they had a good view of the spot where the meeting was supposed to take place on the south bank of the river, plugged in two sets of earphones into the receiver to check the sound and readied the digital camera with a 150-600 mm zoom lens.

After 30 minutes of waiting a black SUV arrived from the park's gravel road into the 50-metre-across boat landing area that extended about 15 metres back from the shore line. Four men, probably Brinkman's security guards, immediately got out of the vehicle and deployed in different directions to determine if anyone was nearby. About 30 seconds later they returned to the vehicle and gathered in a rough circle in front of it. After another ten minutes four identical black SUVs drove up the gravel road and parked at the four corners of the open space. Out of each a driver first appeared, looked around, got nods from the security guards in the middle of the clearing and then four back doors opened and one man got out of each vehicle. Choy, watching the scene unfold through the telephoto lens, quickly identified Brinkman and Baxter but did not recognize either of the other two men. He was surprised that Turner was not one of the four "leaders" of the far right.

As the four men walked towards a picnic table not far from where the first SUV had parked, the eight security guards took up positions that created a rectangular perimeter around them.

"Can you hear anything they're saying," whispered Choy.

"Not yet," answered Goodwin. "But I put one of the mikes under the table where they're headed, so we should be good."

Choy began taking photos of the four men, waiting on each until they were in positions where he got a clear head shot. When he got all four, he did something that had become a habit all the way back to the days before digital cameras when he worked on the Peak student newspaper at Simon Fraser University. Over 25 years earlier he had been taking photos of a man and a woman entering a motel room for a story exposing professors who used their positions to have sex with students. He and the woman also working on the story had remained outside the motel room in a car until the two came out. When confronted the professor got extremely angry and tore the camera from Choy's hands, opening the back to expose the roll of film. Ever since, it had been his habit to remove a roll of film, or its equivalent in the digital age, the memory card, once he had important shots and put it in a safe place. In this instance he quickly slipped the memory card into a small, sealable plastic bag and put that in a waterproof pocket inside the wet suit, before putting another memory card in the camera.

As Choy began to take more photos, Goodwin was playing with the receiver, which wasn't yet delivering the sounds of conversation that could be clearly seen taking place 40 metres away.

"Hey," said Choy, while keeping his eye pressed against the camera. "Two of the security guards are pointing in this direction."

"Keep your head down," whispered Goodwin, urgently, as he pressed himself down into the grass.

"Too late," came a voice from behind. "We've been watching since you got here."

Both Choy and Goodwin turned awkwardly to look up. Turner was standing there, pointing a handgun with a silencer on it at them.

14.

The two men sat facing each other, arms bound behind them with nylon cord to steel load-bearing beams in the basement of a 1960s bungalow. A few minutes after the menacingly large security guard with tattoos covering both arms and an oversized neck had secured them and then walked up the stairs, Turner appeared coming down.

He first went to Choy, ripping off the duct tape that had been applied over his mouth.

"You had to fall into their trap?" Turner said, in a voice barely above a whisper. "You've put me in an impossible position. They want blood."

"Who is they?" said Choy.

"There's a leadership battle," answered Turner as he removed the tape covering Goodwin's mouth. "Everyone is manoeuvring to gain an advantage."

"What the fuck's going on?" shouted Goodwin, as soon as the tape was pulled off.

Turner put his index finger in front of his mouth to indicate the need for silence.

"This one claims to be an undercover RCMP agent," Choy said, his voice at a level between the other's two men's whisper and shout.

Turner immediately turned to him and said in an angry whisper: "If you want to live, be quiet and listen."

Goodwin looked at Choy for advice on how to proceed, but received only a sour face, followed by a shrug.

"Listen to me," Turner repeated, again in an urgent whisper, "and don't do anything stupid. I'm going to say some nasty stuff, but you need to trust me. I have a plan to get you out of this mess. Okay?"

Again Goodwin looked at Choy, whose sour look had not disappeared. "Doesn't seem like we have any reasonable alternative," he said in a low voice, but not a whisper.

"You don't."

As Turner said these words someone began to descend the basement stairs. It was the same thick necked goon who had tied them up. He was carrying a large rock.

"We got this from the river," he said, showing it to Turner.

"Perfect," said Turner, taking the 50-pound stone. "And what about the water?"

"John is getting it."

"You told him the water must be from the Bow? It has to be exactly what they would find in their lungs if they drowned in the river. It can't have chlorine or anything else. He understands that?"

"Ya, he understands, I think."

"You think? Well I don't fucking trust him, he's always messing up," said Turner. "You better go and make sure he does it right."

The other man nodded, but didn't move, as he noticed the tape had been removed from the two captives. Turner turned back towards Choy, then looked at Goodwin, showing both of them the rock.

"This is it how it's going down," he said. "First we're going to knock you both unconscious with this rock taken from the river. Then, when John brings back the containers of river water, we're going to drown you in it. Then we're going to dump your bodies, still wearing wetsuits, back in the river, where they'll be found, along with your punctured inner tubes and other stuff and when the autopsies are done , the verdict will be you somehow hit your heads and then drowned in the river."

As Turner finished describing the perfect murder, he gave the other man an exasperated, hurry-up-we-need-the-water, look.

"The sooner Max and John get the water, the sooner we can put you out of your misery."

Max finally climbed back up the stairs as Turner continued talking.

"This is what happens to any commie prick cuckold and lying liberal media type who fucks with us," he said loudly. After moving to the bottom of the stairs and looking up he seemed satisfied no one was listening so he went back to a spot beside Choy.

"Listen carefully, I'm going to buy you some time. When I'm gone, one of you is going to use this to cut the cord." He held up a piece of a Coke bottle. "Which one of you wants it?"

"Me, I'll take it," said Goodwin.

Turner went behind him and put the piece of jagged glass in his right hand.

"The left hand, please," he said.

"Figures," said Turner.

Choy almost smiled, which, given the circumstances, seemed unwise. That he and Goodwin were dependent on this untrustworthy liar made their position anything but amusing. Still, the association between left-handedness and going against the dominant way of thinking had always struck him as a quirky reflection on the conservative mindset. Some people were so intolerant of anything that deviated from "average" that they were bothered by those who used the "wrong" hand.

More important things to think about.

"Who is battling for leadership? Whose trap did we fall into?" Choy said. "Did Goodwin's source set us up?"

"I don't know. Who is his source?"

Goodwin glared at Choy.

"Who is your source?"

"Did she or he set us up?" asked Choy.

"Someone told you about the meeting," said Turner. "Who else could have told us you'd be there?"

It was Choy's turn to give Goodwin an 'I told you so' look.

"I'm not giving you any names," said Goodwin.

"I'm all that stands between you and a cracked skull followed by drowning."

"Fuck you," said Goodwin.

"We don't trust you," said Choy when the supposed undercover cop looked at him. "For all we know this entire thing has been another set-up designed to get us to trust you and reveal the informant in your nest of neo-Nazi, misogynistic, Odin Militia, Proud Boy, Three Percenters."

"This 'entire thing' is designed to get rid of two annoying pests and send a message to the Antifas and nosey journalists."

"Designed by who?" said Choy, sweating because of the wetsuit. And his arms had begun to ache because of their awkward position. "By you. You're the one who wants to get rid of us."

"Of course. That's the role I'm playing."

"'To earn their trust'. I know your story."

"Cops, neo-Nazis, you're all the same," said Goodwin. "Foot soldiers of the fascist state."

"I cannot believe how you're talking to me given the circumstance," said Turner. "Maybe I should just let you die."

"That will look good to your puppet master in Ottawa or Regina or wherever your boss is," said Choy. "Or are you ready to burn that connection?"

"Maybe I tried my best but the situation got out of hand and there was absolutely nothing I could have done to save your pathetic lives."

"Maybe I don't agree with Goodwin's anarchist inspired language, but he's got a point, doesn't he?" said Choy. "The Proud

Boys, Three Percenters, Odin Militia and all the other extreme right groups share an awful lot in common with the politics of a lot of cops, don't they? Law and order, come down hard on crime, let cops hassle people on the street who look like criminals or have brown skin, generally give more power to cops, glorify the military and war, don't trust immigrants, your basic racist view of the world, women are inferior to men …"

"Shut the fuck up will you!" said Turner, trying to contain his anger. "You don't know who cops are and you sure as hell don't realize how dangerous the guys upstairs are. You mess this up it's not on me, understand? They're going to be back with the water any minute now. I have a plan to buy you 20 minutes, maybe a half hour at the outside. You need to free yourself and sneak out, maybe overpower the one guard who will be left upstairs. If you don't manage that while we're gone, I won't be able to do anything more to help, understand?"

"Why don't you just free us now?" said Choy.

"Because I'm not risking my life for you," said Turner. "They catch me and the three of us will be found in the river. Baxter and Dobson already think I'm an informer."

The conversation was interrupted by movement above and men yelling. A few seconds later Max and John walked down the stairs, each carrying a plastic ten gallon gasoline container, which they placed on the floor near the bottom of the stairs.

"I want to bash that one's head," said the guy who must be John as he pointed at Goodwin. "Max can have the journalist."

As John went to pick up the rock, Turner opened the containers of water and made a show of smelling the contents. He stood up and glared at his two partners.

"I can't fucking believe it," he said.

"What?" said Max.

"You fucking assholes! I can't fucking believe you didn't even get this simple job right. You put the water in fucking gas cans! The fucking water stinks of gasoline! I told you, we have to drown them in water exactly like the Bow fucking River. You think the river has gasoline in it? You fucking idiots! Dump this shit out and ditch these cans. We've got to get clean fucking containers and this time I'm going with you so the job gets done right."

The two men looked at each, then back at Turner.

"Come on assholes, we haven't got all fucking day! Dump this shit in the sink over there and let's go!"

As Turner began walking up the stairs, Max and John picked up the cans of water and took them to the corner of the undeveloped basement where there was a laundry sink. Each lifted their cans and poured the contents in. Max headed straight from the sink, container in hand, to the stairs while John first went to Choy, checking the rope binding his hands behind the metal beam and then to Goodwin. He seemed satisfied that they were securely bound, but as he stood up beside Goodwin, he sneered.

"I'm going to enjoy smashing that fucking rock across the side of your head," he said, then disappeared up the stairs.

"You got the glass?" asked Choy, once he could hear footsteps above them.

"I've got it."

"You working on it?"

"As fast as I can."

"Good. Tell me if there's anything I can do to help."

Funny how a person reacts to danger, thought Choy. The first time he faced what he thought were the last few minutes of his life, his brain more or less shut down. The thought of dying was too overwhelming even to contemplate. The second time he faced imminent mortality, everything seemed to slow down — the proverbial life flashing before his eyes — allowing contemplation of the meaning of his existence. This time he felt calm, serene even, as if there was no need to worry.

Instead he thought about the Word file that TwoSpiritPhoenix sent the previous night. It was interesting, but certainly no smoking gun. Ze had connected five different extreme right groups, four of which were based in Western Canada and one in Idaho. All shared at least one person in common: Turner, the supposed RCMP agent. He appeared to be the key figure trying to create one big neo-Nazi gang. But, of course he would have an alternative explanation.

Tied to a post in the basement of a neo-Nazi hideout and still thinking about the story rather than what might happen next. Good.

He imagined being in goal and practicing the progressions.

What's the worst that's going to happen? I'll be dead and unaware of everything. And Rodriguez will still be able to write the story.

Shuffle, T-slide, butterfly, up, shuffle, T-slide, butterfly.

Where is she? Back with the incel kid, probably. Will she know what to do when …

Of course, the thought of never seeing his kids again was troubling. But that thought would only exist as long as he was alive. Once dead all his thoughts would disappear. This was a comforting thought, not a troubling one.

Why are people scared of no longer existing?

Of course he enjoyed being alive, he was not depressed or even overly stressed most of the time. Life was good. Still, the thought of being dead was at least tolerable, and perhaps even comforting.

Does that mean I've come to terms with the possibility of dying? Death no longer frightens me? That's got to be a good thing.

As he was thinking about his mortality Choy heard the sounds of movement and people talking above. He listened carefully to footsteps headed towards the top of the basement stairs, then said: "Someone's coming."

A few seconds later Allan Brinkman came down the stairs, stared at the two captives for a few seconds, shook his head and then listened at the bottom of the stairs for sounds from above.

"These men think I will meekly accept this, but I can't," he said. "Not murder. I mean I don't like journalists and you self-righteous, politically correct Antifa, but to simply allow them to kill you? I have too much to lose."

Goodwin and Choy made eye contact, both communicating the same thought: 'Well get the fuck out of here then and let us escape.'

"So, what are you going to do?" Choy said after a few moments of Brinkman's contemplation. "Order them to let us go."

"I'm not certain they will follow such an order."

"They're your security guards aren't they?"

"I pay them, but ..." His voice trailed off as if his thoughts were elsewhere.

"Neo-Nazi thugs who don't follow their boss's orders?" said Goodwin. "As an advocate of workers' power and a dedicated Antifa, I'm not sure what to think about that."

Again Choy had to suppress a smile because of the inappropriate timing.

"They follow Mr. Turner's orders. 'It's important to maintain the chain of command', he said, and it seemed a good idea at the time."

"You know no one will believe that?" said Choy. "Especially if you're charged with murder."

Brinkman turned to face Choy, his face revealing a certain self-doubt. "I mean, at the appropriate moment, when the time comes, we must act. That's understood. A war is coming and people die in war. That's the way of the world. Violence is the midwife of all significant change."

The bastard is trying to psyche himself into agreeing with killing us!

"But I must think of my position," he continued, now arguing the other side. "If I'm convicted of murder, they will take away all control of my companies and then where will the money come from? The movement will wither on the vine without the necessary funding, just like grapes without enough water."

That's it, convince yourself that being Mr. Money Bags of the far right is more important than killing us.

"I'm not a violent man," he continued. "I understand that is my weakness. Peter explained that very well. The influence of the liberals and cuckservatives — it has made us so soft that we are afraid to use what has always differentiated the strong from the weak, our will to dominate. Instead of a society where the weak look up to and follow the strong, we have become so focused on 'rights for all' that we can no longer tell the weak from the strong, the smart from the stupid or the bold from the timid. All we see is the mushy middle."

This guy flops around more than a chinook salmon just pulled from water.

"When we have the opportunity we must act, to show the world that there are still some real men willing to lead by example."

"Yes, you do need to be strong and bold, and lead by example," said Choy. "Do what you know is right. Untie me and then go upstairs to distract the guard so we can get out of here."

Brinkman looked confused.

"I'm just a messenger, not your enemy and he's just a kid. You think he deserves to die? And even if you'd just as soon see us dead, do you really want to get caught in this bumbling operation? We have someone waiting for us at Prince's Island and when we don't show up, the cops will come looking. People know we were watching you guys. You'll be prime suspects. Is spending the rest of your life in jail really what you want? Even the most expensive lawyers in the world won't be able to save you from this one."

Choy needed to either get Brinkman to untie him or create enough of a distraction that Goodwin could finish cutting the cord.

"And how exactly would killing us help your movement?" he continued. "They're not even planning to take credit for our deaths. They want it to look like a boating accident. Turner is out right now getting water from the river so they can drown us in it and make it look like we fell off our tubes and hit our heads on rocks in a tragic accident. If Turner is successful, the best case scenario for you is we'll be mourned by our friends and family and no one will have a clue that you did anything at all to shut up a liberal journalist and an annoying Antifa. That's if Turner and his goons are successful. If they're not, you'll take the blame because it's your security team that killed us. And if you tell the judge they did it on their own initiative, that you're not guilty, how will that make you look? A boss who can't even control his own workers? A leader who can't lead? Someone who speaks of the need for the weak to follow the strong but is too weak to admit his responsibility for killing a journalist and an Antifa? A strong leader would stop this nonsense immediately. Take charge of a bad situation. Discipline your men. Make it clear who is in charge. Tell them there are going to be acts of violence but it will be at the right moment and you will announce to the world your responsibility. Otherwise, what's the point?"

As he was talking Choy looked at Goodwin, trying to ask with his eyes how close he was to cutting the cord. The facial expressions seemed to indicate close, but he still needed a little more time.

"You've thought about violence a lot, haven't you?" said Choy. "You've imagined how good it would feel to destroy your enemies and remind the world that men of action are destined to rule. You want to be a hero to thousands of men. Isn't that what you imagined? Would this feel like that? Or would it feel like something embarrassing? Something cheap and maybe even wrong? Is that what you want? Manipulated by Turner to make you look weak and stupid?"

"I'm not weak or stupid."

"I'm not saying you are. I'm saying you've been set up and if you don't stop them right now, you will look both."

"I'm not weak or stupid," he repeated.

Choy glanced towards Goodwin whose body language spoke of being very close.

"Prove it by untying me," said Choy.

Just as Brinkman looked like he had made up his mind there was again muffled shouting and people walking across the floor above. Choy and Brinkman looked up, as if they could see what was going on through the floorboards, while Goodwin, who finally finished cutting though the cord, held up his hands in front of him. As Brinkman walked to the bottom of the stairs to greet whoever was coming, Choy noticed that Goodwin's hands were free, but motioned for him to hide that fact from whomever was coming.

"You got the same message I did?" said Brinkman to the person coming down the stairs.

"What's going on?" said a woman's voice.

Choy and Goodwin continued to communicate as best they could without talking while Brinkman was distracted by the visitor. They needed to prepare for whoever was coming and whatever was about to happen.

"Did you approve this?" asked Catherine Baxter, stomping quickly down the stairs. "Were you even asked? Who made the decision to kill them?"

"They were tied up like this when I got here," answered Brinkman. "I was told they were found spying on the meeting and were about to be punished."

"They weren't found; they were lured. Turner knew they would be spying on the meeting because he had information leaked to that one." She looked at Goodwin.

"A trap?" said Brinkman.

She nodded. "He wanted them caught and killed. And you knew nothing about it?"

He shook his head, looking confused and also embarrassed at his obvious impotence.

"You're supposed to be in charge," she said. "We agreed that our belief in capitalism meant your wealth rightfully gave you the most power."

Brinkman's nod looked more like hanging his head in shame.

"Whoever decided to do this didn't bother to tell you?"

He was reduced to a pitiful shake of his head.

"You're pathetic," she said, an intense bitterness in her loud whisper.

"I know."

"You've always been pathetic."

"I know," he repeated, looking at Catherine very much like a puppy who loved its master but could not figure out how to please her.

Choy immediately thought of Robyn, a dominatrix he had written a feature about 15 or so years earlier, back when the *Sun* had a weekend 'magazine' whose editor was interested in stories about the "wild side of Vancouver", as he put it. The dominatrix had given him some pretty "wild" quotes to go along with even "wilder" photos that, of course, never made it into print because the powers-that-were decided there was a limit to wildness in a family newspaper. The details of the resulting brouhaha between the editor-in-chief, publisher and assistant managing editor in charge of the magazine somehow were leaked to the *Georgia Straight*, a long-time alternative Vancouver weekly, which led to the "resignation" of the assistant managing editor, one of the brightest and best journalists Choy had ever had the pleasure to work with.

The look of authoritative disgust on Catherine's face was very much like Robyn's in what was planned to be the magazine cover photo.

"Assert yourself," she said, more as an order than as a suggestion, but still whispered, as if it were too embarrassing to say fully out loud.

"Yes."

"What do you mean, 'yes'? Give the order, don't obey it."

He nodded his head instead.

"Be decisive. Be a leader."

Another nod, but he looked lost.

"Tell me what to do. Order me," she hissed, urgently.

He looked at her, lost, unable to articulate anything other than acceptance of her orders.

Choy remembered a quote from Robyn about how she saw the role of a dominatrix. It went something like: "I liberate a man from his sense of inadequacy by humiliating him into doing what he has wanted all along to do."

"Decide what needs to be done and order me to do it," she said, in a drill-sergeant-like voice that was still a whisper. "Now!"

Brinkman looked towards Choy, then at Goodwin, before looking directly into Catherine's eyes. "I order you to tell me what your opinion is," he finally said, a hint of triumph in his voice. "A good leader always seeks the opinions of others before making his decision."

"Be decisive," she barked.

"Are you questioning my authority to demand your opinion?" he barked right back.

"No sir," she answered quickly, as if cowed into submission.

"Well then?" he said, waiting for an answer.

"Yes sir." She hesitated momentarily before continuing. "My opinion is that we have a dilemma. On the one hand we need to be seen as decisive, willing to act, willing to ruthlessly destroy our enemies so the people will understand and admire our strength. On the other hand, if we act before we are ready, before we have the strength to succeed, we risk losing our resources and credibility."

"Yes," said Brinkman, nodding at her assessment. "And what is your opinion regarding our current state of readiness? Do we have the strength to succeed?"

"In my opinion, sir, we do not yet have the strength to succeed," she answered. "Our current connections in government are weak, the number of sympathizers in the police and military are not sufficient and too many people still believe the fake news spewed out by the liberal media. In my opinion, sir, the tasks we must focus on today are destroying people's trust in the fake news media, building our own networks of information, helping to elect sympathetic politicians as planned and continuing our work inside the police and military."

"Yes," he said, once again agreeing with her assessment.

"You can see in the United States how much life can be breathed into our movement when sympathizers are in positions of power. Perhaps if we were there it might make sense to kill these two and send a message."

"It would make sense if we were there, at least in certain counties or maybe states," he answered with some authority in his tone. "But not here, not now. If we were to go ahead with this operation, all that has been accomplished in the past few years would be put at risk."

"Yes sir," she said. "You are most certainly right, sir."

"Untie this one," he said, pointing at Choy. "And then he can release his anarchist comrade."

"Yes sir," she said, moving quickly to free Choy's hands.

"And we must get to the bottom of who is trying to undermine my authority," he continued. "I appoint you as my investigator and empower you with whatever resources you need to conduct an inquiry."

"Yes sir," she said, throwing the cord that had been around Choy's wrists to the floor and then indicating with her head for him to untie Goodwin's hands.

"If we don't follow the chain of command our organization will fall apart," said Brinkman. "We'll be no better than this anarchist Antifa."

Both he and Catherine turned to watch Choy pretend to untie Goodwin.

"Of course we'll need to take decisive action against whoever is responsible," said Catherine.

"We must take decisive action against whoever is responsible," he repeated almost word for word.

"Make an example," she said.

"Make an example," he repeated. "I order you to include a section about the need for making an example in your report."

"Yes, of course," she said. "An excellent idea, sir. The men will admire your clarity and firmness."

As Choy and Goodwin stood beside the post that the younger man had been 'liberated' from, not quite sure what to do with their newfound 'freedom', the sounds of people entering the house came from above. Brinkman looked at Catherine, then up at the unfinished ceiling, then back to Catherine, panic in his eyes.

"Have they come back?" he said. "Mr. Turner?"

"I will go find out, sir," she answered, as if following an order.

"Yes, go find out," he said.

As Catherine headed up the stairs, Brinkman watched her. When she disappeared he turned to Choy and Goodwin, as if waiting for them to tell him what to do. The three men took turns staring at each other, no one saying a word.

"What the fuck did he do?" Turner said angrily as he stomped down the stairs, followed by Catherine, then the goons named John and Max.

Turner went straight to Brinkman and stood so close that there was no more than an inch between their faces. The two men stared at each other for at least 15 seconds, Brinkman surprisingly maintaining his composure. Turner turned away first, looking at Choy and Goodwin, then back at Brinkman.

"What's your plan now for dealing with these two?" Turner whispered.

"You never should have trapped them and brought them here," answered Catherine. "You don't have the authority."

Turner gave her a momentary icy glare, barely moving his head. "But they are here and we need to think carefully about what to do with them," he said, keeping his voice down. "What happens if we let them go? Do they go to the police? Will that one write a story about what happened? How will this make us look? Have you considered any of these questions?"

Brinkman kept up his stare for no more than a few seconds before looking at Catherine. "We have considered these questions," he said. "Before we untied them. Tell him what we discussed Catherine."

Everyone looked at her as she began speaking with authority, as if they really had discussed all possible scenarios. "We decided it doesn't matter what they do. If they go to the police, it will be our words against theirs. There will be no evidence of anything other than a car trip from one side of the river to the other. We'll say they have been harassing us and following us and we wanted to teach them a lesson. If the police actually charge us with some crime, we will produce so many stories exposing how the Antifas and the Fake News media always get away with attacking us that we'll gain hundreds of new supporters and thousands in new donations. If this one writes about us, good — the more publicity the better. Our greatest need right now is for more people to hear about us and what we do."

Brinkman looked triumphant. Turner remained impassive.

"What do you think John and Max will think about us letting them go?" Turner said in a voice just loud enough for everyone in the basement to hear. "Or what about Doug upstairs, who has been promised an opportunity, for almost six months now, of carrying out a meaningful action? How happy will they be?"

As Max and John took a few steps towards Choy and Goodwin, Catherine cut them off. "John and Max and Doug understand the importance of chain of command. They know we are nothing without a leader who will guide us to victory. They understand that the time must be right before we act. And they'll get their opportunities for meaningful action soon enough."

The two goons standing in front of Catherine looked towards Turner, who remained in front of Brinkman, calculating whether or not to challenge his supposed boss's authority.

"Is there something you disagree with?" Brinkman said, doing his best to sound like he was in charge.

"Everything is copacetic," answered Turner after a few moments, then motioned with his eyes for his boys to back off.

Catherine smiled slyly at the two goons, with whom there was clearly a history of disagreement. The one named Max looked like he was about to return her smirk, but instead his mouth and lips produced an inaudible "fuck you" before he turned and headed up the stairs with John following.

"Boss," said Turner, as he stepped back from Brinkman. "Could you go upstairs and give the boys a pep talk? They need to hear directly from their leader why letting these two assholes go makes sense and will further our cause."

"Couldn't you go talk to them?" Brinkman answered.

"I talk to them too much. You and Catherine are right, the men need to understand who their leader is. They need to follow you without question and without looking to me for approval. You see how they reacted just now. We cannot allow dual loyalty."

Brinkman immediately looked to Catherine to gauge her reaction to what Turner was saying. She seemed uncomfortable, but how could she disagree with the sentiment, so she nodded, almost imperceptibly.

"Perhaps I should build more of a personal relationship with the men," said Brinkman. "Let them get to know me better."

As Brinkman headed up the stairs, Catherine and Turner took menacing steps towards each other. Then another and another like gunmen with their hands by their sides in a cowboy movie. But rather than the winner being the one with the quickest draw and the truest aim this fight would be settled by verbal bullets.

"I'll squish you, wipe up what remains and flush it down the toilet, if you ever do that again," said Turner.

"Little boy is upset that I out manoeuvred him again?" she retorted.

"A nasty little horsefly with an annoying bite, but don't have any illusions, you're just an insect who can be swatted away anytime I choose."

"Little boy thinks he's so clever, but when we play the game of stab each other in the back, you really are just a beginner. Half the girls in my Grade 5 schoolyard were better at this than you."

"Does your husband know what you're up to?"

"Does yours?"

"Would Mr. Baxter be interested in learning about your relationship with Brinkman and how the men talk about it."

"He'd be interested in that almost as much as learning about how you tried to destroy our group by killing those two and having the police crawl all over us."

"Because of you they call him Mr. Cuck. How do you think he'd react to that little piece of news?"

"How do you think he'd react to proof you are an undercover cop?"

"You're the one who has been leaking inside information to the dimwit Antifa over there."

"You're the one who encouraged Chucky Dobson to get even with that girl hockey player and gave him her address."

As quick as they began the verbal joust, both stopped, seemingly satisfied that mutually assured destruction protected each from the other.

Knowing that too much curiosity killed both cats and journalists Choy decided it was best to interrupt the show before something was said that would cause these lunatics to change their minds regarding the pros and cons of killing him and Goodwin. "As much as I have enjoyed learning your dirty dark secrets, it's time for us to depart, so …" He moved his hand to shoo them away from the spot where they blocked the path upstairs.

As the two combatants turned their intense glares on him, Choy smiled and repeated his hand movements. Much to his amazement they parted without saying a word, leaving an escape route, so he signalled Goodwin to pick up the bag with their belongings and follow him up the stairs. While he half expected Turner to pull a gun and shoot them both in the back, the two men made it into the frozen-in-the-1960s kitchen, where they could hear Brinkman talking to John, Max and Doug in the next room. The door from the kitchen to the back porch was open so they headed that way. But just as they were leaving the house, Peter Baxter and Chucky Dobson entered the yard from a gate at the back corner of the house.

"Waylon, just the guy I was looking for," said Baxter.

"Who let you go?" said Dobson.

The younger man stepped off the sidewalk that ran along the back of the house onto the hard, yellowed lawn that had obviously not been watered in weeks. As he stepped onto the grass he pulled out a military looking handgun that had been tucked into the back of his pants.

"We're going for a little ride," Baxter said, smiling like a used car salesman.

Dobson pointed his gun back towards the gate from which he and Baxter had just emerged.

15.

"You need to check with your leader," said Choy. "Brinkman let us go."

"Shut up," said Dobson, who was sitting in the front seat of the car but twisted around so he could watch and point his gun at the two men in the rear.

"It was his direct order to let us go," said Goodwin. "You're going to be in big trouble with your Fuhrer if you do anything to harm us."

"Give me a reason, any reason, to pull this trigger you pussy whipped, Antifa cock-sucking scum," said Dobson.

"Who said anyone was going to harm you?" said Baxter, placing his hand on Dobson's upper arm to calm him, while keeping his eyes on the road.

"Like Ginger said, your boss is going to be pissed if you hold us against our will."

"We didn't hear any order," said Dobson. "And who says we only do what Brinkman tells us anyway?"

Choy knew these extreme right groups were unstable at the best of times because members competed to be the next Hitler. Violence often resulted from opposing messianic impulses. Brinkman's leadership was obviously in question on numerous fronts.

"Mr. Goodwin, you are an anarchist are you not?" said Baxter.

"What's it to you?" he answered.

"Some people say I'm a right wing anarchist, so perhaps we have something in common."

"I have nothing in common with Nazis, except confrontation."

"We share a belief that violence is sometimes necessary. 'Propaganda of the deed' is, I believe, what you anarchists call it."

"What about it?"

"Sometimes it is good to learn from our opponents, for example the right learning from the left about the use of violence."

"Bullshit. The right has always used violence, mostly state violence. The police break up strikes and kill people of colour simply for being who they are. The prison industrial complex jails half of young black men in the USA and almost the same percentage of aboriginal men in Canada. The military attacks entire countries that step out of line with American capitalist hegemony. The left's violence has always been in response to the right's violence and the right has always used state violence to do its bidding."

"See, there is another point of agreement between us. I too am against state violence and in fact the very idea of the state. The global elites are trying to use their governments and their violence to impose a single multicultural world order to rule over us and turn us into slaves."

"What's your point?" said Goodwin.

"My point is you should not simply view us as the enemy. Perhaps we could be allies in certain fights, for example against the global world order."

"We don't agree on what constitutes the global world order," said Goodwin, "so how the hell could we be allies fighting it."

"Let's define it as the existing social order," he answered.

"You said 'multicultural world order', ten seconds ago. You're a pack of racists, we don't work with you, we fight against you."

"Perhaps for strategic reasons you should reconsider."

"Racism is a way of dividing and conquering the working class and other oppressed people."

"I agree, that's why we want each race to have their own homeland, so they cannot be divided and conquered."

"Spare me your simple-minded, bullshit, racist White nationalism."

"You really should consider my proposal," said Baxter.

"You do know I'm Jewish?" said Goodwin.

"Yes and I admire the state of Israel very much," he said. "In fact the Jewish Nation State law that is being debated in the Knesset right now could be a model for the White Nation State. We also have much in common with the Jewish Defence League and sometimes work closely with them, as we could with you."

"I'm an anti-Zionist Jew and have never thought a 'state for the Jewish people' is a good idea," said Goodwin. "I don't believe the state is a solution to anything but if you have one it certainly can't favour one religion or ethnic group over another. We have absolutely nothing in common."

"But we do. And to prove our good intentions, I am going to drop you off at your apartment."

Choy recognized the LRT bridge crossing the Bow River as Baxter prepared to turn left into the Sunnyside neighbourhood where Goodwin lived.

"And what makes you think I won't call the police and tell them you have kidnapped Waylon?"

"Because you do not believe in the state, so why would you call the police? You didn't the other night when … And besides, Mr. Choy is not our prisoner, he is being offered an exclusive interview, information that I'm sure he will find most interesting."

Choy glanced up at the rear view mirror where he caught Baxter looking at him.

The guy plans to use me as part of an internal battle with Brinkman, Turner and maybe even his own wife.

"Put the gun away," Choy said to Dobson. "I don't do interviews with a gun pointed at me or my friend."

"Charles," instructed Baxter, "do as he says."

While Dobson looked annoyed, he didn't resist the order.

"I believe this is your building," said Baxter.

Goodwin made eye contact with Choy, silently asking him what he should do.

"Go, I'll be fine," said Choy. "If I turn up dead, you'll be witness to my last known location and who I was with."

"You sure?"

"If they wanted to kill me or do me harm, there'd be much better ways of going about it."

The truth? Choy was intrigued by what Baxter might say and the thought of a revealing interview easily outweighed any concerns about his own safety. He had a good story, but what if it might become an even better story with one more interview? Besides, he had survived enough threats to his life that they now seemed almost a normal part of being a journalist. Whether this was good or bad would be the subject of later deliberations.

Right now, I have an interview to do.

***

"I'm going to be brutally honest with my questions and I expect you to be the same with your answers," said Choy, having gotten out of the wetsuit and into regular clothes, sitting on a chair in his hotel suite, where he had insisted the interview be conducted, partly so that the front desk clerk and the lobby cameras would see who accompanied him and partly because his notepads and other tools of his trade were there.

"I wouldn't have it any other way," said Baxter. "Honesty is always the best policy."

"Let's stop right there," said Choy, aggressively. "You demonstrably do not believe, or act as if, honesty is always the best policy. I've already experienced your lies and obfuscations."

While Baxter's twitch revealed an annoyance, the permanent smile never faded. "Let me rephrase that: Honesty is the best policy, except when manipulation and deceit are necessary to a winning strategy."

"A sentiment that Leo Strauss would have approved."

"You are familiar with Strauss?"

"Familiar enough," Choy said. "Political philosophy has long been an interest of mine."

"Excellent, perhaps then we can have a more intelligent conversation than would be possible with most journalists."

"Perhaps," he answered, but his look towards Dobson suggesting the presence of such a person would limit the intellectual sophistication of the conversation.

"Do not underestimate Charles," said Baxter. "I assure you that under his well-practised dumb rich kid nerd demeanour, there lurks a crafty and well educated political philosopher."

Choy found this funny enough that an involuntary smile immediately appeared on his face. But when he glanced towards the kid there was a brief flicker of deceptive intelligence in his eyes.

"Yes, he's that good," said Baxter, noting Choy's glance. "But, if we're going to be brutally honest, let's both acknowledge that journalists are often among the most easily fooled members of society, especially the ones who are earnest rather than cynical. But, of course I would not include either of us in the latter category."

"So, you consider yourself both cynical and a journalist?" asked Choy, "Can you elucidate?"

"What more is there to say?"

"Did you get into journalism because you were cynical? Or did you become cynical as a result of being a journalist?"

"Definitely the former," answered Baxter. "Journalism has always been a means to an end for me, which is true for many of us. The most common of those ends is to earn a living. Ernest Hemingway working for the *Toronto Star*. The journalist who wants to write novels is a cliché. But so is the crusading journalist who wants to change the world. Our so-called profession is a means to an end for them as well."

"Do you consider yourself a crusading journalist?"

"Of course. We come in three basic types: Those who simply follow orders, always trying to figure out what pleases their boss; Those who suffer from the illusion that objectivity, fairness and neutrality are possible and desirable; Those who want to change the world in one way or another and use their journalism to that end. The first two types are, in reality, mere drones doing the bidding of a Queen Bee and her hive, which in this case is the owner of the media outlets that employ them and the existing social-economic system."

"You don't think it's possible to be objective and fair while trying to change the world?"

"Perhaps in some perfect imaginary world where everyone is equal and altruistic, but that world can never exist because that is not how we are," said Baxter. "The best we can hope for is a well-ordered, efficient world that provides the most for many."

"That's the goal of your journalistic crusade? A well-ordered, efficient world that provides the most for many?"

"I'm aware that compared to the grand visions of Marx's socialist perfection or the numerous pseudo philosophical attempts to argue for a political economy of perfect capitalist competition this seems a rather limited ambition. But my goal at least possesses the possibility of success, unlike the utopian schemes of others."

"So your fundamental philosophical outlook is based on what you perceive is possible?"

"I am a radical conservative," said Baxter. "I believe what is and what was defines what is possible. We look to the past and the present to determine how best to move forward."

"Someone of the philosophical lineage that goes back to Edmund Burke and Joseph de Maistre?"

"Exactly," answered Baxter. "Our tradition came about as a response to the radical dreamers who believed they could reshape human nature. We were the people who said, 'no you can't' and have obviously been proven correct."

"The world was better off when aristocracies were in charge?" asked Choy.

"You ask that with incredulity in your voice, as if you can't imagine someone preferring a time before democracy. But what has one person one vote really gotten us? Chaos, ugliness, Donald Trump."

"You don't like Donald Trump? I thought all you alt-right types love him."

"He has been a great help to our movement and we need more politicians like him," said Baxter as Dobson reacted to the conversation for the first time with an enthusiastic nod. "But he is also a symptom of the disease that is democracy. He is the crassness necessary to attract stupid people to vote for good policies. I have been grooming Charles here for the past three years to follow a similar path. It is sad to see the direction that it has been necessary to push him — it's not easy for a smart boy from a good family to become crude, unsophisticated, a bully, but that's what democracy demands to attract the uneducated masses. Donald Trump demonstrates that someone like him is necessary in order to use democracy to get rid of democracy."

What a great quote.

Choy quickly wrote it down and circled it on his notepad, while thinking about the best direction to steer the interview.

"That is your goal? To fool people into electing someone who will end democracy and reinstate some form of aristocratic rule?"

"That's not exactly how we formulate the project," said Baxter, "but in the spirit of brutal honesty, your paraphrasing of our means and end is not wholly inappropriate."

Wow. He actually admits this.

"We believe in the aristocracy of wealth that capitalism creates, a legitimate aristocracy that must prove itself every generation, an aristocracy that already exists, but as Marxists would say, is not yet class conscious."

"A White aristocracy of wealth?"

"Each race will have their own. And we will compete with each on the global level."

"The record of tax cuts for the rich, the accumulation of wealth by a tiny minority and the general neoliberal world order, in contrast to the disappearance of unions seems to suggest your new aristocracy is a hell of a lot more class conscious than the working class," said Choy, surprising himself by saying 'working class' which had generally been considered out of bounds in all his years at the *Vancouver Sun*.

"Which proves our point about the competency of ordinary people to run their own lives as they see fit," said Baxter. "And proves my point about the actual existence of an aristocracy that has not yet proclaimed itself the ruling class. It is our job to make them understand this is necessary."

"And you think people will simply accept that?"

"Which people are we talking about?" said Dobson, speaking for the first time. "Our supporters or the socialist, pussy whipped cucks who we will crush."

"In his unique crude way Charles has answered your question, but I would offer this further elucidation," said Baxter. "Human nature being what it is, most people prefer the certainty of a strong leader over the uncertainty of competing political parties.

This has been proven time and time again, so we foresee the majority ultimately supporting our cause. As for the minority who may disagree, this is why we must capture state power ahead of the transition to our oligarchy of the best and brightest. As your anarchist friend would say, we will use state power to crush that minority."

"I thought you told Ginger you shared his dislike of the state and its repressive apparatus?"

"I do and once we have crushed our enemies, we will no longer have the need for it," said Baxter. "Aristocratic states were generally much less powerful than the republican or parliamentary ones that replaced them, let alone the communist states that then replaced the so-called democracies. And that is because people accepted aristocracies as the natural order. When people have accepted and settled into their place in the new natural order there will be no need for repression. Do you think it is simply a coincidence that most aristocracies had little need for a standing army or for permanent police forces? Democracy requires a powerful repressive force because it goes so strongly against the natural order and therefore must compel people to do what does not come instinctively. We will reverse that by reversing democracy."

"And creating ethno-religious states all across the planet?" said Choy. "Are you really going to argue that's a recipe for smaller, weaker repressive state apparatuses? Sounds to me like a recipe for chaos and war as countries fight over which land belongs to whom. Isn't that what history tells us about nationalism taken to its logical conclusions?"

"I am not denying a period of chaos and violence will be necessary. But we are already living in a period of low level civil war. Better that we have the fight that will ultimately happen and settle who gets what so we can finally begin to once again live in peace and harmony."

"You're saying war is the way to peace and harmony? Sounds an awful lot like Hitler and look how that turned out."

"If Hitler had won we would have had peace and harmony by now," said Dobson, interrupting for the second time.

"'War is the continuation of politics with other means'; the properly translated Clausewitz quote is an accurate description of how human beings have acted for many millennium," said Baxter. "Like it or hate it, war has always been with us and always will be. Violence is the natural way of settling disputes."

"Just like women being inferior to men is natural?" asked Choy, who couldn't help his ironic tone. "Because they aren't as good at waging war as men?"

"Women are inferior to men for many more reasons than that," answered Dobson. "Yes, they're weaker, but they're also governed by emotion rather than logic, easily manipulated, not as smart, prone to mental breakdowns, flighty, weak-willed, and much too talkative."

"And you're saying no men suffer from these faults?"

"In men they are seen as faults, but in women they are defining characteristics," said Dobson, smirking.

"And you agree with this analysis?" Choy looked at Baxter. "That's why you're comfortable using hatred of women as an organizing tool?"

"We don't hate women," Baxter answered. "We love them when they accept their proper place in society."

While Choy was intrigued by the thought processes that comprised Baxter's blend of neo-Fascist ideologies, and generally liked to keep the interviewee talking, he also felt that so far the conversation had been too friendly. It was time to get nasty. He turned to Dobson. "Is that how you justify beating Emma Murphy with a hockey stick? Keeping women in their proper place? 'Violence is the ultimate way of settling disputes?' She had a dispute with you and you settled it with violence?"

Dobson smiled and almost nodded, but Baxter's look prevented him from actually speaking.

"Charles has an ironclad alibi for the time that assault occurred, as I'm sure the police have informed you," he said.

"Given to him by his uncle and you."

"The salient point being Charles will not be charged with any crime, but even if he were, there's no way he would be found guilty. And even if he were to be found guilty what do you think millions of young men around the world, fed up with feminism and homosexuality would think of silencing a feminist lesbian hockey player who broke into a private chatroom where forlorn and loveless men were discussing their feelings?"

"You're saying Chucky would be a hero for millions of young men? I think you exaggerate the number by a factor of a thousand."

"Like the liberal media, drinking its own bathwater, believing people think like them, has always underestimated us, you fail to understand the anger of men who have lost their traditional, rightful place in the world. Feminism, female empowerment, pushy broads, are the best recruiting tools we have on the right."

Is he the intellectual leader of this bunch?

"When we talk to these boys and explain the connections between multiculturalism, feminism, the suppression of White nationalism and their inability to find a good wife, they get it right away."

Listening to these words made Choy think about the conversation with his son about a teacher unfairly choosing a girl over him in order to help her self-confidence, and also about what happened to Emma. He felt a wave of sadness. He had believed the world was making progress, that it was a better place for most people than it had been 50 or 100 years earlier, but now doubted that. What if these extreme right-wing nuts won? Hadn't Donald Trump proven it was possible? Could Chucky Dobson really get away with his crime? What sort of life was awaiting his daughter?

"So, you're proud of what you did?" Choy decided to say to the young man sitting six feet away from him. "If you truly are, tell me what you did. Describe how and why you did it. I'll write it all down, put it in my story and make you famous. That's the object of this conversation, right? That's why you want me to interview you?"

Be honest and upfront with these guys.

Choy turned back to Baxter.

"You want my help making Chucky famous? I'll do it, but only if both of you tell me the truth. Remember, you promised honesty."

"There you go," said Baxter, "confusing truth and honesty, like so many journalists do."

Choy chose to stare at him rather than ask the obvious question, which Baxter clearly wanted him to ask. The guy got satisfaction from his simplistic sophistry and, while it might be necessary to play along in a general sense for the sake of a successful interview, this specific bit of fallacious reasoning was going to be especially annoying because it involved important journalistic principles.

"Truth is always relative, but honesty never is," Baxter finally said, unable to hold his narcissistic, self-proclaimed cleverness inside. "Honesty is said to be the best policy, while truth is much too complicated to ever be reduced to a simple program. Faith can be a critical component of defining an individual's truth, but honesty is much less open to interpretation. While we can define our own truth, our level of honesty is always judged by others."

Choy continued to stare blankly for a few seconds past the triumphant smile. The longer he spent with this man, the shallower he seemed to be. Or perhaps this was cover for the depth of his deviousness. He didn't have a good read.

"I have no idea what the words you just said mean," Choy said, shaking his head. "And quite frankly I'm not interested in you explaining them. All I want is for you to tell me what you promised. What's going on with your neo-Nazis grouplets? Why were you meeting this morning? Who is really in charge? What are you planning? Why did you get your wife to tell me that story about a planned bombing at the chuckwagon races? Answer these questions and we'll be done. I'll write a story and maybe the *Herald* or some other publication will be interested in it, hard to tell without knowing what you're going to tell me."

He paused and looked first at Baxter then at Dobson.

"Or, if you tell me the truth about what happened in Emma's apartment," Choy continued, "I can guarantee you the *Globe and Mail*, *Star*, *National Post*, *Herald*, CBC, probably even the *New York Times*, and every other media outlet across North America will be interested in the story I write. You give me that story and I promise to make sure anything and everything you say will be included, no matter how much I disagree with it. Millions of people will learn about you and the reasons why you did what you did."

As soon as Choy said these words he regretted them, not because they were untrue, or even misleading in any way, but because they were an accurate reflection of how far he was willing to go to get a good story. He was willing to give voice to an evil fascist intent on destroying democracy. He and Rodriguez already had a good story. He didn't need any more from Dobson or Baxter. On the other hand, a better story, one with an actual confession and the gory details would get better play.

Of course a professional journalist always strives for the best possible story.

Then why do I feel so guilty?

How far one should be willing to go as part of his or her professional responsibility had been a recurring argument that had gnawed away the ties that bound together his marriage. It started when his ex-wife agreed to represent a man accused of murdering his girlfriend. Or maybe it began when Helena moved from labour to criminal law two years after becoming a lawyer. When they dated during law school she was going to change the world but then decided to become an actor in the theatre of criminal court instead.

Whenever the argument began it always followed the same basic pattern. Details of some horrific crime would appear in the newspaper and he would ask Helena, "could you really represent someone who raped a six-year-old" or whatever shockingly bad deed the person was accused of and she would answer, "that's what lawyers do, they defend people accused of crimes." This would be followed by statements about the critical importance of everyone having the right to representation in court, whether they were guilty or not, then he would argue that was all bullshit because, in fact, only people with money received effective representation and that law was primarily about protecting property. "How is that any different from journalism?" she would ask and describe a world where rich people and corporations could buy journalists by the dozens to influence the so-called 'objective' reporting of the news. Yes, he would retort, but at least journalists don't have to defend child rapists — to which she would respond, no, just presidents who start wars and corporate executives who make decisions to throw thousands of people out of work, destroying entire communities. Both would then agree that their jobs sometimes could be a little like prostitution and they would laugh, at least for the first dozen or so times the discussion arose. But he would always try to get in the last word by saying, "I could never defend someone I knew was guilty, just like I could never work in public relations or advertising" and the smiles by the end of conversations became fewer. As their relationship deteriorated they seldom discussed her clients and their cases because such conversations would always end with the sorts of words exchanged that one could never really take back.

Why did the thought of my wife defending bad people bother me so much? Was it because, like she said, I want to believe life is simple? That people can choose to be pure and always stand by their principles?

He had wanted to believe people could choose between right and wrong, good and bad, but now realized that's seldom how the world works. Most of the time all you can really control is whether or not you do your job well. Beyond that narrow focus for most of us decisions belong to someone else.

He would be doing his job well if he got the story about how a neo-Nazi incel, close to the Alberta provincial opposition party, attacked a female university hockey player and justified it in the name of building a political movement to overthrow democracy, becoming a hero to many young men in the process. But what if, by writing that story, he spread the message that these Nazis wanted spread and contributed to the growth of their movement? How would that be any different from a lawyer defending a murderer or rapist who she knew was guilty?

While he was thinking about the morality of journalism, Baxter and Dobson were looking at each other, communicating with facial expressions.

"We're going to need some time to think about this," Baxter finally said.

"Me too," said Choy. "I'll give you until tomorrow to decide. I have to get out of this hotel and back to Vancouver after that."

"Okay," said Baxter. "We'll be in touch."

I'm sure you will, Choy thought as they left. He needed a shower, to at least symbolically wash away the stench of just doing his job. Also known as the banality of evil.

16.

"Do you know what a Rowhammer attack is?"

"No," answered Choy.

"It's a way of carefully testing weaknesses in a security chip set. It takes time and can't be rushed or you risk discovery," said TwoSpiritPhoenix. "These people you are investigating ..."

"Neo-Nazis."

"These neo-Nazis are very security conscious and have state-of-the-art systems," ze said. "Very similar to the RCMP. In fact, I'd guess the person or persons responsible went to school in Ottawa."

"You mean trained by the RCMP?"

"CSIS, CSE or the NSA. Definitely people who worked with Five Eyes," ze said. "They've already got protection from malware NSA let go rogue."

NSA was the world's largest electronic spying network and the CSE Canada's version of that. 'Five Eyes' were the national security agencies of the USA, Canada, Britain, Australia and New Zealand. A few years before he left the *Sun*, Choy had interviewed an author about his book on privacy in the 21st century who had explained some of the ways governments watched us. The five countries spied on each other and then shared the information to get around legislation that limited internal national surveillance.

This could mean the incels and White nationalists were even more infiltrated by authorities than he thought, or that the extreme right wing recruitment of police had been successful. Or a little of both.

"But you did get in?" said Choy.

"Of course," ze said. "They're good, but they're not creative. They believe their Manichean technology is invulnerable like the manufacturer tells them, even though there's always a way for someone like me, an expert in the spaces between. Even with computer chips, no two are ever exactly the same. If you have a well-developed sense of nuance there can be weaknesses to exploit, subtle differences that can enable pathways and voila."

"What did you find?"

"Everything you wanted. Even more. Their servers and everything on them belong to me. I could wreak havoc or shut them down completely."

"No, or at least not yet. We can't let them know we're watching."

"They're full of hate. You should see the chatroom discussions about women and people like me."

"I want to see it. You have it all?"

"We have it all. There's a new folder on your desktop. The entire history of the incel chatroom, the four associated White nationalist and alt-right chatrooms, internal emails, phone messages, everything. Did you know two of their chatrooms are aimed at young non-white men who hate feminism?"

"You're kidding!" said Choy.

"These people are clever, or maybe devious is the better word. They use hatred of women to stream these young men into different extreme right groups. And you know what's really weird?"

"What?"

"It's like a lot of the propaganda on these sites has a feminine touch."

"What do you mean?"

"It's hard to explain. It's really just a feeling I have. I think a woman was involved in writing this stuff."

Catherine?

Choy immediately thought of Catherine Baxter's claim to be the brains behind the operation.

"Check for yourself," ze said. "You can monitor all their sites in real time."

"Fantastic. You're brilliant."

"Mostly I'm just thorough," ze answered. "Thorough, persistent and creative."

"As good a definition of brilliant as I've ever heard."

"Thank you."

Zirs voice was soft, gentle and husky. Choy had never asked if ze had once been designated a man or a woman, because it didn't seem any of his business, but guessed zirs birth certificate read 'male' because of the voice. Not that it made any difference. But it was probably significant in ways he did not understand. If he ever had the opportunity, after the two of them became truly comfortable with each other, it would be interesting to ask what it felt like to be a transsexual. It might even make a good story.

I'm addicted to looking for stories to write.

Choy decided to change the subject, or at least to think about something other than his obsession with storytelling. "If the neo-Nazis hacked me, won't they see what's on my desktop and know we hacked them?" he asked.

"There's no sign of them getting onto your computer," ze said. "The software I put on your laptop is excellent, almost hack proof. You just need to continue following my instructions. And even if they did get in, nothing is really on your machine, it's all encrypted on a server that would take the world's largest super computer 18 months to break into. But my system is updated at least every six months and new passwords every three months. Plus, we never exchange files or communicate in the same way twice in a row. So we're as safe as technology made by humans can ever be."

As with other personal matters, Choy had never asked where ze had learned the craft of hacking, but based on knowledge possessed and comments made, he guessed it was at one of Canada's security agencies. A further supposition, based on nothing more than an active imagination, was that ze had been a he back then but had to quit when whatever spy agency he was working for discovered his secret.

Why do I assume his gender transition was a secret? Why do I assume ze no longer works for whatever security agency ze once worked for?

"I have complete confidence in whatever you tell me," said Choy.

"A much better rule of thumb is to never have complete confidence in what people tell you," ze responded.

"Sounds slightly paranoid."

"If you had half the experiences I have in these matters you wouldn't say that. Trust me on this one."

"I have complete confidence in whatever you tell me."

"You're funny."

"Perhaps, but mostly I'm just a good reporter — at least I try to be — and that requires people trust me. The funny thing about earning someone's trust — it only happens after they believe you trust them. Would you trust me if you thought I didn't trust you?"

"Who says I trust you?" ze said.

Choy smiled, even though the person he was smiling at couldn't see him.

"I do, but how do you really know that?" ze continued. "And don't say because I told you so, because people are liars."

"Are you a liar?" asked Choy.

"Some people are liars. And you can never tell which ones."

"True enough, but what's your point?"

"Be careful. These people you are dealing with are dangerous and well connected to people in positions of power. People with guns and other weapons and permission to use them. They've almost killed one person already and they are not the least bit sorry. In fact, they seem proud of what they've done."

"I'm always careful."

"I don't think you are."

"I appreciate your concern. I don't understand why you care about me, but I am glad you do."

"You helped a close friend. Someone like me. Someone who shared the worst pain I've ever experienced."

Choy was almost certain he knew who ze was talking about. A story for the *Vancouver Sun* near the end of his time at the news-paper.

"I was just doing my job, helping to uncover the truth. It's what journalists do."

"Not enough of them. Most just tell stories the rich and powerful want them to tell. I should know."

What does ze mean by that?

"Why do you know about journalists?"

The silence suggested ze was thinking about whether or not to tell him something.

"I've got to go now," ze finally said. "You need to look at what I sent you. You need to expose these people."

"Yes."

Ze hung up.

He should expose these people. But how could he do that if it meant giving them the publicity they craved? How could he let them say whatever they wanted, twisting the truth and telling outright lies? Was any story worth allowing people like them to use him?

Maybe all that I need to expose them is in the files ze sent me and what Rodriguez and I have already learned. Maybe we won't need their cooperation at all.

It wouldn't be the first time he caught a lucky break. Serendipity was often the best friend of a journalist.

***

Three hours of looking through the material that TwoSpiritPhoenix sent proved frustrating because while over-the-top hatred for women, gays, and certain ethnic minorities, as well as outright fascism was revealed in all its ugliness, there was little that could link specific individuals to illegal activities. Certainly the racism, sexism and anti-gay bigotry that was on display would cause the police to investigate the websites for violations of Canada's hate laws, but there was no evidence that could help prove who attacked Emma or the two women in Abbotsford.

Choy had the makings of a very good article — an expose of the emerging Canadian neo-Nazi movement and its connections to the misogynist world of incels — but it was not the story he had set out to write. He had wanted to expose the person who attacked Emma, to write something that would force the police to investigate and hopefully charge whoever had hit her across the head with a goalie stick. It was frustrating to be almost certain who did it, but unable to prove it without a confession, something that seemed possible only if he collaborated with the neo-Nazis, offering them the publicity they desired.

Of course I could simply lie to them, have whoever publishes the piece edit out all the quotes or whatever else that portrays them in a sympathetic light. But the problem is telling the horrible truth about them inevitably portrays them in a sympathetic light to some people.

The problem with lying to these people wasn't so much danger as it was unethical. But why should that concern him?

Is lying to liars unethical?

It would at least blur the line between him and them.

Why does that seem the worst thing I can be accused of? Being unethical.

The truth was only bad journalists acted unethically and he was someone with principles, someone dedicated to the highest professional standards. And someone who knew that sticks and stones could break his bones, but names, when they were deserved, would really hurt you.

As Choy was pondering his ethical dilemma, there was a knock at the hotel room door. During the few seconds it took to place his right hand on the doorknob whoever it was had pounded on the door twice more. It was Catherine Baxter, who rushed straight into his bedroom as soon as he opened the door.

"What … where …"

He froze momentarily, confused, but not completely surprised, given her previous behaviour. He followed her into the room where she was standing beside the bed, unbuttoning a light blue blouse, one foot out of the high heel shoe she had been wearing a few seconds before.

"What are you doing?"

She ignored his question. After undoing the last button she pulled at the blouse, freeing it from her dark blue skirt, dropping it on the floor and slipped off her other shoe. She tried to look straight into Choy's eyes but his sight was aimed a little lower, towards the white bra, with embroidered, almost transparent cups that revealed more of her breasts than they covered up.

"What's going on?" Choy said, his voice louder and slightly higher pitched.

Instead of answering, she pulled down the zipper at the side of her skirt and began wiggling her hips so that the garment fell to the floor, leaving her standing there in bra and panties with her eyes fixed on his.

"Why …" he said, flustered and unsure what to do. "I am not participating in this."

He wanted to turn and walk away but was confused as he watched her reach both hands behind herself to unhook the bra, which she held in place in front for a few seconds, then let it slip down below her breasts, before twirling it with one hand over her head. They were not exactly his kind of breasts, but they were nice to look at, nonetheless. She smiled in what he assumed was an attempt to be sexy, but her stylized stripper moves seemed more inappropriate and discomforting than sexy.

"I'm not participating in this," he repeated as he walked the few steps to Rodriguez's bedroom and pounded on the door. "Bal, I need you out here, now. Bal! Hurry please."

As he looked back towards his bedroom, Choy could see a completely naked Catherine pulling a negligee from the handbag she had placed on his bed. As she noticed him looking at her she held up the gown in front of her, demonstrating that it was completely see-through, then pulled it away in what she clearly thought was a sexually enticing manner. But rather than producing arousal, her strange behaviour was causing him tremendous anxiety.

"Take a picture of me," she said, posing.

When Choy didn't pull out his cellphone, she grabbed hers and turned to take a selfie that would have him in the background staring at her.

"Come on, let's have some fun!" she said, backing up towards him and snapping photos.

As he stood in front of the door to Rodriguez's bedroom, she continued backing up until her buttocks touched his. She giggled and he froze. She turned and threw her arms around his neck, while continuing to take selfies and smiling for the camera.

She's setting me up.

As he tried to disentangle himself from the crazy woman in order to knock on Bal's door again, she opened it.

"What's going on?" Rodriguez said, dressed in pyjamas and not completely awake.

"Baxter … Catherine," he mumbled. "She's …"

"Who is this?" said a surprised Catherine.

When Rodriguez saw the scene in front of her, a 95 per cent naked woman with her arms around Choy's neck, she muttered, "what the fuck!"

Distracted by the presence of someone else in the hotel suite, Catherine let go of Choy and he retreated into the living room. Both women followed.

"She showed up here a few minutes ago, headed straight for my bedroom and took off her clothes," said Choy. "Baxter's wife."

"What the fuck!" Rodriguez repeated, this time louder.

"Yes, that the idea," said Catherine, reacting to the last word Rodriguez spoke. "Let's do a threesome with me, you and whoever your cute little friend is."

Catherine continued to take selfies as she spread one arm wide as if inviting Rodriguez to embrace her. Choy was embarrassed, uncomfortable and, if he were completely honest, a little aroused — all at the same time — by the sight of this woman's breasts, hips, and shaved pubic area provocatively uncovered by the sheer white-lace negligee that dangled above. One region of his brain was warring with another; the one further up the evolutionary scale that wanted him to look away lost the battle to the more primal that reveled in sexual desire. Perhaps if he had had more time to react, the higher region would have won out, but what happened next banished the more evolutionary advanced part of his favourite vital organ into the background by flooding his body with a fight-or-flight hormonal cascade.

As Catherine was advancing, someone once more began pounding loudly and aggressively on the door to the suite. A voice was yelling "I know you're in there. I know you're in there."

Choy looked towards the door, then back at Rodriguez who looked at him, then at Catherine whose faux sexual come-hither look suddenly disappeared, turning immediately into one of panic. "It's my husband," she said, in a quiet voice that Rodriguez and Choy could barely hear.

Of course it's her husband. This is a set-up.

Rodriguez looked back at Choy who had taken the few steps to the door and was in the process of opening it. As the doorknob was turned, he was thrown back by the force of someone pushing the other side and Baxter crashed into the hallway, a gun in his hand. "Where is she?" he said.

He waved the gun wildly, first pointing it towards his wife in the living room and then at Choy who slowly sank to a seated position on the hallway floor. But when he saw Rodriguez, who was standing behind Catherine, Baxter stiffened, momentarily immobilized.

His eyes met Rodriguez's then Choy's before fixing on his wife. After a brief hesitation Baxter charged forward, pushing Rodriguez out of the way to face his wife who stood there, more exposed than just plain naked, gun pointed loosely in her direction. After a moment he turned, looking over at Rodriguez who had moved a few steps back towards the kitchen and then at Choy who remained seated on the floor, back against the hall wall across from the entrance door, eyes wide, ready to act as the fight-or-flight hormones had taken control of his body.

"Why is my wife naked in your hotel room?" he said, gun pointed in Choy's direction.

"I honestly don't know." Choy said as calmly as he could under the circumstance. He had read dozens, maybe hundreds of stories about men killing wives and lovers in exactly this sort of situation, so was expecting a bullet to enter his body at any moment.

"Why is my wife naked in your hotel room?"

"I was doing some work and she knocked on the door a few minutes ago and I let her in. She marched straight into the bedroom and began taking off her clothes. I didn't know what to do, so I knocked on Bal, my intern's door, waking her up. Catherine started taking pictures with her phone and walking around, like that. That's all I know. Honest."

Baxter turned back to Rodriguez, who nodded. He then turned to his wife. They looked at each other for a few moments. He looked more and more troubled while she grew angry.

"I wanted him to fuck me," she said, an ugly tone in her voice. "To humiliate you like you've humiliated me."

Baxter stared at his wife, then momentarily glanced at Choy.

"I've seen the way he looks at me," Catherine said, walking towards her husband, then slipped past him. "He desires me and he treats me better than you do."

She walked into the hallway, past the corner where Choy was sitting on the floor, back against the wall. She turned to face him.

"You like the way I look, don't you?" she said, pirouetting to show off her body.

Choy tried to focus on the doorknob, but again that primitive part of his brain took control of his eyes and they scanned Catherine from head to ten toes and especially parts in between.

"I can see the desire in your eyes," she said. "A woman can sense it in a man."

Then suddenly her seductive smile went cold as she turned to her husband, who stared at her from the living room.

"He can't get it up anymore, unless he humiliates me," she said. "A soft, wrinkly, little boy's penis, not a real man, unless …"

"Don't," said Baxter, pointing the gun at his wife.

At first Choy thought she was scared by the gun, but after a moment's hesitation Catherine lifted up her negligee above her hips

"He made me shave down there even though it gets very itchy and he makes me pretend I'm 12 years old, playing doctor with him. I told him I didn't want to but that just makes him more excited. Then he wanted to watch me shave myself, even though I cried, begging him to not to insist. But that also just made him more excited."

"Don't," Baxter repeated, looking over at Choy, then at Rodriguez who had reappeared from the kitchen, then back at Catherine before re-emphasizing he could shoot her at any moment, by aiming the gun at her head.

"I've called the police," said Rodriguez, as she stepped into the living room to show Baxter her cellphone. "The 911 operator is listening now so put down the gun."

"You wouldn't believe what he's made me do over the years," continued Catherine. "On our wedding night, when I was a virgin, that was the only time our sex was ever normal. At first it was oral sex he wanted, which made me gag, but he kept on insisting and convinced me I shouldn't feel humiliated by that, because everyone was doing it. And then all sorts of other things, he always told me I would do them if I loved him and was a good, obedient wife. It wasn't until he made me have sex with another man, so he could watch, and all the things he wanted to put inside me, that I knew it wasn't normal. That I knew it was all about humiliation for him. That's what arouses him."

Rodriguez continued to hold up the phone so the 911 operator could hear and Baxter could see that someone outside was listening. But he paid no attention, instead looked back and forth from Choy to Catherine.

"He's even aroused right now, because of what I'm saying and doing. Aren't you? He knows how humiliating it is for me to admit all this in front of strangers."

Both Rodriguez and Choy looked into Baxter's eyes and knew what his wife was saying was true. Catherine looked at each in turn.

"You can see it in the way he looks, can't you?"

She turned her head back so that she was once again staring into her husband's eyes.

"You want to rape me, don't you?" she said quietly. "The thought of forcing me is the only thing that excites you now, isn't it? Or how about if Mr. Choy and I ..."

She put her arms around Choy, pressing her breasts up against him as her husband pointed the gun at them. Then she slowly lowered herself until falling to her knees, touching his chest and stomach while doing so until she was kneeling in front of him, her face an inch away from his belt buckle.

What the fuck do I do?

For a few moments Choy thought he was about to be a dead man, but Baxter didn't pull the trigger. Instead he lowered the gun and the words that came out of him were whiny and pathetic. "Catherine," he said, breathing heavily. "Please stop. This isn't going to work."

"You tell me it's all my fault, that I'm frigid, but ..."

Choy finally disentangled himself from Catherine, who was staring at her husband, anger growing in her eyes.

"You are pathetic," she said, standing. "You had the opportunity but couldn't do it."

What is she talking about?

"She's mentally ill," Baxter said. "She makes things up. You can see that, right? She has hallucinations."

Shooting me. He had his opportunity to shoot me.

"I am sick, but I don't make things up," she answered quickly.

"Catherine, we need to get you to a doctor," Baxter said as he flipped the safety switch of his gun and made a show of putting it in a holster that hung from leather straps under his shirt, in the small of his back.

"Why don't you give the gun to me, instead of putting it there?" said Choy as he stood on the other side of the room.

Baxter quickly jabbed his right hand at him, index finger pointed straight out, to signal 'back off!'.

"He tries to control every aspect of my life, that's why I'm sick," said Catherine, who now looked defeated rather than defiant. "Do you know what's it like to have someone telling you what to do all the time? Someone who is not even half as smart as you are."

"Catherine, why don't you go into the bedroom and put some clothes on," said her husband, reaching out his left hand in her direction.

"Don't you dare touch me!" she screamed and backed up.

"You're naked, worse than naked, and you're embarrassing yourself," he said, trying to sound gentle and in charge. "Ask them, him and her, they're both embarrassed for you."

Catherine looked at Choy, who tried to remain impassive, and then at Rodriguez, before shaking her head. "I don't care. Why should I care? Why should I be embarrassed? I'm just doing what you told me."

Baxter studied his wife carefully, then glanced at Choy. His right hand moved ever so slightly back towards the gun.

"The police are coming, won't you find that embarrassing?" he asked his wife, again using a gentle voice. "If you get your clothes this young woman can tell the dispatcher that there's no longer a need for the police to come. I've put the gun away; you're putting your clothes on and everything is under control."

"This was all his idea, he told me to come here and take off my clothes," Catherine said abruptly turning to Choy, before looking back with tired eyes, at her husband. "I'm so pathetic that

I once again did what I was told. He was going to shoot you. That was his plan, but then this other woman was here. He should have just shot you anyway. I gave him the opportunity. I said the words we planned. I played my part perfectly."

Choy watched as Baxter seemed to be deciding whether or not to grab his gun again.

"He said no jury would find him guilty if he shot a man who was having sex with his wife," she continued, looking down at her feet as if ashamed of what she was saying. "He said such a trial would be good for his political profile."

"Catherine, do you want me to get your clothes from the bedroom?" said Baxter. "I can help you get dressed."

"He wanted me to have sex with you, so he could watch and then shoot you," she said, mostly to herself. "And then he was going to shoot me as well."

She looked into his eyes as if realizing this for the first time. Baxter's fingers wrapped around the pistol's grip.

"You were going to shoot me too, weren't you?" she said. "No jury would convict you of killing your naked wife in another man's hotel room."

Baxter looked at Choy, then at Rodriguez and back at his wife. "You're delusional," he said.

Choy made eye contact with Rodriguez, then looked at Baxter's hand touching the gun behind his back, trying to send a message that he was going to try grabbing it.

"You've tried to convince me I don't see what I see or hear what I hear, but I see, I hear and I remember, despite what you say."

"Catherine, please put some clothes on."

She sneered at him and quickly let what little clothing she had on fall to the floor.

"Catherine!"

"These men he hangs around with, they believe European women should have babies to prevent the Great Replacement. They think that's all we're good for. I'm the smartest one, their natural leader, but babies are all I'm good for. And he doesn't give me credit for anything. Not for the good or the bad."

Husband and wife made eye contact.

"Do you know that I was the one who assaulted your friend Emma?" she said, looking at Choy. "But he even tries to take away credit for that."

Now she really had the attention of everyone in the room.

"He sent me there to talk with her. 'Have sex if you have to,' he said. He wanted me to have sex with her. He wanted to watch two women doing it. We were waiting outside when that horrible protégé of his was inside, trying to intimidate Emma, but she stood her ground and he came out whimpering like a little puppy. So my husband told me to go in and have sex with her. But Emma never wanted me. She didn't even want to talk about sex, but about the things those men were writing in the chatrooms my husband ran. She told me about what happened to her grandmother, who she loved as much as her own mother. She asked me how I could live with a man who encouraged young, lonely boys to talk like that about women, who was using their loneliness and anger to manipulate and turn them into neo-Nazis. She was so friendly and energetic, like a little girl making a new best friend."

"So why did you hit her with a goalie stick?" asked Rodriguez.

"I told her the incel chatrooms were my idea," Catherine said. "Attract the young men who were desperate for sex and manipulate them. Choose the right ones, the ones full of anger. Make them do an initiation that excites them, rape works the best, and keep a record. Then they will always do what you tell them. And it worked beautifully. We have hundreds of potential new recruits. It was all my idea, but no one gives me any credit."

She glared one more time at her husband, then turned to Rodriguez.

"They all think it was his idea because he's a man. 'The husband thinks and the wife does.' That's his favourite saying even though he knows I'm smarter than him. He knows it."

"But why did you hit her with a hockey stick?" Rodriguez asked again.

Catherine shook her head, then sat on the couch. She stared blankly ahead for a few seconds and then began to cry. She looked up at Rodriguez and said: "Are you married?"

Rodriguez shook her head.

"My entire life— my father, mother, uncles, aunts, husband, everyone — has told me a wife must obey her husband. I know there are people with other opinions, but … He told me we had to shut her up. I asked her nicely and she laughed. We argued and she called me a Nazi whore, which I did my best to take as a compliment, but … I threatened her, but that didn't work either. Then I told her … that if she wanted we could have sex. I thought that was ridiculous, but my husband said dykes were like men — sex addicts — so maybe he was right, I didn't really know. But she …"

She began to sob.

"What did she do?" asked Rodriguez.

"She looked sad and asked me why I was saying this and I told her the truth."

"Because of your husband?" Rodriguez said.

Catherine nodded.

"Then what?"

"I was crying and she began to comfort me. She was nice to me. Not in a sexual way, in a nice way. She acted like a friend."

Choy and Rodriguez waited for her bout of sobbing to end, while her husband mostly stared at the floor, looking up only once.

"I don't know why I did it," Catherine said, after she had pulled herself together enough to talk. "We were talking, like two good women friends might — I'm just guessing there because I've never had a woman friend since we married— and the thought of my husband, all those other men, laughing at me for being friends with a dyke took over my mind. They would have made jokes, belittled me. And so when she wasn't looking, she was sitting at the kitchen table pouring another cup of tea, I grabbed the goalie stick that was leaning against the wall and swung it as hard as I could at her head. She fell over. Blood pooling on the floor. But I walked out quickly with the stick and told my husband Emma was no longer a problem. We burned the stick, but later when he found out exactly what happened, he got angry, not because I did it, but because I wanted to give myself up to the police. He was angry, not because I might go to jail, but because I was a woman. He wanted 'to take credit for silencing the Antifa dyke' were his exact words or let his sick protégé become a hero to the other sick men by saying he did it."

She stared at her husband, but he continued to look at the floor, fingers on his right hand twitching near the gun grip.

"I'm sorry. I'm really sorry."

Choy thought she was saying sorry for her assault on Emma, but she may have been saying sorry to Baxter, he wasn't sure. She began sobbing again, this time for only a few moments. A second after becoming silent, she looked up at Rodriguez.

"Can you help me to the bedroom, please. I need to get dressed," she said calmly.

As Catherine stood up and Rodriguez moved towards her, Choy noticed Baxter wrap his fingers tightly around the gun and flip open the holster strap with his thumb. At that exact moment there was once again aggressive knocking at the door.

"It's the police," came a deep and loud voice. "Open the door immediately. Open the door, now."

As Rodriguez opened the door, Baxter reattached the holster strap and moved both his hands so that they were in front of him.

17.

Rodriguez sat in the front seat of Choy's convertible as they drove on the TransCanada highway towards Banff.

"Beautiful sight," said Choy as they came over the crest of a big hill, framing the foothills and the Rocky Mountains behind them like a tourist poster. "Been making this drive since I was six years old and every time I still feel a thrill about heading into the mountains."

"It is a magnificent sight," she answered, but with little enthusiasm.

"What's wrong?" They had grown close enough and she was easy enough to read that he felt comfortable assuming something was bothering her.

"I feel bad leaving so quickly, with so many unanswered questions."

"You wanted to stay for the Stampede? I thought you said rodeos should be banned because of cruelty to animals."

"Paying $650 a night to stay in a hotel to be around people dressed in cowboy hats, getting drunk and then waking up hungover early the next morning to have pancake breakfast isn't exactly my idea of fun, even aside from the rodeo part of it," she responded.

"Catherine?" he asked.

She nodded and looked sad.

"We have a great story," said Choy. "You did a great job. You should be proud of yourself."

"Emma," said Rodriguez. "They think her last operation was a success. If we could have stayed a few more days ..."

"I could be weeks, months, even years."

"There's so many loose ends," said Rodriguez.

"You want to be a journalist you better get used to that. 'All the news that we can gather in one shift that fits, and fills the spaces between the ads' — that's what we used to say when I worked for the *Sun*. It's even worse in TV."

"I don't want to be a TV journalist. Too shallow of a medium."

"Good for you."

"I want to write books. Tell important stories from start to finish. Help people understand what's going on in the world."

"Again, good for you. But it's rare to get a story where there's a beginning, middle and end. Especially if you're writing the first draft of history. The best you can usually do is get most of the bits and pieces right. If you want to write books like that you'll have to stick with things that happened at least a few years ago, not current events. They're never neat and tidy. And I'm almost certain the same is true of actual history."

She was silent for a few moments before asking: "Don't you want to know more about why Catherine did it? Or if she did it?"

"You don't believe what she told us?"

"What did she tell us? That her husband's misogyny made her mentally ill, so she wasn't really responsible for her actions?"

"You don't buy that?"

"At one level sure, but isn't accepting that as an explanation just another form of misogyny? I mean, women are so weak they can be made to do anything by their domineering husbands. Isn't that the message? Women are too frail to stand up for themselves."

"There are both frail women and frail men who are taken advantage of by domineering personalities," said Choy. "Who are most of the incels? Maybe even most of the neo-Nazis? Weak, vulnerable people who are abused and manipulated for political ends."

"Was that any kind of defence at the Nuremberg trials?"

The reference to the trials of Nazis after the Second World War surprised Choy. Bal seemed so young. Maybe his own misogyny or at least some kind of ageism was showing.

"So you don't have sympathy for Catherine?" he said.

"I have plenty of sympathy, but just because you're a victim doesn't absolve you from responsibility for your own actions. If she hit Emma across the head with a goalie stick Emma is the victim who should get most of our sympathy."

"You know that when I'm writing this story, I will go out of my way to be as sympathetic as possible to everyone. That includes Baxter and Chucky and Turner."

"Why?"

"Because that's what good journalists do," he said. "We let the people in our stories, as much as possible, have their own voice."

"Thought you didn't like the whole 'he said, she said' form of journalism?"

"I don't. But not because it lets each side speak for itself, but because that's all it does. A good story needs the objective facts, as well as the spin from all sides. So, 'Donald Trump says the moon may be made of blue cheese and Donald Trump says everyone thinks the USA is the greatest country in the world. Democratic House leader says Donald Trump is pathological liar and an ignorant buffoon.' If that's all your story is, you're only uncovering a very shallow and insignificant truth: The words of politicians. To help your readers really understand the world you need to include the verifiable facts about the subject the politicians are disagreeing about and offer possible reasons why they may be saying what they're saying."

"So we let the neo-Nazis and incels and misogynists speak but make them look like ignorant fools by including the truth about what they do and say," said Rodriguez, who was obviously not convinced.

"And expose how dangerous they are."

"Really? I see very little evidence that this is what journalists actually do," she said. "Much more likely to be just 'he said, she said' and the reality-based comment gets exactly the same weight as the made-up-because-it-fits-with-my-politics lie."

"No doubt there's a lot of bad journalism out there."

"Honestly, you think that's all it is? Bad journalism? You don't think the corporations who own the media, big business and governments want journalism to be the way it is? They certainly don't want you questioning them or the journalism they're selling. And most journalists just go along with it."

"What is it with you young people? You're just like my daughter, calling herself a Marxist. If you want a job there are certain compromises you must make, certain things you can't write or say. Number 1 being never criticize your employer. Is that so onerous? Does it undermine the principles of journalism? Or is just common sense? If you're going to be a journalist, you can't take sides, especially against your boss."

"I disagree," said Rodriguez. "To be a good journalist you have to take a side. The side of truth. The side where facts matter. The side of ordinary people. 'Comfort the afflicted and afflict the comfortable.' Don't you believe in that?"

"Sure, but you have to do it carefully."

"How is that possible?"

"It's hard," said Choy shrugging. "Reality is complex. Working in the real world for a pay cheque is a lot more complicated than what they teach in J-school. Working for me is easy in comparison."

"That's why I became a nurse before I started on journalism. I figured having a steady outside income would make me more independent."

She's smart. Smarter than I was at her age.

"Independence might be another word for marginalized," he answered. "Working for a big media company is a balancing act. On the one hand you have to compromise and be careful. On the other hand they offer a big audience. Is it better to write for a thousand or a million?"

"Telling the truth to a thousand is better than lying to a million," she retorted.

"Is it?" he asked, because he was not sure. "Maybe."

It felt weird to be the conservative one in a conversation, even though it seemed to be happening more and more with his children. Was he really getting more conservative or were they becoming more radical? He expected Rodriguez to continue talking, to go after him the way his daughter would, but instead, she went silent, staring straight ahead, the mountains growing larger as the car got closer. Maybe it was similar with people's politics. As you got closer and closer to death, the less important radical change seemed to be. The barriers to that change grew larger and larger, until that was all you could see. Young people were radical because they hadn't experienced how difficult real change is. They naively thought the mountains could be easily climbed. On the other hand maybe young people were in better shape, with more energy and mountain climbing was an eagerly sought after adventure. For young people mountains were not an insurmountable barrier, but rather something pretty to look at, while driving through them or climbing over.

She's sleeping again and doesn't seem the least interested in looking at mountains.

The truth was most young people have no real sense of aesthetics.

God I'm becoming a cranky old man.

He needed to use this quiet time to focus on exactly how to write the story and where to pitch it, but his thoughts drifted.

Bal was right, it was unsatisfying to have questions unanswered. But maybe the material TwoSpiritPhoenix sent will provide more details.

Sullivan is a good guy and I should keep in touch.

Will Emma ever wake up?

A half hour later Rodriguez opened her eyes and immediately began speaking. "What if Catherine is not crazy but rather really clever? What if the whole getting naked and admitting to assaulting Emma was a diversion? What if she really is the brains behind the whole bunch of neo-Nazis and calculated that, because she's a woman and apparently crazy, she won't serve much time for the crime, unlike Chucky, or her husband?"

What if she's Adolph Hitler's distant relative?

His actual response was a dismissive shrug.

"What if there's no such thing as misogyny?" he added a few seconds later, extending his peripheral vision as much as he could to see Rodriguez's reaction.

She briefly thought about his words, before continuing. "Okay, I agree that it seems likely Catherine is mentally ill and that she did what she said she did. I agree that the men in her life are a pack of vicious woman haters so her story is plausible, but how can we know for certain? How can you write that she's guilty?"

"I won't. I'll only write what happened, what she and the rest of them did and said. If she goes to trial we'll report the verdict. The readers can make up their own minds about her ultimate guilt or innocence."

"I guess," she said sounding disappointed after a few moments of thought. "But that's not as satisfying as being certain who did it."

"How many innocent people have been convicted of crimes?" said Choy.

"What's your point?"

"Journalists need to keep open minds. In the real world we write about not everything is black and white, good guys and bad guys. There's shades of grey, doubt, best guesses, suggestive behaviour, mistakes, lies, deception, good cops and bad cops, good reporters and bad reporters."

"Are you 'mansplaining' the world to me?"

"I'm experiencedjournalistsplaining to you," Choy said, a little offended, but not too much. "You did ask to be my intern?"

"Well actually, to get through the program I have to intern for a month," she said. "It's not optional. And you seemed the best of a meagre selection of unpaid choices."

Choy let his eyes wander from the highway to Rodriguez. She was smiling.

"You have a strange sense of humour," he said.

"Surely the daughter you have described has you well trained and used to being teased about male privilege."

"You never teased me on the drive to Calgary."

"I didn't know you then. We weren't close enough for me to feel comfortable teasing you."

"Maybe it was better that way," he said, trying his best to look serious, but then couldn't help smiling.

Again, both occupants of the front seat went silent, each lost in unshared thoughts.

Choy liked this young woman who was self-reliant, hard-working and unafraid of the world. He hoped Samantha would be just like her. Bal would make a great investigative reporter, if she was able to find some media outlet willing to hire her.

It really was a mystery why any young person wanted to be a journalist given the dearth of jobs. To be successful today maybe it took someone like Bal, an independent self-starter, someone who could go out and make a reputation for herself on her own, as a freelancer, to attract enough attention that some media outlet would offer her a job.

Not like the old days.

Thinking about the conditions facing young journalists was not pleasant, especially since there was one sitting beside him. Being a newspaper reporter at a big city daily was a very good job, 30 years ago. But these kids would never experience that.

On the other hand, the life and jobs they have will seem normal to them. They will learn to cope and survive, some becoming excellent journalists, while others settle for just keeping their jobs. And is that so different from when I started?

There would certainly be a lot fewer jobs for journalists. The latest data showed the number of North American newspaper reporters had fallen by more than half in the past 15 years and that layoffs were continuing. Shrinking newsrooms had become such a longstanding fact of journalistic life that it was hardly newsworthy anymore.

I really do need to use this quiet time to reflect on the story. Concentrate.

He needed to write a quick feature. Three, four thousand words in a quality publication, a taste of what might come for a book publisher. If Emma were to die, the book title could be 'Who Killed Emma Murphy?'

If she doesn't die?

The thought this story might be more saleable if Emma died was both distracting from what he needed to think about and profoundly unsettling.

If books and stories are commodities to be sold, writers must inevitably also be salespeople.

It was almost impossible to think this was a good thing, although he did try, momentarily.

Maybe the problem is unfettered capitalism, like Samantha announced at the dinner table a few weeks ago. The commodification of social necessities like news goes against any real democracy.

Jesus, Samantha has gotten into my head with her juvenile Marxist view of the world.

He needed to focus on work. He normally was good at that, but today seemed incapable of concentrating. Perhaps it was the passenger, whose eyes were once again closed. Her presence was distracting. But compared to a newsroom? Maybe he had gotten used to working alone these past few years and simply wasn't as good at filtering out distractions.

"What are you going to write about the connection between incels and neo-Nazis?" said Rodriguez, immediately after opening her eyes again.

"Back to the land of the living?" said Choy. "What do you mean?"

"What do you think the connection is between fascism and misogyny?"

"I think Emma would say that the first fascism was misogyny," he answered, deflecting the question because he was unsure of what his opinion might be.

"Exactly," said Rodriguez, sitting up straight and suddenly looking alert. "Thinking about how these White supremacists use the incel website as a recruiting tool, made me realize how much misogyny is fascist-like. I mean, women are defined as sub-human — inferior, untrustworthy, stupid, emotional — just like the Nazis talked about Jews or Roma or Russians."

"You sure you never took a Women's Studies course?"

"Nursing, journalism, that's it after high school," she answered. "Everything I know about feminism is from the university of life under male domination. I mean there was always a tension in my family. Growing up it always seemed because my dad was Latin and my mother European, but in hindsight maybe it had more to do with her being a feminist and him an authoritarian male chauvinist."

"But not a pig?"

"I love my father. But there's no doubt he thinks women are inferior to men, that wives should do what their husbands tell them and sons take precedence over daughters."

"That must have been tough."

"No tougher than what billions of other women face around the world," she said, then realized something from hearing her own words. "You know what? I take it back. Misogynists are not like fascists. It's the other way around. And misogyny is worse than fascism because it is everywhere. It's so ingrained we don't even see it for what it is. Unlike fascism, which we supposedly fought a war against, misogyny is completely unremarkable, because it is everywhere."

"So, maybe we should fight a war against it?" said Choy, who was familiar with this line of argument because it could have been his daughter speaking the same words.

Why when women talk about misogyny does it always feel like a personal attack?

"Sending an army to fight misogyny is like ordering foxes to defend the hen house or pyromaniacs to put out the fire."

"You definitely have a way with words," said Choy smiling. "Maybe you should help me with the magazine feature and the book I plan on writing."

"How could we do that?" Rodriguez quickly asked, obviously keen on the idea. "Would you assign me to write a certain part? Or would we sit in the same room together writing alternating sentences?"

"The former is more likely than the latter."

"Of course," she said slightly embarrassed. "I mean writing is such a personal thing, you can't really do it together, not at the same time."

"I was thinking more about the problem of a woman working with her male oppressor," Choy said, then regretted it when he saw the look on her face.

"My oppressor? No, I never meant that you were a misogynist or a male chauvinist. You've been nothing but great to me. You never once hit on me or made me uncomfortable, even though we were staying in the same apartment. I mean you did have a few occasions where you treated me like your 16-year-old daughter, but on the whole you worked with me more like a colleague than a teacher. You seem to be genuinely interested in my opinion. If anything, I feel like you've helped me see what misogyny really is rather than acted like a male chauvinist."

"If any of that's true it's almost certainly due to my daughter Samantha," he said, smiling. "I was just kidding, trying to make a joke."

"Oh."

"Not about wanting you to help me with the writing, but about the 'male oppressor' part. That was just me trying for a little levity."

"Of course."

A silence grew again, this time an uncomfortable one.

Funny I never even considered the possibility that I was a male chauvinist before.

Choy had always thought of himself a 21st century man, which without pondering the subject extensively, meant he tried to treat women the same as men and he loved his daughter as much as his son, as well as being supportive and expecting both to be good at whatever they chose to do. Was there anything else? He did think women were different from men. And they were, weren't they? Of course they were. Different body parts, different hormones, different size, different biological roles. But different didn't mean inferior. Women, on average, were better at some things than men and vice versa. The important point was that society shouldn't focus on differences, but rather make sure everyone had the opportunity to succeed in whatever it was they were good at, whether they were men or women. But he definitely self-identified as a man and that was different from being a woman. And he had participated in conversations where men were making fun of women as too emotional or too talkative or too feminine. If someone made similar generalizations about the 'Chinese' or the 'Arabs" he would have objected, or at least not participated so …

Does that make me one? A male chauvinist?

He didn't think so, but maybe he didn't do enough to combat it. Maybe he should have a serious conversation with Sam about this.

He looked over at Rodriguez whose eyes were closed again. What was she thinking? Hopefully about how best to write the story, just as he should be. But she probably wasn't. She was probably thinking about what a male chauvinist he really was.

Or maybe that's what I'm thinking.

This time it appeared Rodriguez had actually fallen asleep. They were well past Golden and getting close to Revelstoke where it would be necessary to stop for gas. Choy kind of wished she would wake up and keep him company. He liked discussing the story with her and listening to her views about journalism, sexism and life in general. Late 40-year-olds need to stay in close touch with youth to stay fresh.

And then he thought about one such youth, Emma, and became sad. But that had the effect of focusing on the story again, which was good.

When he pulled into the gas station Rodriguez didn't stir, but as he pulled out she woke and sat up.

"I'm not convinced Catherine did it," she immediately said.

"How do you sleep like that?" said Choy. "One minute you're out and the next you're engaged in debate."

"Try working 12-hour night shifts, then go to school during the day and you'll learn to get some sleep whenever and wherever you can."

"Not sure I would."

"Did you hear me?"

"We'll never be one hundred percent certain, unless Emma wakes up from her coma and remembers what happened," said Choy.

"Even if she were to wake up, the doctors say she probably won't remember the last few days before she was hit, so that's not very likely," she answered.

"You coming with me to Calgary was not very likely, but it still happened," said Choy.

"You didn't want me?"

He shook his head. "I didn't want an intern, or at least an unpaid one. I was doing a favour for Doug."

"You're welcome to pay me."

He smiled. "It's not a viable business model, but I guess I could." Then he had a thought. "Or how about this? We write the feature and the book together and you get 25 percent of whatever we sell them for?"

"How about 50 percent if we write them together?"

Choy had another thought, an even better one.

"How about you write your version of the story, from a woman's point of view, and I write mine, from a man's point of view, and then we combine them, interweaving the narratives? And then we split the proceeds 60-40?"

"50-50"

"You do realize you have absolutely no bargaining power?" said Choy. "Legally speaking I effectively own you while you're my intern. We both signed the papers from Langara."

"Said the man with all the power, because of the male-created legal system," she answered, with a twinkle in her eye.

She had him and he knew it.

Guilt, it works every time. I really am a liberal sucker.

"Fuck it. Okay, 50-50, if you can write as well as I think you can."

"And who will be the judge of that?"

"Okay, I submit. 50-50, 50-50. 50-50, all the way."

She smiled and threw her arms around him. "I take back all the bad things I was thinking about you," she said, hugging him.

"Hey, I'm driving."

She unwrapped her hands that had been on his neck and settled back into the passenger side bucket seat, a big grin on her face.

"What bad things?" he asked.

"Your daughter is lucky to have a father like you."

It was a corny thing to say, but Choy liked it anyway. The words made him feel good because they acknowledged that he was trying to be the best person, the best father he could be.

"Do you want to pull over and take the top down?" he said. "Looks like the sun has come out."

"That would be perfect," said Rodriguez.

At the next wide shoulder, he pulled the car over. As the soft top travelled its route into storage, she seemed eager to say something else. "Doesn't it scare you?"

"What?"

"Having a daughter in a world with these incel neo-Nazis. I mean the worst insult they can come up with is to call another man a "cuck" — they constantly refer to liberals and socialists as cuckolds. They believe 'their woman' should belong to them, like some sex slave."

He nodded.

"Are they so afraid of our sexuality? Is that what it is?"

How am I supposed to answer that?

He shrugged.

"Are most men like that, but they just don't tell us?"

"No!" he said quickly, but then realized he didn't know the answer. "I don't think so. But how the hell would I know what most men think? Hard enough to figure out what I think."

She scrunched her face while looking at him, then relaxed.

"And these incels who hate women but want to have sex with us. What's that all about? How can anyone think hating women is a good strategy if you want to have sex with us?"

"Maybe these guys really do want a sex slave, not a partner."

"But isn't sex so much better when it is consensual and passionate? Don't these guys know what they're missing?"

"Probably not."

Rodriguez shook her head as he put the car in gear.

It was going to be great to have the top down, a friend in the front seat, driving through the mountains of British Columbia back home to Vancouver.

18.

The fifth time Choy heard from Emma Murphy was a week later when his cellphone vibrated while he was on his second long day of going over the discussion from incel chatrooms that TwoSpiritPhoenix had sent him. He had already found some incredible quotes to use in the 'investigative exclusive' the *Toronto Star* had tentatively agreed to run but was diligently searching for even better ones.

"Mr. Choy?"

The screen said it was Caroline Murphy, but the voice was not the mother. It was her daughter.

"Emma? Is it you?"

"Yes. I came out of the coma yesterday afternoon. I would have called earlier but the doctors wouldn't let me."

"It is so good to hear your voice," said Choy, who walked quickly into the living room where Rodriguez had set up her "office" in the far corner. "How are you feeling?"

Choy mouthed the words, "it's Emma" as his intern looked up at him. She leapt to her feet as she whispered, "speaker phone" then parked herself right beside him on the couch.

"I feel strange," said Emma, her voice coming out of the cellphone speakers. "Like I'm looking at things and listening through a long pipe or the wrong end of a telescope. People, stuff that I see, even my own thoughts, are far away. The doctors say it could be a few months before my brain adjusts."

"I am so happy you're okay," said Choy.

"I'm awake, but that doesn't mean I'm okay," Emma responded. "I have to stay in hospital for at least another week. And the doctors told me I'll never be able to play hockey again, so I don't know if I'll be able to give you those goalie lessons I owe you."

Choy looked at Rodriguez as neither knew what to say.

"Do you believe everything the doctors tell you?" Rodriguez said, breaking the silence.

"You two haven't met," he said. "Emma Murphy, meet Bal Rodriguez. She's my intern who has been helping me with the investigation and now writing the story."

"Hi," said Rodriguez.

"My mother told me about you. Thank you for helping her."

"Thank you for coming out of the coma," said Rodriguez.

"Maybe you're right about the doctors and hockey," said Emma. "I could at least try."

Choy frowned.

"I didn't mean there's anything you should be doing right now," said Rodriguez. "You're going to need a lot of rest for the next while."

"My mother told me you are a nurse."

"A nurse and a journalist," she responded.

"If she's as good of a nurse as she is a journalist, you should listen to whatever health advice she offers," said Choy.

"I talked with Detective Sullivan," said Emma. "After the medical staff and my mother he was the first one to see me. You know he has four daughters?"

"I do," said Choy.

"He seems to like you," she added. "He said you're the only journalist he'd ever invite to meet his daughters."

Choy smiled.

"He also said that your and Bal's work was critical to making the arrests," Emma continued. "'Something unique' in his experience."

"We got lucky, that's all Emma," said Choy. "These alt-right, Neo-Nazi groups are always at each other's throats and we happened to be able to take advantage of that."

"You know I can't remember anything after leaving Vancouver," said Emma. "I was so mad at you for not coming with me to the police. Funny, that's the last thing I remember and almost the first thing I thought of when I woke up."

"Maybe you had to come out of your coma to tell me off," said Choy.

"Maybe," she answered. "The detective didn't know what happened with those two women in Abbotsford."

"They're still in pretty rough shape," said Rodriguez.

"But there's been three arrests," said Choy. "And two suspensions from the police force. Did Sullivan tell you about the undercover cops?"

"Yes and it didn't surprise me," said Emma. "But do you think they will be found guilty? Courts seem to …"

"Protect cops?" said Rodriguez. "They sure do."

"Who knows what will happen?" said Choy. "It's going to be months before they even go to trial. The cops and neo-Nazis will have good lawyers. They still have a lot of money behind them."

"But at least those incel websites will likely be shut down," said Rodriguez. "You should be proud that your work was the beginning of the end for them."

"Thinking about that, remembering through the wrong end of a telescope, it seems so far away."

"You did good work," said Rodriguez. "You helped uncover a little bit of the truth."

"Hey, if you ever decide to drop hockey and acting in favour of journalism, apparently I now take on interns."

"Paid interns," added Rodriguez.

"I'll keep that in mind."

Choy and Rodriguez were sharing a smile.

"So how is your daughter doing?" said Emma.

"Great. She'd really like to meet you," said Choy. "So when you come to Vancouver to give me those goalie lessons you owe me, you'll have to save some time for Samantha."

"I'd love that."

"She wants to interview you for her school newspaper," said Choy. "She's doing a series called 'Women Heroes'."

"I don't feel much like a hero."

"Well you are," said Rodriguez. "A successful warrior in the war again misogyny."

"That's the angle Sam wants to take," said Choy.

"And she's right," added Rodriguez.

"Thank you."

"No. Thank you." Choy and Rodriguez spoke the same words at the same time.

The End

Other FAKE NEWS Mysteries

(Available on Amazon)

American Spin

War on Drugs

Other novels by Gary Engler

(Available on Amazon)

The Year We Became US

About the Author

Gary Engler is a former journalist, local union official, marine engineer, apprentice millwright, postal worker, truck driver, playwright, audio-visual technician, and assembly-line worker. Earning money from writing while attending St. Francis High School in Calgary in the late 1960s got him hooked on literary endeavours even while he worked at various real jobs. His first professional theatrical production was Sudden Death Overtime at Factory Theatre Lab in Toronto in 1974. His first published novel was The Year We Became Us (Fernwood 2012 and Spanish language translation, Cuba 2016). He also spent 20 years as a reporter, feature writer and editor at the Vancouver Sun.